J.M. Coetzee

THE MASTER OF PETERSBURG

VINTAGE BOOKS
London

Published by Vintage 2004

6 8 10 9 7

First published in Great Britain in 1994 by
Secker & Warburg

First published by
Vintage in 1999

Vintage
Random House, 20 Vauxhall Bridge Road,
London SW1V 2SA

www.vintage-books.co.uk

Addresses for companies within The Random House Group Limited can be found at:
www.randomhouse.co.uk/offices.htm

The Random House Group Limited Reg. No. 954009

A CIP catalogue record for this book
is available from the British Library

ISBN 9780099470373

The Random House Group Limited makes every effort to ensure that the papers used in its books are made from trees that have been legally sourced from well-managed and credibly certified forests. Our paper procurement policy can be found at:
www.rbooks.co.uk/environment

Printed and bound in Great Britain by
Cox & Wyman Ltd, Reading, Berkshire

Contents

I

Petersburg

October, 1869. A droshky passes slowly down a street in the Haymarket district of St Petersburg. Before a tall tenement building the driver reins in his horse.

His passenger regards the building dubiously. 'Are you sure this is the place?' he asks.

'Sixty-three Svechnoi Street, that's what you said.'

The passenger steps out. He is a man in late middle age, bearded and stooped, with a high forehead and heavy eyebrows that lend him an air of sober self-absorption. He wears a dark suit of somewhat démodé cut.

'Wait for me,' he tells the driver.

Beneath scarred and peeling exteriors the older houses of the Haymarket still retain some of their original elegance, though most have by now become rooming-houses for clerks and students and working-folk. In the spaces between them, sometimes sharing walls with them, have been erected rickety wooden structures of two or even three storeys, warrens of rooms and cubicles, the homes of the very poorest.

No. 63, one of the older dwellings, is flanked on both sides by structures of this kind. Indeed, a web of beams and struts crosses its face at mid-level, giving it a hemmed-in look. Birds have nested in the crooks of the reinforcing, and their droppings stain the façade.

A band of children who have been climbing the struts to lob stones into puddles in the street, then leaping down to retrieve them, pause in their game to inspect the stranger. The three youngest are boys; the fourth, who seems to be their leader, is a girl with fair hair and striking dark eyes.

'Good afternoon,' he calls out. 'Do any of you know where Anna Sergeyevna Kolenkina lives?'

The boys make no response, staring at him unyieldingly. But the girl, after a moment, lets fall her stones. 'Come,' she says.

The third floor of No. 63 is a warren of interconnecting rooms giving off from a landing at the head of the stairs. He follows the girl down a dark, hook-shaped passageway that smells of cabbage and boiled beef, past an open washroom, to a grey-painted door which she pushes open.

They are in a long, low room lit by a single window at head-height. Its gloom is intensified by a heavy brocade on the longest wall. A woman dressed in black rises to face him. She is in her middle thirties; she has the same dark eyes and sculpted eyebrows as the child, but her hair is black.

'Forgive me for coming unannounced,' he says. 'My name . . .' He hesitates. 'I believe my son has been a lodger of yours.'

From his valise he takes an object and unwraps the white napkin around it. It is a picture of a boy, a daguerreotype in a silvered frame. 'Perhaps you recognize him,' he says. He does not give the picture into her hands.

'It is Pavel Alexandrovich, Mama,' whispers the child.

'Yes, he stayed with us,' says the woman. 'I am very sorry.' There is an awkward silence. 'He was a lodger here since April,' she resumes. 'His room is as he left it, and all his belongings, except for some things that the police took. Do you want to see?'

'Yes,' he says hoarsely. 'If there is rent owed, I am of course responsible.'

His son's room, though really only a cubicle partitioned off from the rest of the apartment, has its own entrance as well as a window on to the street. The bed is neatly made up; for the rest, there is a chest of drawers, a small table with a lamp, a chair. At the foot of the bed is a suitcase with the initials P. A. I. embossed on it. He recognizes it: a gift of his to Pavel.

He crosses to the window and looks out. On the street the droshky is still waiting. 'Will you do something for me?' he asks the girl. 'Will you tell the driver he can go now, and will you pay him?'

The child takes the money he gives her and leaves.

'I would like to be by myself for a while, if you don't mind,' he tells the woman.

The first thing he does when she has left is to turn back the covers of the bed. The sheets are fresh. He kneels and puts his nose to the pillow; but he can smell nothing but soap and sun. He opens the drawers. They have been emptied.

He lifts the suitcase on to the bed. Neatly folded on top is a white cotton suit. He presses his forehead to it. Faintly the smell of his son comes to him. He breathes in deeply, again and again, thinking: his ghost, entering me.

He draws the chair to the window and sits gazing out. Dusk is falling, deepening. The street is empty. Time passes; his thoughts do not move. *Pondering*, he thinks – that is the word. This heavy head, these heavy eyes: lead settling into the soul.

The woman, Anna Sergeyevna, and her daughter are having supper, sitting across the table from each other with the lamp between them. They fall silent when he enters.

'You know who I am?' he says.

She looks steadily at him, waiting.

'You know, I mean, that I am not Isaev?'

'Yes, we know. We know Pavel's story.'

'Don't let me interrupt your meal. Do you mind if I leave the suitcase behind for the time being? I will pay to the end of the month. In fact, let me pay for November too. I would like to keep the room, if it isn't promised.'

He gives her the money, twenty roubles.

'You don't mind if I come now and then in the afternoons? Is there someone at home during the day?'

She hesitates. A look passes between her and the child. Already, he suspects, she is having second thoughts. Better if he would take the suitcase away and never come back, so that the story of the dead lodger could be closed and the room freed. She does not want this mournful man in her home, casting darkness all about him. But it is too late, the money has been offered and accepted.

'Matryosha is at home in the afternoons,' she says quietly. 'I will give you a key. Could I ask you to use your own entrance? The door between the lodger's room and this one doesn't lock, but we don't normally use it.'

'I am sorry. I didn't realize.'

Matryona.

For an hour he wanders around the familiar streets of the Haymarket quarter. Then he makes his way back across Kokushkin Bridge to the inn where, under the name Isaev, he took a room earlier in the day.

He is not hungry. Fully dressed, he lies down, folds his arms, and tries to sleep. But his mind goes back to No. 63, to his son's room. The curtains are open. Moonlight falls on the bed. He is there: he stands by the door, hardly breathing, concentrating his gaze on the chair in the corner, waiting for the darkness to thicken, to turn into another kind of darkness, a darkness of presence. Silently he forms his lips over his son's name, three times, four times.

He is trying to cast a spell. But over whom: over a ghost or over himself? He thinks of Orpheus walking backwards step by step, whispering the dead woman's name, coaxing her out of the entrails of hell; of the wife in graveclothes with the blind, dead eyes following him, holding out limp hands before her like a sleepwalker. No flute, no lyre, just the word, the one word, over and over. When death cuts all other links, there remains still the name. Baptism: the union of a soul with a name, the name it will carry into eternity. Barely breathing, he forms the syllables again: *Pavel.*

His head begins to swim. 'I must go now,' he whispers or thinks he whispers; 'I will come back.'

I will come back: the same promise he made when he took the boy to school for his first term. *You will not be abandoned*. And abandoned him.

6 He is falling asleep. He imagines himself plunging down a long waterfall into a pool, and gives himself over to the plunge.

2

The cemetery

They meet at the ferry. When he sees the flowers Matryona is carrying, he is annoyed. They are small and white and modest. Whether Pavel has a favourite among flowers he does not know, but roses, whatever roses cost in October, roses scarlet as blood, are the least he deserves.

'I thought we could plant it,' says the woman, reading his thoughts. 'I brought a trowel. Bird's-foot: it flowers late.' And now he sees: the roots are indeed wrapped in a damp cloth.

They take the little ferryboat to Yelagin Island, which he has not visited in years. But for two old women in black, they are the only passengers. It is a cold, misty day. As they approach, a dog, grey and emaciated, begins to lope up and down the jetty, whining eagerly. The ferryman swings a boathook at it; it retreats to a safe distance. Isle of dogs, he thinks: are there packs of them skulking among the trees, waiting for the mourners to leave before they begin their digging?

At the gatekeeper's lodge it is Anna Sergeyevna, whom he still thinks of as *the landlady*, who goes to ask directions, while he waits outside. Then there is the walk through the avenues of the dead. He has begun to cry. *Why now?* he thinks, irritated with himself. Yet the tears are welcome in their way, a soft veil of blindness between himself and the world.

'Here, Mama!' calls Matryona.

They are before one mound of earth among many mounds with cross-shaped stakes plunged into them bearing shingles with painted numbers. He tries to close his mind to this one number, *his* number, but not before he has seen the 7s and the 4s and has thought: Never can I bet on the seven again.

This is the moment at which he ought to fall on the grave. But it is all too sudden, this particular bed of earth is too strange, he cannot find any feeling for it in his heart. He mistrusts, too, the chain of indifferent hands through which his son's limbs must have passed while he was still in Dresden, ignorant as a sheep. From the boy who still lives in his memory to the name on the death certificate to the number on the stake he is not yet prepared to accept the train of fatality. *Provisional*, he thinks: there are no final numbers, all are provisional, otherwise the play would come to an end. In a while the wheel will roll, the numbers will start moving, and all will be well again.

The mound has the volume and even the shape of a recumbent body. It is, in fact, nothing more or less than the volume of fresh earth displaced by a wooden chest with a tall young man inside it. There is something in this that does not bear thinking about, that he thrusts away from him. Taking the place of the thought are galling memories of what he was doing in Dresden all the time that, here in Petersburg, the procedure of storing, numbering, encasing, transporting, burying was following its indifferent course. Why was there no breath of a presentiment in the Dresden air? Must multitudes perish before the heavens will tremble?

Among images that return is one of himself in the bathroom of the apartment on Lärchenstrasse, trimming his beard in the mirror. The brass taps on the washbasin gleam; the face in the mirror, absorbed in its task, is the face of a stranger from the past. Already I was old, he thinks. Sentence had been pronounced; and the letter of sentence, addressed to me, was on its way, passing from hand to hand, only I did not know it. *The joy of your life is over:* that is what the sentence said.

The landlady is scraping a small hole at the foot of the mound. 'Please,' he says, and gestures, and she moves aside.

Unbuttoning his coat, unbuttoning his jacket, he kneels, then pitches awkwardly forward till he lies flat upon the mound, his arms extended over his head. He is crying freely, his nose is streaming. He rubs his face in the wet earth, burrows his face into it.

When he gets up there is soil in his beard, in his hair, in his eyebrows. The child, to whom he has paid no attention, stares with wondering eyes. He brushes his face, blows his nose, buttons his clothes. What a Jewish performance! he thinks. But let her see! Let her see one is not made of stone! Let her see there are no bounds!

Something flashes from his eyes toward her; she turns away in confusion and presses against her mother. Back to the nest! A terrible malice streams out of him toward the living, and most of all toward living children. If there were a newborn babe here at this moment, he would pluck it from its mother's arms and dash it against a rock.

Herod, he thinks: now I understand Herod! Let breeding come to an end!

He turns his back on the pair of them and walks off. Soon he has left behind the newer quarter of the graveyard and is roaming among the old stones, among the long-dead.

When he returns the bird's-foot has been planted.

'Who is going to take care of it?' he asks sullenly.

She shrugs. The question is not for her to answer. It is his turn now, it is for him to say: I will come every day to tend it, or to say: God will take care of it, or else to say: No one is going to take care of it, it will die, let it die.

The little white flowers toss cheerfully in the breeze.

He grips the woman's arm. 'He is not here, he is not dead,' he says, his voice cracking.

'No, of course he is not dead, Fyodor Mikhailovich.' She is matter-of-fact, reassuring. More than that: she is, at this moment, motherly, not only toward her daughter but toward Pavel too.

Her hands are small, her fingers slim and rather childish, yet her figure is full. Absurdly, he would like to lay his head on her breast and feel those fingers stroke his hair.

The innocence of hands, ever-renewed. A memory comes back to him: the touch of a hand, intimate in the dark. But whose hand? Hands emerging like animals, without shame, without memory, into the light of day.

'I must make a note of the number,' he says, avoiding her eyes.

'I have the number.'

Where does his desire come from? It is acute, fiery:

he wants to take this woman by the arm, drag her behind the gatekeeper's hut, lift her dress, couple with her.

He thinks of mourners at a wake falling on the food and drink. A kind of exultation in it, a brag flung in the face of death: Us you do not have!

They are back at the jetty. The grey dog slinks cautiously up to them. Matryona wants to stroke it but her mother discourages her. There is something wrong with the dog: an open, angry sore runs up its back from the base of its tail. It whimpers softly all the time, or else drops suddenly on its hindquarters and attacks the sore with its teeth.

I will come again tomorrow, he promises: I will come alone, and you and I will speak. In the thought of returning, of crossing the river, finding his way to his son's bed, being alone with him in the mist, there is a muted promise of adventure.

3

Pavel

He sits in his son's room with the white suit on his lap, breathing softly, trying to lose himself, trying to evoke a spirit that can surely not yet have left these surroundings.

Time passes. From the next room, through the partition, come the hushed voices of the woman and child and the sounds of a table being laid. He puts the suit aside, taps on the door. The voices cease abruptly. He enters. 'I will be leaving now,' he says.

'As you can see, we are about to have supper. You are welcome to join us.'

The food she offers is simple: soup, and potatoes with salt and butter.

'How did my son come to lodge with you?' he asks at a certain point. Still he is careful to call him *my son*: if he brings forth the name he will begin to shake.

She hesitates, and he understands why. She could say: He was a nice young man; we took to him. But *was* is the obstacle, the boulder in her path. Until there is a way of circumventing the word in all its starkness, she will not speak it in front of him.

‘A previous lodger recommended him,’ she says at last. And that is that.

She strikes him as dry, dry as a butterfly’s wing. As if between her skin and her petticoat, between her skin and the black stockings she no doubt wears, there is a film of fine white ash, so that, loosened from her shoulders, her clothes would slip to the floor without any coaxing.

He would like to see her naked, this woman in the last flowering of her youth.

Not what one would call an educated woman; but will one ever hear Russian spoken more beautifully? Her tongue like a bird fluttering in her mouth: soft feathers, soft wing-beats.

In the daughter he detects none of the mother’s soft dryness. On the contrary, there is something liquid about her, something of the young doe, trusting yet nervous, stretching its neck to sniff the stranger’s hand, tensed to leap away. How can this dark woman have mothered this fair child? Yet the telltale signs are all there: the fingers, small, almost unformed; the dark eyes, lustrous as those of Byzantine saints; the fine, sculpted line of the brow; even the moody air.

Strange how in a child a feature can take its perfect form while in the parent it seems a copy!

The girl raises her eyes for an instant, encounters his gaze exploring her, and turns away in confusion. An angry impulse rises in him. He wants to grip her arm and shake her. Look at me, child! he wants to say: Look at me and learn!

His knife drops to the floor. Gratefully he fumbles for it. It is as if the skin has been flayed from his face, as if, despite himself, he is continually thrusting upon the two of them a hideous bleeding mask.

The woman speaks again. 'Matryona and Pavel Alexandrovich were good friends,' she says, firmly and carefully. And to the child: 'He gave you lessons, didn't he?'

'He taught me French and German. Mostly French.'

Matryona: not the right name for her. An old woman's name, the name of a little old woman with a face like a prune.

'I would like you to have something of his,' he says. 'To remember him by.'

Again the child raises her eyes in that baffled look, inspecting him as a dog inspects a stranger, hardly hearing what he says. What is going on? And the answer comes: She cannot imagine me as Pavel's father. She is trying to see Pavel in me and she cannot. And he thinks further: To her Pavel is not yet dead. Somewhere in her he still lives, breathing the warm, sweet breath of youth. Whereas this blackness of mine, this beardedness, this boniness, must be as repugnant as death the reaper himself. Death, with his bony hips and his inch-long teeth and the rattle of his ankles as he walks.

He has no wish to speak about his son. To hear him spoken of, yes, yes indeed, but not to speak. By arithmetic, this is the tenth day of Pavel being dead. With every day that passes, memories of him that may still be floating in the air like autumn leaves are being trodden into the mud or caught by the wind and borne up into the blinding heavens. Only he wants to gather and conserve those memories. Everyone else adheres to the order of death, then mourning, then forgetting. If we do not forget, they say, the world will soon be nothing but a huge library. But the very thought of Pavel being forgotten enrages him, turns him into an old bull, irritable, glaring, dangerous.

He wants to hear stories. And the child, miraculously, is about to tell one. 'Pavel Alexandrovich' – she glances toward her mother to confirm that she may utter the dead name – 'said he was only going to be in Petersburg a little while longer, then he was going to France.'

She halts. He waits impatiently for her to go on.

'Why did he want to go to France?' she asks, and now she is addressing him alone. 'What is there in France?'

France? 'He did not want to go to France, he wanted to leave Russia,' he replies. 'When you are young you are impatient with everything around you. You are impatient with your motherland because your motherland seems old and stale to you. You want new sights, new ideas. You think that in France or Germany or England you will find the future that your own country is too dull to provide you with.'

The child is frowning. He says *France*, *motherland*, but she hears something else, something underneath the words: rancour.

'My son had a scattered education,' he says, addressing not the child now but the mother. 'I had to move him from school to school. The reason was simple: he would not get up in the mornings. Nothing would wake him. I make too much of it, perhaps. But you cannot expect to matriculate if you do not attend school.'

What a strange thing to say at a time like this! Nevertheless, turning to the daughter, he plunges on. 'His French was very undependable – you must have noticed that. Perhaps that is why he wanted to go to France – to improve his French.'

'He used to read a lot,' says the mother. 'Sometimes

the lamp would be burning in his room all night.' Her voice remains low, even. 'We didn't mind. He was always considerate. We were very fond of Pavel Alexandrovich – weren't we?' She gives the child a smile that seems to him like a caress.

Was. She has brought it out.

She frowns. 'What I still don't understand . . .'

An awkward silence falls. He does nothing to relieve it. On the contrary, he bristles like a wolf guarding its cub. Beware, he thinks: at your own peril do you utter a word against him! I am his mother and his father, I am everything to him, and more! There is something he wants to stand up and shout as well. But what? And who is the enemy he is defying?

From the depths of his throat, where he can no longer stifle it, a sound breaks out, a groan. He covers his face with his hands; tears run over his fingers.

He hears the woman get up from the table. He waits for the child to retire too, but she does not.

After a while he dries his eyes and blows his nose. 'I am sorry,' he whispers to the child, who is still sitting there, head bowed over her empty plate.

He closes the door of Pavel's room behind him. Sorry? No, the truth is, he is not sorry. Far from it: he is in a rage against everyone who is alive when his child is dead. In a rage most of all against this girl, whom for her very meekness he would like to tear limb from limb.

He lies down on the bed, his arms tight across his chest, breathing fast, trying to expel the demon that is taking him over. He knows that he resembles nothing so much as a corpse laid out, and that what he calls a demon may be nothing but his own soul flailing its wings. But being alive is, at this moment, a kind of nausea. He wants to be dead. More than that: to be extinguished, annihilated.

As for life on the other side, he has no faith in it. He expects to spend eternity on a river-bank with armies of other dead souls, waiting for a barge that will never arrive. The air will be cold and dank, the black waters will lap against the bank, his clothes will rot on his back and fall about his feet, he will never see his son again.

On the cold fingers folded to his chest he counts the days again. Ten. This is what it feels like after ten days.

Poetry might bring back his son. He has a sense of the poem that would be required, a sense of its music. But he is not a poet: more like a dog that has lost a bone, scratching here, scratching there.

He waits till the gleam of light under the door has gone out, then quietly leaves the apartment and returns to his lodgings.

During the night a dream comes to him. He is swimming underwater. The light is blue and dim. He banks and glides easily, gracefully; his hat seems to have gone, but in his black suit he feels like a turtle, a great old turtle in its natural element. Above him there is a ripple of movement, but here at the bottom the water is still. He swims through patches of weed; slack fingers of water-grass brush his fins, if that is what they are.

He knows what he is in search of. As he swims he sometimes opens his mouth and gives what he thinks of as a cry or call. With each cry or call water enters his mouth; each syllable is replaced by a syllable of water. He grows more and more ponderous, till his breastbone is brushing the silt of the river-bed.

Pavel is lying on his back. His eyes are closed. His hair, wafted by the current, is as soft as a baby's.

From his turtle-throat he gives a last cry, which seems to him more like a bark, and plunges toward the boy. He wants to kiss the face; but when he touches his hard lips to it, he is not sure he is not biting.

This is when he wakes.

Following old habit, he spends the morning at the little desk in his room. When the maid comes to clean, he waves her away. But he does not write a word. It is not that he is paralysed. His heart pumps steadily, his mind is clear. At any moment he is capable of picking up the pen and forming letters on the paper. But the writing, he fears, would be that of a madman – vileness, obscenity, page after page of it, untameable. He thinks of the madness as running through the artery of his right arm down to the fingertips and the pen and so to the page. It runs in a stream; he need not dip the pen, not once. What flows on to the paper is neither blood nor ink but an acid, black, with an unpleasing green sheen when the light glances off it. On the page it does not dry: if one were to pass a finger over it, one would experience a sensation both liquid and electric. A writing that even the blind could read.

In the afternoon he returns to Svechnoi Street, to Pavel's room. He closes the inner door to the apartment and props a chair against it. Then he lays the white suit out on the bed. By daylight he can see how grimy the cuffs are. He sniffs the armpits and the smell comes clearly: not that of a child but of another man, fullgrown. He inhales it again and again. How many breaths before it fades? If the suit were shut up in a glass case, would the smell be preserved too?

He takes off his own clothes and puts on the white suit. Though the jacket is loose and the trousers too long, he does not feel clownish in it.

He lies down and crosses his arms. The posture is theatrical, but wherever impulse leads he is ready to follow. At the same time he has no faith in impulse at all.

He has a vision of Petersburg stretched out vast and low under the pitiless stars. Written in a scroll across the heavens is a word in Hebrew characters. He cannot read the word but knows it is a condemnation, a curse.

A gate has closed behind his son, a gate bound sevenfold with bands of iron. To open that gate is the labour laid upon him.

Thoughts, feelings, visions. Does he trust them? They come from his deepest heart; but there is no more reason to trust the heart than to trust reason.

From somewhere to somewhere I am in retreat, he thinks; when the retreat is completed, what will be left of me?

He thinks of himself as going back into the egg, or at least into something smooth and cool and grey. Perhaps it is not just an egg: perhaps it is the soul, perhaps that is how the soul looks.

There is a rustling under the bed. A mouse going about its business? He does not care. He turns over, draws the white jacket over his face, inhales.

Since the news came of his son's death, something has been ebbing out of him that he thinks of as firmness. I am the one who is dead, he thinks; or rather, I died but my death failed to arrive. His sense of his own body is that it is strong, sturdy, that it will not yield of its own accord. His chest is like a barrel with sound staves. His heart will go on beating for a long time. Nevertheless, he has been tugged out of human time. The stream that carries him still moves forward, still has direction, even purpose; but that purpose is no longer life. He is being carried by dead water, a dead stream.

He falls asleep. When he wakes it is dark and the whole world is silent. He strikes a match, trying to gather his fuddled wits. Past midnight. Where has he been?

He crawls under the covers, sleeps intermittently. In the morning, on his way to the washroom, smelly, dishevelled, he runs into Anna Sergeyevna. With her hair under a kerchief, in big boots, she looks like any market-woman. She regards him with surprise. 'I fell asleep, I was very tired,' he explains. But it is not that. It is the white suit, which he is still wearing.

'If you don't mind, I will stay here in Pavel's room till I leave,' he goes on. 'It will only be for a few days.'

'We can't discuss it now, I'm in a hurry,' she replies. Clearly she does not like the idea. Nor does she give her consent. But he has paid, there is nothing she can do about it.

All morning he sits at the table in his son's room, his head in his hands. He cannot pretend he is writing. His mind is running to the moment of Pavel's death. What he cannot bear is the thought that, for the last fraction of the last instant of his fall, Pavel knew that nothing could save him, that he was dead. He wants to believe Pavel was protected from that certainty, more terrible than annihilation itself, by the hurry and confusion of the fall, by the mind's way of etherizing itself against whatever is too enormous to be borne. With all his heart he wants to believe this. At the same time he knows that he wants to believe in order to etherize himself against the knowledge that Pavel, falling, knew everything.

At moments like this he cannot distinguish Pavel from himself. They are the same person; and that person is no more or less than a thought, Pavel thinking it in him, he thinking it in Pavel. The thought keeps Pavel alive, suspended in his fall.

It is from knowing that he is dead that he wants to protect his son. As long as I live, he thinks, let me be the one who knows! By whatever act of will it takes, let me be the thinking animal plunging through the air.

Sitting at the table, his eyes closed, his fists clenched, he wards the knowledge of death away from Pavel. He thinks of himself as the Triton on the Piazza Barberini in Rome, holding to his lips a conch from which jets a constant crystal fountain. All day and all night he breathes life into the water. The tendons of his neck, caught in bronze, are taut with effort.

4

The white suit

November has arrived, and the first snow. The sky is filled with marsh-birds migrating south.

He has moved into Pavel's room and within days has become part of the life of the building. The children no longer stop their games to stare when he passes, though they still lower their voices. They know who he is. Who is he? He is misfortune, he is the father of misfortune.

Every day he tells himself he must go back to Yelagin Island, to the grave. But he does not go.

He writes to his wife in Dresden. His letters are reassuring but empty of feeling.

He spends his mornings in the room, mornings of utter blankness which come to have their own insidious and deathly pleasure. In the afternoons he walks the streets, avoiding the area around Meshchanskaya Street and the Voznesensky Prospekt where he might be recognized, stopping for an hour at a tea-house, always the same one.

In Dresden he used to read the Russian newspapers. But he has lost interest in the world outside. His world has contracted; his world is within his breast.

Out of consideration for Anna Sergeyevna he returns to the apartment only after dusk. Till called to supper he stays quietly in the room that is and is not his.

He is sitting on the bed with the white suit on his lap. There is no one to see him. Nothing has changed. He feels the cord of love that goes from his heart to his son's as physically as if it were a rope. He feels the rope twist and wring his heart. He groans aloud. 'Yes!' he whispers, welcoming the pain; he reaches out and gives the rope another twist.

The door behind him opens. Startled, he turns, bent and ugly, tears in his eyes, the suit bunched in his hands.

'Would you like to eat now?' asks the child.

'Thank you, but I would prefer to be by myself this evening.'

Later she is back. 'Would you like some tea? I can bring it to you.'

She brings a teapot and sugar-bowl and cup, bearing them solemnly on a tray.

'Is that Pavel Alexandrovich's suit?'

He puts the suit aside, nods.

She stands at arm's length watching while he drinks. Again he is struck by the fine line of her temple and cheekbone, the dark, liquid eyes, the dark brows, the hair blonde as corn. There is a rush of feeling in him, contradictory, like two waves slapping against each other: an urge to protect her, an urge to lash out at her because she is alive.

Good that I am shut away, he thinks. As I am now, I am not fit for humankind.

He waits for her to say something. He wants her to speak. It is an outrageous demand to make on a child, but he makes the demand nevertheless. He raises his eyes to her. Nothing is veiled. He stares at her with what can only be nakedness.

For a moment she meets his gaze. Then she averts her eyes, steps back uncertainly, makes a strange, awkward kind of curtsy, and flees the room.

He is aware, even as it unfolds, that this is a passage he will not forget and may even one day rework into his writing. A certain shame passes over him, but it is superficial and transitory. First in his writing and now in his life, shame seems to have lost its power, its place taken by a blank and amoral passivity that shrinks from no extreme. It is as if, out of the corner of an eye, he can see clouds advancing on him with terrific speed, stormclouds. Whatever stands in their path will be swept away. With dread, but with excitement too, he waits for the storm to break.

At eleven o'clock by his watch, without announcing himself, he emerges from his room. The curtain is drawn across the alcove where Matryona and her mother sleep, but Anna Sergeyevna is still up, seated at the table, sewing by lamplight. He crosses the room, sits down opposite her.

Her fingers are deft, her movements decisive. In Siberia he learnt to sew, out of necessity, but he cannot sew with this fluid grace. In his fingers a needle is a curiosity, an arrow from Lilliput.

'Surely the light is too poor for such fine work,' he murmurs.

She inclines her head as if to say: I hear you, but also: What do you expect me to do about it?

'Has Matryona been your only child?'

She gives him a direct look. He likes the directness. He likes her eyes, which are not soft at all.

'She had a brother, but he died when he was very young.'

'So you know.'

'No, I don't know.'

What does she mean? That an infant's death is easier to bear? She does not explain.

'If you will allow me, I will buy you a better lamp. It is a pity to ruin your eyesight so early.'

She inclines her head as if to say: Thank you for the thought; I will not hold you to your promise.

So early: what does *he* mean?

He has known for some time that when the words that come next come, he will not try to stop them. 'I have a hunger to talk about my son,' he says, 'but even more of a hunger to hear others talk about him.'

'He was a fine young man,' she offers. 'I am sorry we knew him for a short time only.' And then, as if realizing this is not enough: 'He used to read to Matryona at bedtime. She looked forward to it all day. There was a real fondness between them.'

'What did they read?'

'I call to mind *The Golden Cockerel* and Krylov. He taught her some French poems too. She can still recite one or two.'

'It's good that you have books in the house.' He gestures toward a shelf on which there must be twenty or thirty volumes. 'Good for a growing child, I mean.'

'My husband was a printer. He worked in a printer's shop. He read a lot, it was his recreation. These are only a few of his books. Sometimes the apartment would be overflowing, while he was alive. There was no space for all of them.' She hesitates. 'We have a book of yours. *Poor Folk*. It was one of my husband's favourites.'

There is a silence. The lamp begins to flicker. She turns it down and lays aside her sewing. The farther corners of the room sink into shadow.

'I had to ask Pavel Alexandrovich not to invite friends to his room in the evenings,' she says. 'I regret that now. It was after they kept us awake, talking and drinking late into the night. He had some quite rough friends.'

'Yes, he was democratic in his friendships. He could speak to ordinary people about things close to their hearts. Ordinary people have a hunger for ideas. He never spoke down to them.'

'He didn't speak down to Matryosha either.'

The light grows dimmer, the wick begins to smoke. A salve of words, he thinks, rubbed over the sore places. But do I want to be healed?

'He was a serious person, despite his youth,' he presses on. 'He thought about Russia, about the conditions of our existence here. He was concerned about things that matter to ordinary folk.'

There is a long pause. Tribute, he thinks: I am paying tribute, however lamely, however belatedly, and trying to extort tribute from her too. And why not!

'I have been wondering about something you said the other day,' she says ruminatively. 'Why did you tell me that story about Pavel oversleeping?'

'Why? Because, unimportant as it may seem now, it marred his life. Because of his late sleeping I had to remove him from school, from one school after another. That was why he did not matriculate. So in the end he found himself here in Petersburg on the fringes of student society, where he had no real business, where he did not properly belong. It was not just sluggishness. Nothing would wake him – shouting, shaking, threats, pleas. It was like trying to wake a bear, a hibernating bear!'

'I understand that. Some children never settle down at school. But I meant something else. Forgive me for saying so, but what struck me when you told the story was how angry with him you still seemed to be.'

'Of course I was angry! His mother died, you must remember, when he was fifteen. It was not easy to bring him up alone. I had better things to do than to coax a boy of that age out of bed. If Pavel had finished his schooling like everyone else, none of this would have happened.'

'This?'

He waves an arm impatiently, as if to dismiss the apartment, the city of Petersburg, even the great dark canopy of the night above them.

She gives him a quiet, steady look; and under that look it begins to come home to him what he has said. A trembling overtakes him, starting in his right hand. He gets up and paces across the room, clasping his hands behind him. Something is on its way, something whose name he is trying to avoid. He tries to speak, but his voice emerges strangled. I am behaving like a character in a book, he thinks. But even jeering at himself does not help. His shoulders heave. Soundlessly he begins to cry.

In a book, the woman would respond to his grief with a surge of pity. This woman does not. She sits at the table in the flickering light, her head averted, her sewing in her lap. It is late, there is no one to see them, the child is sleeping.

Damn the heart, he tells himself! Damn this emotionalism! The touchstone is not the heart and how the heart feels, but death and how the dead boy feels!

At this moment the clearest of visions comes to him, a vision of Pavel smiling at him, at his peevishness, his tears, his histrionics, at what lies behind the histrionics too. The smile is not of derision but on the contrary of friendliness and forgiveness. *He knows!* he thinks: *He knows and does not mind!* A wave of gratitude and joy and love passes over him. *Now there is sure to be a fit!* he thinks too, but does not care. No longer holding back the tears, he feels his way back to the table, buries his head in his arms, and lets loose howl after howl of grief.

No one strokes his hair, no one murmurs a consoling word in his ear. But when at last, fumbling for his handkerchief, he raises his head, the girl Matryona is standing before him observing him intently. She wears a white nightdress; her hair, brushed out, lies over her shoulders. He cannot fail to notice the budding breasts. He tries to give her a smile, but her expression does not change. *She knows too*, he thinks. She knows what is false, what is true; or else by staring deep enough means to know.

He collects himself. Through the last of the tears his gaze locks on to hers. In that instant something passes between them from which he flinches as though pierced by a red-hot wire. Then her mother's arm enfolds her; a whispered word passes; she withdraws to her bed.

5

Maximov

'Good morning. I have come to claim' (he is surprised at how steady his voice is) 'some belongings of my son's. My son was involved in an accident last month, and the police took charge of certain items.'

He unfolds the receipt and passes it across the counter. Depending on whether Pavel gave up the ghost before or after midnight, it is dated the day after or the day of Pavel's death; it names simply 'letters and other papers.'

The sergeant inspects the receipt dubiously. 'October 12th. That's less than a month ago. The case won't be settled yet.'

'How long will it take to settle?'

'Could be two months, could be three months, could be a year. It depends on the circumstances.'

'There are no circumstances. There is no crime involved.'

Holding the paper at arm's length, the sergeant leaves the room. When he returns, his air is markedly more surly. 'You are, sir, – ?'

'Isaev. The father.'

'Yes, Mr Isaev. If you will take a seat, you will be attended to in a short while.'

His heart sinks. He had hoped simply to be handed Pavel's belongings and walk out of this place. What he can least afford is that the police should turn their attention on him.

'I can wait only a short while,' he says briskly.

'Yes, sir, I'm sure the investigator in charge will see you soon. Just take a seat and make yourself comfortable.'

He consults his watch, sits down on the bench, looks around with pretended impatience. It is early; there is only one other person in the ante-room, a young man in stained housepainter's overalls. Sitting bolt upright, he seems to be asleep. His eyes are closed, his jaw hangs, a soft rattle comes from the back of his throat.

Isaev. Inside him the confusion has not settled. Should he not drop the Isaev story at once, before getting mired in it? But how can he explain? 'Sergeant, there has been a slight mistake. Things are not entirely as they appear to be. In a sense I am not Isaev. The Isaev whose name I have for reasons of my own been using, reasons I won't go into here and now, but perfectly good reasons, has been dead for some years. Nevertheless, I brought up Pavel Isaev as my son and love him as my own flesh and blood. In that sense we bear the same name, or ought to. Those few papers he left behind are precious to me. That is why I am here.' What if he made this admission unprompted, and all the while they had suspected nothing? What if they had been on the point of giving him the papers, and now pulled up short? 'Aha, what is this? Is there more to the case than meets the eye?'

As he sits vacillating between confessing and pressing on with the imposture, as he takes out his watch and glances at it crossly, trying to seem like an impatient *homme d'affaires* in this stuffy room with a stove burning in a corner, he has a premonition of an attack, and in the same movement recognizes that an attack would be a device, and the most childish of devices at that, for extricating himself from a fix, while somewhere to the side falls the nagging shadow of a memory: surely he has been here before, in this very ante-room or one like it, and had an attack or a fainting fit! But why is it that he recollects the episode only so dimly? And what has the recollection to do with the smell of fresh paint?

'This is too much!'

His cry echoes around the room. The dozing house-painter gives a start; the desk-sergeant looks up in surprise. He tries to cover his confusion. 'I mean,' he says, lowering his voice, 'I can't wait any longer, I have an appointment. As I said.'

He has already stood up and put on his coat when the sergeant calls him back. 'Councillor Maximov will see you now, sir.'

In the office into which he is conducted there is no high bench. Save for a huge sofa in imitation leather, it is furnished in nondescript government issue. Councillor Maximov, the judicial investigator in Pavel's case, is a bald man with the tubby figure of a peasant woman, who fusses till he is comfortably seated, then opens the bulky folder before him on the desk and reads at length, murmuring to himself, shaking his head from time to time. 'Sad business . . . Sad business . . .'

At last he looks up. 'My sincerest condolences, Mr Isaev.'

 Isaev. Time to make up his mind!

'Thank you. I have come to ask for my son's papers to be returned. I am aware that the case has not been closed, but I do not see how private papers can be of any interest to your office or of any relevance to – to your proceedings.'

'Yes, of course, of course! As you say, private papers. But tell me: when you talk of papers, what exactly do you mean? What do the papers consist in?'

The man's eyes have a watery gleam; his lashes are pale, like a cat's.

'How can I say? They were removed from my son's room, I haven't seen them yet. Letters, papers . . .'

'You have not seen them but you believe they can be of no interest to us. I can understand that. I can understand that a father should believe his son's papers are a personal matter, or at least a family matter. Yes, indeed. Nevertheless, there is an investigation in progress – a mere formality, perhaps, but called for by the law, therefore not to be dismissed with a snap of the fingers or a flourish of the hand, and the papers are part of that investigation. So . . .'

He puts his fingertips together, lowers his head, appears to sink into deep thought. When he looks up again he is no longer smiling, but wears an expression of the utmost determination. 'I believe,' he says, 'yes, I do believe I have a solution that will satisfy both parties. Since the case is not closed – indeed, it has barely been opened – I cannot return the papers themselves to you. But I am going to let you see them. Because I agree, it is unfair, most unfair, to whisk them off at such a tragic time and keep them from the family.'

With a sudden, startling gesture, like a card-player playing an all-conquering card, he sweeps a single leaf out of the folder and places it before him.

It is a list of names, Russian names written in Roman script, all beginning with the letter A.

'There is some mistake. This is not my son's handwriting.'

'Not your son's handwriting? Hmm.' Maximov takes back the page and studies it. 'Then have you any idea whose handwriting this might be, Mr Isaev?'

'I don't recognize the handwriting, but it is not my son's.'

From the bottom of the file Maximov selects another page and advances it across the desk. 'And this?'

He does not need to read it. How stupid! he thinks. A flush of dizziness overtakes him. His voice seems to come from far away. 'It is a letter from myself. I am not Isaev. I simply took the name – '

Maximov is waving a hand as if to chase away a fly, waving his words away, waving for silence; but he masters the dizziness and completes his declaration.

'I took the name so as not to complicate matters – for no other reason. Pavel Alexandrovich Isaev is my stepson, my late wife's only child. But to me he is my own son. He has no one but me in the world.'

Maximov takes the letter from his slack grasp and peruses it again. It is the last letter he wrote from Dresden, a letter in which he chides Pavel for spending too much money. Mortifying to sit here while a stranger reads it! Mortifying ever to have written it! But how is one to know, *how is one to know*, which day will be the last?

' "Your loving father, Fyodor Mikhailovich

 Dostoevsky," ' murmurs the magistrate, and looks up. 'So let me be clear, you are not Isaev at all, you are Dostoevsky.'

'Yes. It has been a deception, a mistake, stupid but harmless, which I regret.'

'I understand. Nevertheless, you have come here purporting – but need we use that ugly word? Let us use it gingerly, so to speak, for the time being, for lack of a better – purporting to be the deceased Pavel Alexandrovich Isaev's father and applying to have his property released to you, while in fact you are not that person at all. It does not look well, does it?'

'It was a mistake, as I say, which I now bitterly regret. But the deceased *is* my son, and I am his guardian in law, properly appointed.'

'Hm. I see here he was twenty-one, getting on for twenty-two, at the time of decease. So, strictly speaking, the writ of guardianship had expired. A man of twenty-one is his own master, is he not? A free person, in law.'

It is this mockery that finally rouses him. He stands up. 'I did not come here to discuss my son with strangers,' he says, his voice rising. 'If you insist on keeping his papers, say so directly, and I will take other steps.'

'Insist on keeping the papers? Of course not! My dear sir, please be seated! Of course not! On the contrary, I would very much like you to examine the papers, for your own sake and for ours too. The guidance you could give us would be appreciated, deeply appreciated. To begin with, let us take this item.' He lays before him a set of half a dozen leaves written on both sides, the complete list of names of which he has already seen the first page, the A's. 'Not your son's handwriting, is it?'

'No.'

'No, we know that. Any idea whose handwriting it is?'

'I do not recognize it.'

'It belongs to a young woman at present resident abroad. Her name is not relevant, though if I mentioned it I think you would be surprised. She is a friend and associate of a man named Nechaev, Sergei Gennadevich Nechaev. Does the name mean anything to you?'

'I do not know Nechaev personally, and I doubt very much that my son knew him. Nechaev is a conspirator and an insurrectionist whose designs I repudiate with the utmost force.'

'You do not know him personally, as you say. But you have had contact with him.'

'No, I have not had contact with him. I attended a public meeting in Switzerland, in Geneva, at which numerous people spoke, Nechaev among them. He and I have been together in the same room – that is the sum of my acquaintance with him.'

'And when was that?'

'It was in the autumn of 1867. The meeting was organized by the League for Peace and Freedom, as the body calls itself. I attended openly, as a patriotic Russian, to hear what might be said about Russia from all sides. The fact that I heard this young man Nechaev speak does not mean that I stand behind him. On the contrary, I repeat, I reject everything he stands for, and have said so many times, in public and in private.'

'Including the welfare of the people? Doesn't Nechaev stand for the welfare of the people? Isn't that what he is striving for?'

'I fail to understand the force of these questions. Nechaev stands first and foremost for the violent overthrow of all the institutions of society, in the name of a principle of equality – equal happiness for all or, if not that, then equal misery for all. It is not a principle that he attempts to justify. In fact he seems to despise justification in general as a waste of time, as useless intellection. Please don't try to associate me with Nechaev.'

'Very well, I accept the reproof. Though I am surprised, I might add – I would not have thought of you as a martinet for principles. But to business. The list of names you see in front of you – do you recognize any of them?'

'I recognize some of them. A handful.'

'It is a list of people who are to be assassinated, as soon as the signal is given, in the name of the People's Vengeance, which as you know is the clandestine organization that Nechaev has brought into being. The assassinations are meant to precipitate a general uprising and to lead to the overthrow of the state. If you turn to the end, you will come to an appendix which names entire classes of people who are thereupon, in the wake of the overthrow, to suffer summary execution. They include the entire higher judiciary and all officers of the police and officials of the Third Section of the rank of captain and higher. The list was found among your son's papers.'

Having delivered this information, Maximov tilts his chair back and smiles amicably.

'And does that mean that my son is an assassin?'

'Of course not! How could he be when no one has been assassinated? What you have there is, so to speak, a draft, a speculative draft. In fact, my opinion – my opinion as a private individual – is that it is a list such as a young man with a grudge against society might concoct in the space of an afternoon, perhaps as a way of showing off to the very young woman to whom he is dictating – showing off his power of life and death, his completely illusory power. Nevertheless, assassination, the plotting of assassination, threats against officialdom – these are serious matters, don't you agree?'

'Very serious. Your duty is clear, you don't need my advice. If and when Nechaev returns to his native country, you must arrest him. As for my son, what can you do? Arrest him too?'

'Ha ha! You will have your joke, Fyodor Mikhailovich! No, we could not arrest him even if we wanted to, for he has gone to a better place. But he has left things behind. He has left papers, more papers than any self-respecting conspirator ought to. He has left behind questions too. Such as: Why did he take his life? Let me ask you: Why do *you* think he took his life?'

The room swims before his eyes. The investigator's face looms like a huge pink balloon.

'He did not take his life,' he whispers. 'You understand nothing about him.'

'Of course not! Of your stepson and the vicissitudes of his existence I understand not a whit, nor do I pretend to. What I hope to understand in a material, investigative sense, however, is what drove him to his death. Was he threatened, for instance? Did one of his associates threaten to disclose him? And did fear of the consequences unsettle him so deeply that he took his own life? Or did he perhaps not take his life at all? Is it possible that, for reasons of which we are still ignorant, he was found to be a traitor to the People's Vengeance and murdered in this particularly unpleasant way? These are some of the questions that run through my mind. And that is why I took this lucky opportunity to speak to you, Fyodor Mikhailovich. Because if you do not know him, having been his stepfather and for so long his protector, in the absence of his natural parents, who does?

'Then, as well, there is the question of his drinking. Was he used to heavy drinking, or did he take to it recently, because of the strains of the conspiratorial life?'

'I don't understand. Why are we talking about drinking?'

'Because on the night of his death he had drunk a great deal. Did you not know that?'

He shakes his head dumbly.

'Clearly, Fyodor Mikhailovich, there is a great deal you do not know. Come, let me be candid with you. As soon as I heard you had arrived to claim your stepson's papers, stepping, so to speak, into the lion's den, I was sure, or almost sure, that you had no suspicion of anything untoward. For if you had known of a connection between your stepson and Nechaev's criminal gang, you would surely not have come here. Or at least you would have made it plain from the outset that it was only the letters between yourself and your stepson that you were claiming, nothing else. Do you follow?'

'Yes – '

'And since you are already in possession of your stepson's letters to you, that would have meant you wanted only the letters written by you to him. But why – '

'Letters, yes, and everything else of a private nature. What can be the point of your hounding him now?'

'What indeed! . . . So tragic . . . But to return to the matter of the papers: you use the expression "of a private nature." It occurs to me that in today's circumstances it is hard to know what "of a private nature" means any longer. Of course we must respect the deceased, we must defend rights your stepson is no longer in a position

to defend, in this case a right to a certain decent privacy.
The prospect that after our decease a stranger will come sniffing through our possessions, opening drawers, breaking seals, reading intimate letters – such would be a painful prospect to any of us, I am sure. On the other hand, in certain cases we might actually prefer a disinterested stranger to perform this ugly but necessary office. Would we be easy at the thought of our more intimate affairs being opened up, when emotions are still raw, to the unsuspecting gaze of a wife or a daughter or a sister? Better, in certain respects, that it be done by a stranger, someone who cannot be offended because we are nothing to him, and also because he is hardened, by the nature of his profession, to offence.

'Of course this is, in a sense, idle talk, for in the end it is the law that disposes, the law of succession: the heirs to the estate come into possession of the private papers and everything else. And in a case where one dies without naming an heir, rules of consanguinity take over and determine what needs to be determined.

'So letters between family members, we agree, are private papers, to be treated with the appropriate discretion. While communications from abroad, communications of a seditious nature – lists of people marked down to be murdered, for instance – are clearly not private papers. But here, now, here is a curious case.'

He is leafing through something in the file, drumming on the desk with his fingernails in an irritating way. 'Here's a curious case, *here's* a curious case,' he repeats in a murmur. 'A story,' he announces abruptly. 'What shall we say of a story, a work of fiction? Is a story a private matter, would you say?'

'A private matter, an utterly private matter, private to the writer, till it is given to the world.'

Maximov casts him a quizzical look, then pushes what he has been reading across the desk. It is a child's exercise book with ruled pages. He recognizes at once the slanted script with its trailing loops and dashes. Orphan writing, he thinks: I will have to learn to love it. He places a protective hand over the page.

'Read it,' says his antagonist softly.

He tries to read but he cannot concentrate; the more he tries, the more he sees only details of penmanship. His eyes are blurred with tears too; he dabs with a sleeve to prevent them from falling and blotting the page. 'Trackless wastes of snow,' he reads, and wants to correct the cliché. Something about a man out in the open, something about the cold. He shakes his head and closes the book.

Maximov reaches across and tugs it gently from him. He turns the pages till he finds what he wants, then pushes it back across the desk. 'Read this part,' he says, 'just a page or two. Our hero is a young man convicted of treasonous conspiracy and sent to Siberia. He escapes from prison and finds his way to the home of a landowner, where he is hidden and fed by a kitchenmaid, a peasant girl. They are young, romantic feelings develop between them, and so forth. One evening the landowner, who is portrayed as a gross sensualist, tries to force his attentions on the girl. This is the passage I suggest you read.'

Again he shakes his head..

Maximov takes the book back. 'The young man can bear the spectacle no longer. He comes out of his hiding-place and intervenes.' He begins to read aloud.

'"Karamzin" – that is the landowner – "turned upon him and hissed, 'Who are you? What are you doing here?' Then he took in the tattered grey uniform and the broken leg-shackle. 'Aha, one of those!' he cried – 'I'll soon take care of you!' He turned and began to lumber out of the room." That is the word used, "lumber," I like it. The landowner is described as a pug-faced brute with hairy ears and short, fat legs. No wonder our young hero is offended: age and ugliness pawing maiden beauty! He picks up a hatchet from beside the stove. "With all the force at his command, shuddering even as he did so, he brought the hatchet down on the man's pale skull. Karamzin's knees folded beneath him. With a great snort like a beast's he fell flat on the scrubbed kitchen floor, his arms spread out wide, his fingers twitching, then relaxing. Sergei" – that is our hero's name – "stood transfixed, the bloody hatchet in his hand, unable to believe what he had done. But Marfa" – that is the heroine – "with a presence of mind he did not expect, snatched up a wet rag and pushed it under the dead man's head so that the blood would not spread." A nice touch of realism, don't you think?

'The rest of the story is sketchy – I won't read on. Perhaps, once the obscene Karamzin has been polished off, our author's inspiration began to dwindle. Sergei and Marfa drag the body off and drop it down a disused well. Then they set off together into the night "full of resolution" – that is the phrase. It is not clear whither they intend to flee. But let me mention one last detail. Sergei does not leave the murder weapon behind. No, he takes it with him. What for, asks Marfa? I quote his reply. "Because it is the weapon of the Russian people, our means of defence and our means of revenge." The bloody axe, the people's revenge – the allusion could not be clearer, could it?'

He stares at Maximov in disbelief. 'I can't believe my ears,' he whispers. 'Do you really intend to construe this as evidence against my son – a story, a fantasy, written in the privacy of his room?'

'Oh dear, no, Fyodor Mikhailovich, you misunderstand me!' Maximov throws himself back in his chair, shaking his head in seeming distress. 'There can be no question of hounding your stepson (to use your word). His case is closed, in the sense that matters most. I read you his fantasy, as you like to call it, simply to indicate how deeply he had fallen under the influence of the Nechaevites, who have led astray heaven knows how many of our more impressionable and volatile young people, particularly here in Petersburg, many of them from good families too. Quite an epidemic, I would say, Nechaevism. An epidemic, or perhaps just a fashion.'

'Not a fashion. What you call Nechaevism has always existed in Russia, though under other names. Nechaevism is as Russian as brigandage. But I am not here to discuss the Nechaevites. I came for a simple reason – to fetch my son's papers. May I have them? If not, may I leave?'

'You may leave, you are free to leave. You have been abroad and returned to Russia under a false name. I will not ask what passport you are carrying. But you are free to leave. If your creditors discover you are in Petersburg they are of course equally free to take such steps as they may decide on. That is none of my business, that is between you and them. I repeat: you are free to leave this office. However, I caution you, I cannot positively conspire with you to maintain your deception. I take that as understood.'

'At this moment nothing could be less important to me than money. If I am to be harried for old debts, then so be it.'

'You have suffered a loss, you are despondent, that is why you take such a line. I understand fully. But remember, you have a wife and child who depend on you. If only for their sake, you cannot afford to abandon yourself to fate. As regards your request for these papers, with regret I must say, no, they cannot yet be surrendered to you. They are part of a police matter in which your stepson is linked to the Nechaevites.'

'Very well. But before I leave, may I change my mind and say one last thing about these Nechaevites? For I at least have seen and heard Nechaev in person, which is more – correct me if I am wrong – than you have.'

Maximov cocks his head interrogatively. 'Please proceed.'

'Nechaev is not a police matter. Ultimately Nechaev is not a matter for the authorities at all, at least for the secular authorities.'

'Go on.'

'You may track down and imprison Sergei Nechaev but that will not mean Nechaevism will be stamped out.'

'I agree. I agree fully. Nechaevism is an idea abroad in our land; Nechaev himself is only the embodiment of it. Nechaevism will not be extinguished till the times have changed. Our aims must therefore be more modest and more practical: to check the spread of this idea, and where it has already spread to prevent it from turning to action.'

'Still you misunderstand me. Nechaevism is not an

 idea. It despises ideas, it is outside ideas. It is a spirit, and Nechaev himself is not its embodiment but its host; or rather, he is under possession by it.'

Maximov's expression is inscrutable. He tries again.

'When I first saw Sergei Nechaev in Geneva, he struck me as an unprepossessing, morose, intellectually undistinguished, and distinctly ordinary young man. I do not think that first impression was wrong. Into this unlikely vehicle, however, there has entered a spirit. There is nothing remarkable about the spirit. It is a dull, resentful, and murderous spirit. Why has it elected to reside in this particular young man? I don't know. Perhaps because it finds him an easy host to go out from and come home to. But it is because of the spirit inside him that Nechaev has followers. They follow the spirit, not the man.'

'And what name does this spirit have, Fyodor Mikhailovich?'

He makes an effort to visualize Sergei Nechaev, but all he sees is an ox's head, its eyes glassy, its tongue lolling, its skull cloven open by the butcher's axe. Around it is a seething swarm of flies. A name comes to him, and in the same instant he utters it: 'Baal.'

'Interesting. A metaphor, perhaps, and not entirely clear, yet worth bearing in mind. Baal. I must ask myself, however, how practical is it to talk of spirits and spirit-possession? Is it even practical to talk about ideas going about in the land, as if ideas had arms and legs? Will such talk assist us in our labours? Will it assist Russia? You say we should not lock Nechaev up because he is possessed by a demon (shall we call it a demon? – *spirit* strikes a false note, I would say). In that case, what *should* we do? After all, we are not a contemplative order, we of the investigative arm.'

There is a silence.

'I by no means want to dismiss any of what you say,' Maximov resumes. 'You are a man of gifts, a man of special insight, as I knew before I met you. And these child conspirators are certainly a different kettle of fish from their predecessors. They believe they are immortal. In that sense it is indeed like fighting demons. And implacable too. It is in their blood, so to speak, to wish us ill, our generation. Something they are born with. Not easy to be a father, is it? I am a father myself, but luckily a father of daughters. I would not wish to be the father of sons in our age. But didn't your own father . . . wasn't there some unpleasantness with your father, or do I misremember?'

From behind the white eyelashes Maximov launches a keen little peep, then without waiting proceeds.

'So I wonder, in the end, whether the Nechaev phenomenon is quite as much of an aberration of the spirit as you seem to say. Perhaps it is just the old matter of fathers and sons after all, such as we have always had, only deadlier in this particular generation, more unforgiving. In that case, perhaps the wisest course would be the simplest: to dig in and outlast them – wait for them to grow up. After all, we had the Decembrists, and then the men of '49. The Decembrists are old men now, those who are still alive; I'm sure that whatever demons were in possession of them took flight years ago. As for Petrashevsky and his friends, what is your opinion? Were Petrashevsky and his friends in the grip of demons?'

Petrashevsky! Why does he bring up Petrashevsky?

'I disagree. What you call the Nechaev phenomenon has a colouring of its own. Nechaev is a man of blood.

 The men you do the honour of referring to were idealists. They failed because, to their credit, they were not schemers enough, and certainly not men of blood. Petrashevsky – since you mention Petrashevsky – from the outset denounced the kind of Jesuitism that excuses the means in the name of the end. Nechaev is a Jesuit, a secular Jesuit who quite openly embraces the doctrine of ends to justify the most cynical abuse of his followers' energies.'

'Then there is something I have missed. Explain to me again: why are dreamers, poets, intelligent young men like your stepson, drawn to bandits like Nechaev? Because, in your account, isn't that all Nechaev is: a bandit with a smattering of education?'

'I do not know. Perhaps because in young people there is something that has not yet gone to sleep, to which the spirit in Nechaev calls. Perhaps it is in all of us: something we think has been dead for centuries but has only been sleeping. I repeat, I do not know. I am unable to explain the connection between my son and Nechaev. It is a surprise to me. I came here only to fetch Pavel's papers, which are precious to me in ways you will not understand. It is the papers I want, nothing else. I ask again: will you return them to me? They are useless to you. They will tell you nothing about why intelligent young men fall under the sway of evildoers. And they will tell *you* least of all because clearly you do not know how to read. All the time you were reading my son's story – let me say this – I noticed how you were holding yourself at a distance, erecting a barrier of ridicule, as though the words might leap out from the page and strangle you.'

Something has begun to take fire within him while he

has been speaking, and he welcomes it. He leans forward, gripping the arms of his chair.

'What is it that frightens you, Councillor Maximov? When you read about Karamzin or Karamzov or whatever his name is, when Karamzin's skull is cracked open like an egg, what is the truth: do you suffer with him, or do you secretly exult behind the arm that swings the axe? You don't answer? Let me tell you then: reading is being the arm and being the axe *and* being the skull; reading is giving yourself up, not holding yourself at a distance and jeering. If I asked you, I am sure you would say that you are hunting Nechaev down so that you can put him on trial, with due process and lawyers for the defence and prosecution and so forth, and then lock him away for the rest of his life in a clean, well-lit cell. But look into yourself: is that your true wish? Do you not truly want to chop off his head and stamp your feet in his blood?'

He sits back, flushed.

'You are a very clever man, Fyodor Mikhailovich. But you speak of reading as though it were demon-possession. Measured by that standard I fear I am a very poor reader indeed, dull and earthbound. Yet I wonder whether, at this moment, you are not in a fever. If you could see yourself in a mirror I am sure you would understand what I mean. Also, we have had a long conversation, interesting but long, and I have numerous duties to attend to.'

'And I say, the papers you are holding on to so jealously may as well be written in Aramaic for all the good they will do you. Give them back to me!'

Maximov chuckles. 'You supply me with the strongest, most benevolent of reasons not to give in to your request,

Fyodor Mikhailovich, namely that in your present mood the spirit of Nechaev might leap from the page and take complete possession of you. But seriously: you say you know how to read. Will you at some future date read these papers for me, all of them, the Nechaev papers, of which this is only a single file among many?'

'Read them for you?'

'Yes. Give me a reading of them.'

'Why?'

'Because you say I cannot read. Give me a demonstration of how to read. Teach me. Explain to me these ideas that are not ideas.'

For the first time since the telegram arrived in Dresden, he laughs: he can feel the stiff lines of his cheeks breaking. The laugh is harsh and without joy. 'I have always been told,' he says, 'that the police constitute the eyes and ears of society. And now you call on me for help! No, I will not do your reading for you.'

Folding his hands in his lap, closing his eyes, looking more like the Buddha than ever, ageless, sexless, Maximov nods. 'Thank you,' he murmurs. 'Now you must go.'

He emerges into a crowded ante-room. How long has he been closeted with Maximov? An hour? Longer? The bench is full, there are people lounging against the walls, people in the corridors too, where the smell of fresh paint is stifling. All talk ceases; eyes turn on him without sympathy. So many seeking justice, each with a story to tell!

It is nearly noon. He cannot bear the thought of returning to his room. He walks eastward along Sadovaya Street. The sky is low and grey, a cold wind blows; there is ice on the ground and the footing is slippery. A gloomy day, a day for trudging with the head lowered. Yet he cannot stop himself, his eyes move restlessly from one passing figure to the next, searching for the set of the shoulders, the lilt to the walk, that belong to his lost son. By his walk he will recognize him: first the walk, then the form.

He tries to summon up Pavel's face. But the face that appears to him instead, and appears with surprising vividness, is that of a young man with heavy brows and a sparse beard and a thin, tight mouth, the face of the young man who sat behind Bakunin on the stage at the Peace Congress two years ago. His skin is cratered with scars that stand out livid in the cold. 'Go away!' he says, trying to dismiss the image. But it will not go. 'Pavel!' he whispers, conjuring his son in vain.

6

Anna Sergeyevna

He has not been to the shop before. It is smaller than he had imagined, dark and low, half beneath street level. YAKOVLEV GROCER AND MERCHANT reads the sign. A bell tinkles when he opens the door. His eyes take a while to adjust to the gloom.

He is the only customer. Behind the counter stands an old man in a dirty white apron. He pretends to examine the wares: open sacks of buckwheat, flour, dried beans, horsefeed. Then he approaches the counter. 'Some sugar, please,' he says.

'Eh?' says the old man, clearing his throat. His spectacles make his eyes seem tiny as buttons.

'I'd like some sugar.'

She emerges through a curtained doorway at the back of the shop. If she is surprised to see him, she does not show it. 'I will attend to the customer, Avram Davidovich,' she says quietly, and the old man stands aside.

'I came for some sugar,' he repeats.

'Sugar?' There is the faintest smile on her lips.

'Five kopeks' worth.'

Deftly she folds a cone of paper, pinches the bottom

shut, scoops in white sugar, weighs it, folds the cone. Capable hands.

'I have just been to the police. I was trying to get Pavel's papers returned to me.'

'Yes?'

'There are complications I didn't foresee.'

'You will get them back. It takes time. Everything takes time.'

Though there is no cause to do so, he reads into this remark a double meaning. If the old man were not hovering behind her, he would reach across the counter and take her hand.

'That is – ?' he says.

'That is five kopeks.'

Taking the cone, he allows his fingers to brush hers. 'You have lightened my day,' he whispers, so softly that perhaps not even she hears. He bows, bows to Avram Davidovich.

Does he imagine it, or has he somewhere before seen the man in the sheepskin coat and cap who, having dawdled on the other side of the road watching workmen unload bricks, now turns, like him, in the direction of Svechnoi Street?

And sugar. Why of all things did he ask for sugar?

He writes a note to Apollon Maykov. 'I am in Petersburg and have visited the grave,' he writes. 'Thank you for taking care of everything. Thank you too for your many kindnesses to P. over the years. I am eternally in your debt.' He signs the note *D.*

It would be easy to arrange a discreet meeting. But he does not want to compromise his old friend. Maykov, ever generous, will understand, he tells himself: I am in mourning, and people in mourning shun company.

It is a good enough excuse, but it is a lie. He is not in mourning. He has not said farewell to his son, he has not given his son up. On the contrary, he wants his son returned to life.

He writes to his wife: 'He is still here in his room. He is frightened. He has lost his right to stay in this world, but the next world is cold, as cold as the spaces between the stars, and without welcome.' As soon as he has finished the letter he tears it up. It is nonsense; it is also a betrayal of what remains between himself and his son.

His son is inside him, a dead baby in an iron box in the frozen earth. He does not know how to resurrect the baby or – what comes to the same thing – lacks the will to do so. He is paralysed. Even while he is walking down the street, he thinks of himself as paralysed. Every gesture of his hands is made with the slowness of a frozen man. He has no will; or rather, his will has turned into a solid block, a stone that exerts all its dumb weight to draw him down into stillness and silence.

He knows what grief is. This is not grief. This is death, death coming before its time, come not to overwhelm him and devour him but simply to be with him. It is like a dog that has taken up residence with him, a big grey dog, blind and deaf and stupid and immovable. When he sleeps, the dog sleeps; when he wakes, the dog wakes; when he leaves the house, the dog shambles behind him.

His mind dwells sluggishly but insistently on Anna Sergeyevna. When he thinks of her, he thinks of nimble fingers counting coins. Coins, stitches – what do they stand for?

He remembers a peasant girl he saw once at the gate of the convent of St Anne in Tver. She sat with a dead baby at her breast, shrugging off the people who tried to remove the little corpse, smiling beatifically – smiling like St Anne, in fact.

Memories like wisps of smoke. A reed fence in the middle of nowhere, grey and brittle, and a wisp of a figure slipping between the reeds, flat, without weight, the figure of a boy in white. A hamlet on the steppes with a stream and two or three trees and a cow with a bell around its neck and smoke trailing into the sky. The back of beyond, the end of the world. A boy weaving through the reeds, back and forth, in arrested metamorphosis, in purgatorial form.

Visions that come and go, swift, ephemeral. He is not in control of himself. Carefully he pushes paper and pen to the far end of the table and lays his head on his hands. If I am going to faint, he thinks, let me faint at my post.

Another vision. A figure at a well bringing a pan to his lips, a traveller on the point of departing; over the rim, the eyes already abstracted, elsewhere. A brush of hand against hand. Fond touch. 'Goodbye, old friend!' And gone.

Why this plodding chase across empty country after the rumour of a ghost, the ghost of a rumour?

Because I am he. Because he is I. Something there that I seek to grasp: the moment before extinction when the blood still courses, the heart still beats. Heart, the faithful ox that keeps the millwheel turning, that casts up not so much as a glance of puzzlement when the axe is raised on high, but takes the blow and folds at the knees and expires. Not oblivion but the moment before oblivion, when I come panting up to you at the rim of the well and we look upon each other for a last time, knowing we are alive, sharing this one life, our only life. All that I am left to grasp for: the moment of that gaze, salutation and farewell in one, past all arguing, past all pleading: 'Hello, old friend. Goodbye, old friend.' Dry eyes. Tears turned to crystals.

I hold your head between my hands. I kiss your brow. I kiss your lips.

The rule: one look, one only; no glancing back. But I look back.

You stand at the wellside, the wind in your hair, not a soul but a body rarefied, raised to its first, second, third, fourth, fifth essence, gazing upon me with crystal eyes, smiling with golden lips.

Forever I look back. Forever I am absorbed in your gaze. A field of crystal points, dancing, winking, and I one of them. Stars in the sky, and fires on the plain answering them. Two realms signalling to each other.

He falls asleep at the table and sleeps through the rest of the afternoon. At suppertime Matryona taps at the door, but he does not waken. They have supper without him.

Much later, after the child's bedtime, he emerges dressed for the street. Anna Sergeyevna, seated with her back to him, turns. 'Are you going out then?' she says. 'Will you have some tea before you go?'

There is a certain nervousness about her. But the hand that passes him the cup is steady.

She does not invite him to sit down. He drinks his tea in silence, standing before her.

There is something he wants to say, but he is afraid he will not be able to get it out, or will even break down again in front of her. He is not in control of himself.

He puts down the empty cup and lays a hand on her shoulder. 'No,' she says, shaking her head, pushing his hand away, 'that is not how I do things.'

Her hair is drawn back under a heavy enamelled clasp. He loosens the clasp and lays it on the table. Now she does not resist, but shakes her hair till it hangs loose.

'Everything else will follow, I promise,' he says. He is conscious of his age; in his voice he hears no trace of the erotic edge that women would once upon a time respond to. Instead there is something to which he does not care to give a name. A cracked instrument, a voice that has undergone its second breaking. 'Everything,' he repeats.

She is searching his face with an earnestness and intentness he cannot mistake. Then she puts aside her sewing. Slipping past his hands, she disappears into the curtained alcove.

He waits, unsure. Nothing happens. He follows her and parts the curtains.

Matryona lies fast asleep, her lips open, her fair hair spread on the pillow like a nimbus. Anna Sergeyevna has half unbuttoned her dress. With a wave of the hand and a cross look in which there is nevertheless a touch of amusement, she orders him out.

He sits down and waits. She emerges in her shift, her feet bare. The veins on her feet stand out blue. Not a young woman; not an innocent surrendering herself. Yet her hands, when he takes them, are cold and trembling. She will not meet his eyes. 'Fyodor Mikhailovich,' she whispers, 'I want you to know I have not done this before.'

She wears a silver chain around her neck. With his finger he follows the loop of the chain till he comes to the little crucifix. He raises the crucifix to her lips; warmly and without hesitation she kisses it. But when he tries to kiss her, she averts her head. 'Not now,' she whispers.

They spend the night together in his son's room. What happens between them happens in the dark from beginning to end. In their lovemaking he is struck above all by the heat of her body. It is not at all as he had expected. It is as if at her core she were on fire. It excites him intensely, and it excites him too that they should be doing such fiery, dangerous work with the child asleep in the next room.

He falls asleep. Sometime in the middle of the night he wakes with her still beside him in the narrow bed. Though he is exhausted, he tries to arouse her. She does not respond; when he forces himself on her, she becomes like a dead thing in his arms.

In the act there is nothing he can call pleasure or even sensation. It is as though they are making love through a sheet, the grey, tattered sheet of his grief. At the moment of climax he plunges back into sleep as into a lake. As he sinks Pavel rises to meet him. His son's face is contorted in despair: his lungs are bursting, he knows he is dying, he knows he is past hope, he calls to his father because that is the last thing left he can do, the last thing in the world. He calls out in a strangled rush of words. This is the vision in its ugly extremity that rushes at him out of the vortex of darkness into which he is descending inside the woman's body. It bursts upon him, possesses him, speeds on.

When he wakes again it is light. The apartment is empty.

He passes the day in a fever of impatience. Thinking

of her, he quivers with desire like a young man. But what possesses him is not the tight-throated *douceur* of twenty years ago. Rather, he feels like a leaf or a seed in the grip of a headlong force, a winged seed drawn up into the highest windstream, carried dizzily above the oceans.

Over supper Anna Sergeyevna is self-possessed and distant, confining her attention to the child, listening single-mindedly to the rambling narrative of her day at school. When she needs to address him, she is polite but cool. Her coolness only inflames him. Can it be that the avid glances he steals at the mother's throat, lips, arms pass the child entirely by?

He waits for the silence that will mean Matryona has gone to bed. Instead, at nine o'clock the light next door is extinguished. For half an hour he waits, and another half-hour. Then with a shielded candle, in his stockinged feet, he creeps out. The candle casts huge bobbing shadows. He sets it down on the floor and crosses to the alcove.

In the dim light he makes out Anna Sergeyevna on the farther side of the bed, her back to him, her arms gracefully above her head like a dancer's, her dark hair loose. On the near side, curled with her thumb in her mouth and one arm cast loosely over her mother, is Matryona. His immediate impression is that she is awake, watching him, guarding her mother; but when he bends over her, her breathing is deep and even.

He whispers the name: 'Anna!' She does not stir.

He returns to his room, trying to be calm. There are perfectly sound reasons, he tells himself, why she might prefer to keep to herself tonight. But he is beyond the reach of his own persuading.

A second time he tiptoes across the room. The two

women have not stirred. Again he has the uncanny feeling that Matryona is watching him. He bends closer.

He is not mistaken: he is staring into open, unblinking eyes. A chill runs through him. She sleeps with her eyes open, he tells himself. But it is not true. She is awake and has been awake all the time; thumb in mouth, she has been watching his every motion with unremitting vigilance. As he peers, holding his breath, the corners of her mouth seem to curve faintly upward in a victorious, bat-like grin. And the arm too, extended loosely over her mother, is like a wing.

They have one more night together, after which the gate closes. She comes to his room late and without warning. Again, through her, he passes into darkness and into the waters where his son floats among the other drowned. 'Do not be afraid,' he wants to whisper, 'I will be with you, I will divide the bitterness with you.'

He wakes sprawled across her, his lips to her ear.

'Do you know where I have been?' he whispers.

She eases herself out from under him.

'Do you know where you took me?' he whispers.

There is an urge in him to show the boy off to her, show him in the springtime of his powers, with his flashing eyes and his clear jaw and his handsome mouth. He wants to clothe him again in the white suit, wants the clear, deep voice to be heard again from his chest. 'See what a treasure is gone from the world!' he wants to cry out: 'See what we have lost!'

She has turned her back to him. His hand strokes her long thigh urgently, up and down. She stops him. 'I must go,' she says, and gets up.

The next night she does not come, but stays with her

daughter. He writes her a letter and leaves it on the table. When he gets up in the morning the apartment is empty and the letter still there, unopened.

He visits the shop. She is at the counter; but as soon as she sees him she slips into the back room, leaving old Yakovlev to attend to him.

In the evening he is waiting on the street, and follows her home like a footpad. He catches her in the entryway.

'Why are you avoiding me?'

'I am not avoiding you.'

He takes her by the arm. It is dark, she is carrying a basket, she cannot free herself. He presses himself against her, drawing in the walnut scent of her hair. He tries to kiss her, but she turns away and his lips brush her ear. Nothing in the pressure of her body answers to him. Disgrace, he thinks: this is how one enters disgrace.

He stands aside, but on the stairway catches up with her again. 'One word more,' he says: 'Why?'

She turns toward him. 'Isn't it obvious? Must I spell it out?'

'What is obvious? Nothing is obvious.'

'You were suffering. You were pleading.'

He recoils. 'That is not the truth!'

'You were in need. It is nothing to be ashamed of. But now it is finished. It will do you no good to go on, and it does me no good either to be used in this way.'

'Used? I am not using you! Nothing could be further from my mind!'

'You are using me to get to someone else. Don't be upset. I am explaining myself, not accusing you. But I don't want to be dragged in any further. You have a wife of your own. You should wait till you are with her again.'

A wife of your own. Why does she drag his wife in? *My*

 wife is too young! – that is what he wants to say – *too young for me as I am now!* But how can he say it?

Yet what she says is true, truer than she knows. When he returns to Dresden, the wife he embraces will be changed, will be infused with the trace he will bring back of this subtle, sensually gifted widow. Through his wife he will be reaching to this woman, just as through this woman he reaches – to whom?

Does he betray what he is thinking? With a sudden angry flush, she shakes his hand from her sleeve and climbs the stairs, leaving him behind.

He follows, shuts himself in his room, and tries to calm himself. The pounding of his heart slows. *Pavel!* he whispers over and over, using the word as a charm. But what comes to him inexorably is the form not of Pavel but of the other one, Sergei Nechaev.

He can no longer deny it: a gap is opening between himself and the dead boy. He is angry with Pavel, angry at being betrayed. It does not surprise him that Pavel should have been drawn into radical circles, or that he should have breathed no word of it in his letters. But Nechaev is a different matter. Nechaev is no student hothead, no youthful nihilist. He is the Mongol left behind in the Russian soul after the greatest nihilist of all has withdrawn into the wastes of Asia. And Pavel, of all people, a foot-soldier in his army!

He remembers a pamphlet entitled 'Catechism of a Revolutionary,' circulated in Geneva as Bakunin's but clearly, in its inspiration and even its wording, Nechaev's. 'The revolutionary is a doomed man,' it began. 'He has no interests, no feelings, no attachments, not even a name. Everything in him is absorbed in a single and total passion: revolution. In the depths of his being he has cut all links with the civil order, with law and morality. He continues to exist in society only in order to destroy it.' And later: 'He does not expect the least mercy. Every day he is ready to die.'

He is ready to die, he does not expect mercy: easy to say the words, but what child can comprehend the fullness of their meaning? Not Pavel; perhaps not even Nechaev, that unloved and unlovely young man.

A memory of Nechaev himself returns, standing alone in a corner of the reception hall in Geneva, glaring, wolfing down food. He shakes his head, trying to expunge it. 'Pavel! Pavel!' he whispers, calling the absent one.

A tap at the door. Matryona's voice: 'Suppertime!'

At table he makes an effort to be pleasant. Tomorrow is Sunday: he suggests an outing to Petrovsky Island, where in the afternoon there will be a fair and a band. Matryona is eager to go; to his surprise, Anna Sergeyevna consents.

He arranges to meet them after church. In the morning, on his way out, he stumbles over something in the dark entryway: a tramp, lying there asleep with a musty old blanket pulled over him. He curses; the man gives a whimper and sits up.

He arrives at St Gregory's before the service is over. As he waits in the portico, the same tramp appears, bleary-eyed, smelly. He turns upon him. 'Are you following me?' he demands.

Though they are not six inches apart, the tramp pretends not to hear or see. Angrily he repeats his question. Worshippers, filing out, glance curiously at the two of them.

The man sidles off. Half a block away he stops, leans

 against a wall, feigns a yawn. He has no gloves; he uses the blanket, rolled into a ball, as a muff.

Anna Sergeyevna and her daughter emerge. It is a long walk to the park, along Voznesensky Prospekt and across the foot of Vasilevsky Island. Even before they get to the park he knows he has made a mistake, a stupid mistake. The bandstand is empty, the fields around the skaters' pond bare save for strutting gulls.

He apologizes to Anna Sergeyevna. 'There's lots of time, it's not yet noon,' she replies cheerfully. 'Shall we go for a walk?'

Her good humour surprises him; he is even more surprised when she takes his arm. With Matryona at her other side they stride across the fields. A family, he thinks: only a fourth required and we will be complete. As if reading his thoughts, Anna Sergeyevna presses his arm.

They pass a flock of sheep huddled in a reed thicket. Matryona approaches them with a handful of grass; they break and scatter. A peasant boy with a stick emerges from the thicket and scowls at her. For an instant it seems that words will pass. Then the boy thinks better of it and Matryona slips back to them.

The exercise is bringing a glow to her cheeks. She will be a beauty yet, he thinks: she will break hearts.

He wonders what his wife would think. His indiscretions hitherto have been followed by remorse and, on the heels of remorse, a voluptuous urge to confess. These confessions, tortured in expression yet vague in point of detail, have confused and infuriated his wife, bedevilling their marriage far more than the infidelities themselves.

But in the present case he feels no guilt. On the contrary, he has an invincible sense of his own rightness.

He wonders what this sense of rightness conceals; but he does not really want to know. For the present there is something like joy in his heart. *Forgive me, Pavel,* he whispers to himself. But again he does not really mean it.

If only I had my life over again, he thinks; if only I were young! And perhaps also: If only I had the use of the life, the youth that Pavel threw away!

And what of the woman at his side? Does she regret the impulse by which she gave herself to him? Had that never happened, today's outing might mark the opening of a proper courtship. For that is surely what a woman wants: to be courted, wooed, persuaded, won! Even when she surrenders, she wants to give herself up not frankly but in a delicious haze of confusion, resisting yet unresisting. Falling, but never an irrevocable falling. No: to fall and then come back from the fall new, remade, virginal, ready to be wooed again and to fall again. A playing with death, a play of resurrection.

What would she do if she knew what he was thinking? Draw back in outrage? And would that be part of the play too?

He steals a glance at her, and in that instant it comes home to him: *I could love this woman*. More than the tug of the body, he feels what he can only call kinship with her. He and she are of the same kind, the same generation. And all of a sudden the generations fall into place: Pavel and Matryona and his wife Anna ranked on the one side, he and Anna Sergeyevna on the other. The children against those who are not children, those old enough to recognize in their lovemaking the first foretaste of death. Hence the urgency that night, hence the heat. She in his arms like Jeanne d'Arc in the flames: the spirit wrestling against its bonds while the body burns away. A struggle with time. Something a child would never understand.

'Pavel said you were in Siberia.'

Her words startle him out of his reverie.

'For ten years. That is where I met Pavel's mother. In Semipalatinsk. Her husband was in the customs service. He died when Pavel was seven. She died too, a few years ago – Pavel must have told you.'

'And then you married again.'

'Yes. What did Pavel have to say about that?'

'Only that your wife is young.'

'My wife and Pavel are of much the same age. For a while we lived together, the three of us, in an apartment on Meshchanskaya Street. It was not a happy time for Pavel. He felt a certain rivalry with my wife. In fact, when I told him she and I were engaged, he went to her and warned her quite seriously that I was too old for her. Afterwards he used to refer to himself as *the orphan*: "The orphan would like another slice of toast," "The orphan has no money," and so forth. We pretended it was a joke, but it wasn't. It made for a troubled household.'

'I can imagine that. But one can sympathize with him, surely. He must have felt he was losing you.'

'How could he have lost me? From the day I became his father I never once failed him. Am I failing him now?'

'Of course not, Fyodor Mikhailovich. But children are possessive. They have jealous phases, like all of us. And when we are jealous, we make up stories against ourselves. We work up our own feelings, we frighten ourselves.'

Her words, like a prism, have only to be shifted slightly

in their angle to reflect a quite different meaning. Is that what she intends?

He casts a glance at Matryona. She is wearing new boots with fluffy sheepskin fringes. Stamping her heels into the damp grass, she leaves a trail of indented prints. Her brow is knitted in concentration.

'He said you used him to carry messages.'

A stab of pain goes through him. So Pavel remembered that!

'Yes, that is true. The year before we were married, on her name-day, I asked him to take a present to her from me. It was a mistake that I regretted afterwards, regretted deeply. It was inexcusable. I did not think. Was that the worst?'

'The worst?'

'Did Pavel tell you of things that were worse than that? I would like to know, so that when I ask forgiveness I know what I have been guilty of.'

She glances at him oddly. 'That is not a fair question, Fyodor Mikhailovich. Pavel went through lonely spells. He would talk, I would listen. Stories would come out, not always pleasant stories. But perhaps it was good that it was so. Once he had brought the past into the open, perhaps he could stop brooding about it.'

'Matryona!' He turns to the child. 'Did Pavel say anything to you – '

But Anna Sergeyevna interrupts him. 'I am sure Pavel didn't,' she says; and then, turning on him softly but furiously: 'You can't ask a child a question like that!'

They stop and face each other on the bare field. Matryona looks away scowling, her lips clamped tight; Anna Sergeyevna glares.

'It is getting cold,' she says. 'Shall we turn back?'

7

Matryona

He does not accompany them home, but has his evening meal at an inn. In a back room there is a card game going on. He watches for a while, and drinks, but does not play. It is late when he returns to the darkened apartment, the empty room.

Alone, lonely, he allows himself a twinge of longing, not unpleasant in itself, for Dresden and the comfortable regularity of life there, with a wife who jealously guards his privacy and organizes the family day around his habits.

He is not at home at No. 63 and never will be. Not only is he the most transient of sojourners, his excuse for staying on as obscure to others as to himself, but he feels the strain of living at close quarters with a woman of volatile moods and a child who may all too easily begin to find his bodily presence offensive. In Matryona's company he is keenly aware that his clothes have begun to smell, that his skin is dry and flaky, that the dental plates he wears click when he talks. His haemorrhoids, too, cause him endless discomfort. The iron constitution that took him through Siberia is beginning to crack; and this spectacle of decay must be all the more distasteful to a child, herself finical about cleanliness, in whose eyes he has supplanted a being of godlike strength and beauty. When her playmates ask about the funereal visitor who refuses to pack his belongings and leave, what, he wonders, does she reply?

You were pleading: when he thinks of Anna Sergeyevna's words he flinches. To have been an object of pity all the time! He goes down on his knees, rests his forehead against the bed, tries to find his way to Yelagin Island and to Pavel in his cold grave. Pavel, at least, will not turn on him. On Pavel he can rely, on Pavel and Pavel's icy love.

The father, faded copy of the son. How can he expect a woman who beheld the son in the pride of his days to look with favour on the father?

He remembers the words of a fellow-prisoner in Siberia: 'Why are we given old age, brothers? So that we can grow small again, small enough to crawl through the eye of a needle.' Peasant wisdom.

He kneels and kneels, but Pavel does not come. Sighing, he clambers at last into bed.

He awakes full of surprise. Though it is still dark, he feels as if he has rested enough for seven nights. He is fresh and invincible; the very tissues of his brain seem washed clean. He can barely contain himself. He is like a child at Easter, on fire for the household to wake up so that he can share his joy with them. He wants to wake her, the woman, he wants the two of them to dance through the apartment: 'Christ is risen!' he wants to call out, and hear her respond 'Christ is risen!' and clash her egg against his. The two of them dancing in a circle with their painted eggs, and Matryosha as well, in her nightdress, stumbling sleepy-eyed and happy amid their legs; and the ghost of the fourth one too, weaving between them, clumsy, big-footed, smiling: children together, newborn, released from the tomb. And over the city dawn breaking, and the roosters in the yards crowing their welcome of the new day.

Joy breaking like a dawn! But only for an instant. It is not merely that clouds begin to cross this new, radiant sky. It is as if, at the moment when the sun comes forth in its glory, another sun appears too, a shadow sun, an anti-sun sliding across its face. The word *omen* crosses his mind in all its dark, ominous weight. The dawning sun is there not for itself but to undergo eclipse; joy shines out only to reveal what the annihilation of joy will be like.

In a single hasty movement he is out of bed. The next few minutes stretch before him like a dark passage down which he must scurry. He must dress and get out of the apartment before the shame of the fit descends; he must find a place out of sight, out of the hearing of decent people, where he can manage the episode as best he can.

He lets himself out. The corridor is in pitch darkness. Stretching out his arms like a blind man, he gropes his way to the head of the stairs and, holding to the banister, taking one step at a time, begins to descend. On the second-floor landing a wave of terror overtakes him, terror without object. He sits down in a corner and holds his head. His hands are smelly from something he has touched, but he does not wipe them. Let it come, he thinks in despair; I have done all I can.

There is a cry that echoes down the stairwell, so loud and so frightful that sleepers are woken by it. As for him, he hears nothing, he is gone, there is no longer time.

When he wakes it is into darkness so dense that he can feel it pressing upon his eyeballs. He has no idea where he is, no idea who he is. He is a wakefulness, a consciousness, that is all. It is as if he has been born a minute ago, born into a world of unrelieved night.

Be calm, says this consciousness, addressing itself, trying to quell its own panic: you have been here before – wait, something will come back.

A body falls vertically through space inside him. He is that body. There is a rush of air: he is the one who feels the rush. There is a throat choked with terror: it is his throat.

Let it die, he thinks: let it die!

He tries to move an arm but the arm is trapped under his body. Stupidly he tries to tug it free. There is a bad smell, his clothes are damp. Like ice forming in water, memories begin at last to coagulate: who he is, where he is; and together with memory an urgent desire to get away from this place before he is discovered in all his disgrace.

These attacks are the burden he carries with him through the world. To no one has he ever confessed how much of his time he spends listening for premonitions of them, trying to read the signs. Why am I accursed? he cries out within himself, pounding the earth with his staff, commanding the rock to yield an answer. But he is not Moses, the rock does not split. Nor do the trances themselves provide illumination. They are not visitations. Far from it: they are nothing – mouthfuls of his life sucked out of him as if by a whirlwind that leaves behind not even a memory of darkness.

He rises and gropes his way down the last flight of stairs. He is shivering, his whole body is cold. Dawn is breaking as he emerges into the open. It has been snowing. Over the fallen snow lies a haze of pulsing scarlet. The colour is not in the snow but in his eyes; he cannot get rid of it. An eyelid twitches so irritatingly that he claps a cold hand over it. His head aches as though a fist were clenching and unclenching inside it. His hat is lost somewhere on the stairway.

Bareheaded, in soiled clothes, he trudges through the snow to the little Church of the Redeemer near Kameny Bridge and shelters there till he is sure Matryona and her mother have gone out. Then he returns to the apartment, warms water, strips naked, and washes himself. He washes his underwear too, and hangs it in the washroom. Fortunate for Pavel, he thinks, that he did not have to suffer the falling sickness, fortunate he was not born of me! Then the irony of his words bursts in upon him and he gnashes his teeth. His head thunders with pain, the red haze still colours everything. He lies down in his dressing-gown, rocks himself to sleep.

An hour later he awakes in an angry and irritable mood. Cones of pain seem to go back from his eyes into his head. His skin is like paper and tender to the touch.

Naked under his dressing-gown, he pads through Anna Sergeyevna's apartment, opening cupboards, looking through drawers. Everything is in order, neat and prim.

In one drawer, wrapped in scarlet velveteen, he finds a picture of a younger Anna Sergeyevna side by side with a man whom he takes to be the printer Kolenkin. Dressed in his Sunday best, Kolenkin looks gaunt and old and tired. What kind of marriage could it have been for this intense and darkly handsome young woman? And why is the picture stuck away in a drawer? Putting it back, he deliberately smudges the glass, leaving his thumbprint over the face of the dead man.

As a child he used to spy on visitors to the household and trespass surreptitiously on their privacy. It is a weakness that he has associated till now with a refusal to accept limits to what he is permitted to know, with the reading of forbidden books, and thus with his vocation. Today, however, he is not inclined to be charitable to himself. He is in thrall to a spirit of petty evil and knows it. The truth is, rummaging like this through Anna Sergeyevna's possessions while she is out gives him a voluptuous quiver of pleasure.

He closes the last drawer and roams about restlessly, not sure what next to do.

He opens Pavel's suitcase and dons the white suit. Hitherto he has worn it as a gesture to the dead boy, a gesture of defiance and love. But now, looking in the mirror, he sees only a seedy imposture and, beyond that, something surreptitious and obscene, something that belongs behind the locked doors and curtained windows of rooms where men in wigs and skirts bare their rumps to be flogged.

It is past midday and his head still aches. He lies down, pressing an arm across his eyes as if to ward off a blow. Everything spins; he has the sensation of falling into endless blackness. When he comes back he has again lost all sense of who he is. He knows the word *I*, but as he stares at it it becomes as enigmatic as a rock in the middle of a desert.

Just a dream, he thinks; at any moment I will awake and all will be well again. For an instant he is allowed to believe. Then the truth bursts over him and overwhelms him.

The door creaks and Matryona peers in. She is clearly surprised to see him. 'Are you sick?' she asks, frowning.

He makes no effort to reply.

'Why are you wearing that suit?'

'If I don't, who will?'

A flicker of impatience crosses her face.

'Do you know the story of Pavel's suit?' he says.

She shakes her head.

He sits up and motions her to the foot of the bed. 'Come here. It is a long story, but I will tell you. The year before last, while I was still abroad, Pavel went to stay with his aunt in Tver. Just for the summer. Do you know where Tver is?'

'It's near Moscow.'

'It's on the way to Moscow. Quite a big town. In Tver there lived a retired officer, a captain, whose sister kept house for him. The sister's name was Maria Timofeyevna. She was a cripple. She was also weak in the head. A good soul, but not capable of taking care of herself.'

He notices how quickly he has fallen into the rhythms of storytelling. Like a piston-engine, incapable of any other motion.

'The captain, Maria's brother, was unfortunately a drunkard. When he was drunk he used to ill-treat her. Afterwards he would remember nothing.'

'What did he do to her?'

'He beat her. That was all. Old-fashioned Russian beating. She did not hold it against him. Perhaps, in her simplicity, she thought that is what the world is: a place where you get beaten.'

He has her attention. Now he turns the screw.

'That is how a dog must see the world, after all, or a horse. Why should Maria be different? A horse does not understand that it has been born into the world to pull carts. It thinks it is here to be beaten. It thinks of a cart as a huge object it is tied to so that it cannot run away while it is being beaten.'

'Don't . . . ,' she whispers.

He knows: she rejects with all her soul the vision of the world he is offering. She wants to believe in goodness. But her belief is tentative, without resilience. He feels no mercy toward her. *This is Russia!* he wants to say, forcing the words upon her, rubbing her face in them. In Russia you cannot afford to be a delicate flower. In Russia you must be a burdock or a dandelion.

'One day the captain came visiting. He was not a particular friend of Pavel's aunt, but he came anyway and brought his sister too. Perhaps he had been drinking. Pavel was not at home at the time.

'A visitor from Moscow, a young man who wasn't familiar with the situation, got into conversation with Maria and began to draw her out. Perhaps he was only being polite. On the other hand, perhaps he was being mischievous. Maria got excited, her imagination began to run away with her. She confided to this visitor that she was betrothed, or, as she said, "promised." "And is your fiancé from the district?" he inquired. "Yes, from nearby," she replied, giving Pavel's aunt a coy smile (you must think of Maria as a tall, gangling woman with a loud voice, by no means young or pretty).

'To keep up appearances, Pavel's aunt had then to pretend to congratulate her, and to pretend to congratulate the captain too. The captain was of course in a fury with his sister, and, as soon as he got her home again, beat her without mercy.'

'Wasn't it true, then?'

'No, it wasn't true at all, except in her own mind. And – it now emerged – the man she was convinced was going to marry her was none other than Pavel. Where she got the idea I don't know. Maybe he gave her a smile one day, or complimented her on her bonnet – Pavel had a kind heart, that was one of the nicest things about him, wasn't it? And maybe she went home dreaming about him, and in no time dreamed she was in love with him and he with her.'

As he speaks he watches the child sidelong. She wriggles and for a moment actually puts her thumb in her mouth.

'You can imagine what fun Tver society had with the story of Maria and her phantom suitor. But now let me tell you about Pavel. When Pavel heard the story, he went straight out and ordered a smart white suit. And the next thing he did was to call on the Lebyatkins, wearing his white suit and bearing flowers – roses, I believe. And though Captain Lebyatkin didn't at first take kindly to it, Pavel won him over. To Maria he behaved very considerately, very politely, like a complete gentleman, though he was not yet twenty. The visits went on all summer, till he left Tver and came back to Petersburg. It was a lesson to everyone, a lesson in chivalry. A lesson to me too. That is the kind of boy Pavel was. And that is the history of the white suit.'

'And Maria?'

'Maria? Maria is still in Tver, as far as I know.'

'But does she know?'

'Does she know about Pavel? Probably not.'

'Why did he kill himself?'

'Do you think he killed himself?'

'Mama says he killed himself.'

'No one kills himself, Matryosha. You can put your life in danger but you cannot actually kill yourself. It is more likely that Pavel put himself at risk, to see whether God loved him enough to save him. He asked God a question – Will you save me? – and God gave him an answer. God said: No. God said: Die.'

'God killed him?'

'God said no. God could have said: Yes, I will save you. But he preferred to say no.'

'Why?' she whispers.

'He said to God: If you love me, save me. If you are there, save me. But there was only silence. Then he said: I know you are there, I know you hear me. I will wager my life that you will save me. And still God said nothing. Then he said: However much you stay silent, I know you hear me. I am going to make my wager – now! And he threw down his wager. And God did not appear. God did not intervene.'

'Why?' she whispers again.

He smiles an ugly, crooked, bearded smile. 'Who knows? Perhaps God does not like to be tempted. Perhaps the principle that he should not be tempted is more important to him than the life of one child. Or perhaps the reason is simply that God does not hear very well. God must be very old by now, as old as the world or even older. Perhaps he is hard of hearing and weak of vision too, like any old man.'

She is defeated. She has no more questions. Now she is ready, he thinks. He pats the bed beside him.

Hanging her head, she slides closer. He folds her within the circle of his arm; he can feel her trembling. He strokes her hair, her temples. At last she gives way and, pressing herself against him, balling her fists under her chin, sobs freely.

'I don't understand,' she sobs. 'Why did he have to die?'

He would like to be able to say: He did not die, he is here, I am he; but he cannot.

He thinks of the seed that for a while went on living in the body after the breathing had stopped, not yet knowing it would never find issue.

'I know you love him,' he whispers hoarsely. 'He knows that too. You have a good heart.'

If the seed could only have been taken out of the body, even a single seed, and given a home!

He thinks of a little terracotta statue he saw in the ethnographic museum in Berlin: the Indian god Shiva lying on his back, blue and dead, and riding on him the figure of a terrible goddess, many-armed, wide-mouthed, staring-eyed, ecstatic – riding him, drawing the divine seed out of him.

He has no difficulty in imagining this child in her ecstasy. His imagination seems to have no bounds.

He thinks of a baby, frozen, dead, buried in an iron coffin beneath the snow-piled earth, waiting out the winter, waiting for the spring.

This is as far as the violation goes: the girl in the crook of his arm, the five fingers of his hand, white and dumb, gripping her shoulder. But she might as well be sprawled out naked. One of those girls who give themselves because their natural motion is to be good, to submit. He thinks of child-prostitutes he has known, here and in Germany; he thinks of men who search out such girls because beneath the garish paint and provocative clothes they detect something that outrages them, a certain inviolability, a certain maidenliness. *She is prostituting the Virgin*, such a man says, recognizing the flavour of innocence in the gesture with which the girl cups her breasts for him, in the movement with which she spreads her thighs. In the tiny room with its stale odours, she gives off a faint, desperate smell of spring, of flowers, that he cannot bear. Deliberately, with teeth clenched, he hurts her, and then hurts her again and again, watching her face all the time for something that goes beyond mere wincing, mere bearing of pain: for the sudden wide-eyed look of a creature that begins to understand its life is in danger.

The vision, the fit, the rictus of the imagination, passes. He soothes her a last time, withdraws his arm, finds a way of being with her as he was before.

'Are you going to make a shrine?' she says.

'I hadn't thought of it.'

'You can make a shrine in the corner, with a candle. Then you can put his picture there. If you like, I can keep the candle lit while you are not here.'

'A shrine is meant to stand forever, Matryosha. Your mother will want to let this room when I am gone.'

'When are you going?'

'I am not sure yet,' he says, evading the trap. And then: 'Mourning for a dead child has no end. Is that what you want to hear me say? I say it. It is true.'

Whether because she picks up a change in his tone or because he has found a raw nerve, she flinches noticeably.

'If you were to die your mother would mourn you for the rest of her life.' And, surprising himself, he adds: 'I too.'

Is it true? No, not yet; but perhaps it is about to be true.

'Then may I light a candle for him?'

'Yes, you may.'

'And keep it burning?'

'Yes. But why is the candle so important to you?'

She wriggles uncomfortably. 'So that he won't be in the dark,' she says at last.

Curious, but that is how he has sometimes imagined it too. A ship at sea, a stormy night, a boy lost overboard. Beating about in the waves, keeping himself somehow afloat, the boy shouts in terror: he breathes and shouts, breathes and shouts after the ship that has been his home, that is his home no longer. There is a lantern at the stern on which he fixes his eyes, a speck of light in a wilderness of night and water. As long as I can see that light, he tells himself, I am not lost.

'Can I light the candle now?' she asks.

'If you like. But we won't put the picture there, not yet.'

She lights a candle and sets it beneath the mirror. Then, with a trustingness that takes him by surprise, she returns to the bed and rests her head on his arm. Together they regard the steady candle-flame. From the street below come the sounds of children at play. His fingers close over her shoulder, he draws her tight against him. He can feel the soft young bones fold, one over another, as a bird's wing folds.

8

Ivanov

He enters sleep, as he enters sleep each night, with the intent of finding his way to Pavel. But on this night he is woken – almost at once, it seems – by a voice, thin to the point of being disembodied, calling from the street below. *Isaev!* the voice calls, over and over, patiently.

The wind in the reeds, that is all, he thinks, and slips gratefully back into sleep. Summertime, the wind in the reeds, a blue sky flecked with high cloud, and he tramping along a stream, whistling, a cane in his hand with which he idly lashes the reeds. A whirr of weaver-birds. He halts, stands still to listen. The song of the grasshoppers ceases too; there is only the sound of his breathing and the reeds shaking in the wind. *Isaev!* calls the wind.

He gives a start and is at once wide awake. It is the dead of night, the whole house is still. Crossing to the window, peering into moonlight and shadow, he waits for the call to be renewed. At last it comes. It has the same pitch, the same length, the same inflection as the word that still echoes in his ears, but it is not a human call at all. It is the unhappy wail of a dog.

Not Pavel, then, calling to be fetched in – only a thing that does not concern him, a dog howling for its father. Well, let the dog-father, whoever he is, go out in the cold and dark and gather in his arms his gross, smelly child. Let him be the one to soothe it and sing to it and lull it to sleep.

The dog howls again. No hint of empty plains and silver light: a dog, not a wolf; a dog, not his son. Therefore? Therefore he must throw off this lethargy! *Because* it is not his son he must not go back to bed but must get dressed and answer the call. If he expects his son to come as a thief in the night, and listens only for the call of the thief, he will never see him. If he expects his son to speak in the voice of the unexpected, he will never hear him. As long as he expects what he does not expect, what he does not expect will not come. Therefore – paradox within paradox, darkness swaddled in darkness – he must answer to what he does not expect.

From the third floor it had seemed easy to find the dog. But when he reaches street level he is confused. Does the crying come from left or from right, from one of the buildings across the street or from behind the buildings or perhaps from a courtyard within one of the buildings? And which building? And what of the cries themselves, which now seem to be not only shorter and lower but of a different timbre altogether – almost not the same cries, in fact?

He searches back and forth before he finds the alley used by the nightsoil carriers. In a branch of this alley he at last comes upon the dog. It is tethered to a drainpipe by a slim chain; the chain has become wrapped around a foreleg, jerking the leg up awkwardly whenever it tightens. At his approach the dog retreats as far as it can, whining. It flattens its ears, prostrates itself, rolls on its back. A bitch. He bends over it, unwinds the chain. Dogs smell fear, but even in the cold he can smell this dog's rank terror. He tickles it behind the ear. Still on its back, it timidly licks his wrist.

Is this what I will be doing for the rest of my days, he wonders: peering into the eyes of dogs and beggars?

The dog gives a heave and is on its feet. Though he is not fond of dogs, he does not draw back from this one but crouches as its warm, wet tongue licks his face, his ears, licks the salt from his beard.

He gives it a last stroke and gets up. In the moonlight he cannot make out his watchface. The dog tugs at its chain, whining, eager. Who would chain a dog outdoors on a night like this? Nevertheless, he does not set it loose. Instead he turns abruptly and departs, pursued by forlorn howls.

Why me? he thinks as he hurries away. Why should I bear all the world's burdens? As for Pavel, if he is to have nothing else, let him at least have his death to himself, let his death not be taken from him and turned into the occasion of his father's reformation.

It is no good. His reasoning – specious, contemptible – does not for one moment take him in. Pavel's death does not belong to Pavel – that is just a trick of language. As long as he is here, Pavel's death is his death. Wherever he goes he bears Pavel with him, like a baby blue with cold ('Who will save the blue baby?' he seems to hear within him, plaintive words that come from he does not know where, in a peasant's singsong voice).

Pavel will not speak, will not tell him what to do. 'Raise up that least thing and cherish it': if he knew the words came from Pavel he would obey them without question. But they do not. *That least thing*: is the least thing the dog, abandoned in the cold? Is the dog the thing he must release and take with him and feed and cherish, or is it the filthy, drunken beggar in his tattered coat under the bridge? A terrible hopelessness comes over him which is connected – how, he does not know – to the fact that he has no idea what time it is, but whose core is a growing certainty that he will never again go out in the night to answer a dog's call, that an opportunity for leaving himself as he is behind and becoming what he might yet be has passed. I am I, he thinks despairingly, manacled to myself till the day I die. Whatever it was that wavered toward me, I was unworthy of it, and now it has withdrawn.

Yet even in the instant of closing the door upon himself he is aware there is still a chance to return to the alley, unchain the dog, bring it to the entryway to No. 63, and make some kind of bed for it at the foot of the stairs – though, he knows, once he has brought it so far it will insist on following him further, and, if he chains it again, will whine and bark till the whole building is roused. *It is not my son, it is just a dog*, he protests. *What is it to me?* Yet even as he protests he knows the answer: Pavel will not be saved till he has freed the dog and brought it into his bed, brought *the least thing*, the beggarmen and the beggarwomen too, and much else he does not yet know of; and even then there will be no certainty.

He gives a great groan of despair. *What am I to do?* he thinks. If I were only in touch with my heart, might it be given to me to know? Yet it is not his heart he has lost touch with but the truth. Or – the other side of the same thought – it is not the truth he has lost touch with at all: on the contrary, truth has been pouring down upon him like a waterfall, without moderation, till now he is drowning in it. And then he thinks (reverse the thought and reverse the reversal too: by such Jesuitical tricks must one think nowadays!): Drowning under the falls, what is it that I need? More water, more flood, a deeper drowning.

Standing in the middle of the snow-covered street, he brings his cold hands to his face, smells the dog on them, touches the cold tears on his cheeks, tastes them. Salt, for those who need salt. He suspects he will not save the dog, not this night nor even the next night, if there is to be a next night. He is waiting for a sign, and he is betting (there is no grander word he dare use) that the dog is not the sign, is not a sign at all, is just a dog among many dogs howling in the night. But he knows too that as long as he tries by cunning to distinguish things that are things from things that are signs he will not be saved. That is the logic by which he will be defeated; and, feeling its iron hardness, he is at his wits' end, like a dog on a chain that breaks the teeth that gnaw it. And beware, beware, he reminds himself: the dog on the chain, the second dog, is nothing in itself, is not an illumination, merely an animal likeness!

With his fists bunched in his pockets, his head bowed, his legs stiff as rods, he stands in the middle of the street feeling the dog's spittle turn to ice on his beard.

Is it possible that at this moment, in the shadowed doorway of No. 63, someone is lurking, watching him? Of the body of the watcher he cannot be sure; even the patch of lighter gloom that he thinks of as the face could be no more than a fleck on the wall. But the longer he stares at it, the more intently a face seems to be staring back at him. A real face? His imagination is full of bearded men with glittering eyes who hide in dark passages. Nevertheless, as he passes into the pitch darkness of the entryway, the sense of another presence becomes so acute that a chill runs down his back. He halts, holds his breath, listens. Then he strikes a match.

In a corner crouches a man, blinking against the light. Though he has a woollen scarf wound around his head and mouth and a blanket over his shoulders, he recognizes the beggar he confronted in the church portico.

'Who are you?' he says, his voice cracking. 'Can't you leave me alone?'

The match goes out. He strikes another.

The man shakes his head firmly. A hand emerges from under the blanket and pushes the scarf aside. 'You can't order me,' he says. There is a smell of putrid fish in the air.

The match goes out. He starts to climb the stairs. But tediously the paradox comes back: *Expect the one you do not expect*. Very well; but must every beggar then be treated as a prodigal son, embraced, welcomed into the home, feasted? Yes, that is what Pascal would say: bet on everyone, every beggar, every mangy dog; only thus will you be sure that the One, the true son, the thief in the night, will not slip through the net. And Herod would agree: make sure – slay all the children without exception.

Betting on all the numbers – is that still gambling? Without the risk, without subjecting oneself to the voice speaking from elsewhere in the fall of the dice, what is left that is divine? Surely God knows that, and will have mercy on the gambler-at-heart! And surely the wife who, when her husband kneels before her and confesses he has gambled away their last rouble and beats his breast and kisses the hem of her dress – the wife who raises him and wipes away his tears and without a word departs to pawn her wedding-ring and returns with money ('Here!') so that he can go back to the gaming-room for the one last bet that will redeem all – surely such a woman is touched with the divine, a woman who stakes on the man who has nothing left, a woman who, when even the wedding-ring is pawned and lost, goes out a second time into the night and comes back with the money for another stake!

Does the woman upstairs, the woman whose name he seems for the moment to have forgotten, whom he even confuses with that *Gnädige Frau* his landlady in Dresden, have the touch of this divinity upon her? He does not know the first thing about her, only the last and most secret thing: how she gives herself. From how a woman gives herself can a man guess how she will give herself to the god of chance? Is such a woman marked by abandon, an abandon that does not care where it leads, to pleasure or to pain, that uses the sensual body only as a vehicle, and only because we cannot live disembodied? Is there a form of lovemaking she stands for in which bodies press against and into and through each other into a darkness in which nothing can be heard but the flapping of bedsheets like wings?

Memories of his nights with her flood back with sudden fullness, and everything that was tangled in him grows straight, pointing like an arrow to her. Desire in all its luxuriousness overwhelms him. *She*, he thinks: *she is the one, it is she whom I want. Therefore . . .*

Therefore, smiling to himself, he hurries back down the stairs and gropes his way to the corner where the man, the hireling, the spy, has made his nest. 'Come,' he says, speaking into the dark, 'I have a bed for you.'

'This is my post, I must stay at my post,' replies the man pawkily.

But nothing can impair his good spirits now. 'The one for whom you are waiting will come, even to the third floor, I assure you. He will knock at the door and wait with patience and refuse to go away.'

There is a long scuffling and a rustling of paper. 'You don't have another light, do you?' says the man.

He strikes a match. Hastily the man stuffs things into a bag and stands up.

Stumbling in the dark like two drunkards, they climb the stairs. At the door of his room he whispers to the man to be quiet and takes his hand to guide him. The hand is unpleasantly pudgy.

Inside, he lights the lamp. It is hard to judge the stranger's age. His eyes are youthful; but in his thin ginger hair and freckled scalp there is something tired and old, and his way of holding himself is that of someone worn down by years and by disgrace.

'Ivanov, Pyotr Alexandrovich,' says the man, drawing his heels together, making a little bow. 'Civil servant, retired.'

He gestures toward the bed. 'Take it.'

'You must be wondering,' says the man, testing the bed, 'how someone of my background comes to be a watcher (that is what we call it in our line: watching).' He lies down, stretches out.

He has a disagreeable presentiment that he has tangled himself with one of those beggars who, unable to juggle or play the violin, feel they must repay alms with the story of their life. 'Please keep your voice down,' he says. 'And take off your shoes.'

'You are the man whose son was killed, aren't you? My deepest condolences. I know some of what you are feeling. Not all, but some. I have lost two children myself. Swept away. Meningetic fever, that is the medical term. My wife has never recovered from the blow. They could have been saved if we had had the money to pay for good doctors. A tragedy; but who cares? Tragedy is all around us nowadays. Tragedy has become the way of the world.' He sits up. 'If you will heed my advice, Fyodor Mikhailovich (you don't mind, do you?), if you will take a word of advice from someone who has been, so to speak, through the mill, you will give in to your grief. Cry like a woman. That is the great secret of womankind, that gives them the advantage over fellows like us. They know when to let go and cry. We don't, you and I. We bottle it up inside us till it becomes like the very devil! And then we go and do something stupid, just to be rid of it for an hour or two. Yes, we do something stupid that we regret forever afterwards. Women aren't like that because women have the secret of tears. We must learn from the fair sex, Fyodor Mikhailovich, we must learn to cry! See, I'm not ashamed to cry: three years, next month, since tragedy struck, and I'm not ashamed to cry!'

And indeed, tears are rolling down his cheeks. He wipes them away with his cuff, but more flow. He seems to have no trouble in talking while he cries. In fact, he seems quite cheerful. 'I believe I will grieve for my lost babies for the rest of my days,' he says.

As Ivanov prattles on about his 'babies,' his attention wanders. Is it simply because he is known to be a writer that people tell him their stories? Do they think he has no stories of his own? He is exhausted, the headache has not gone away. Sitting on the only chair, with birds already beginning to chirp outside, he is desperate to sleep – desperate, in fact, for the bed he has given up. 'We can talk later,' he interrupts testily. 'Go to sleep now, otherwise what is the point of this . . .' He hesitates.

'Of this charity?' fills in Ivanov slyly. 'Is that what you wanted to say?'

He does not reply.

'Because, let me assure you, you need not be ashamed of charity,' the fellow continues softly, 'indeed not. Just as you need not be ashamed of grief. Generous impulses, both of them. They seem to bring us low, these generous impulses of ours, but in truth they exalt us. And He sees them and records each one of them, He who sees into the crevices of our hearts.'

With a struggle he opens his eyelids. Ivanov is sitting in the middle of the bed, cross-legged, like an idol. Charlatan! he thinks. He closes his eyes. When he wakes, Ivanov is still there, sprawled across the bed, his hands folded under his cheek, asleep. His mouth is open; from his lips, small and pink as a baby's, comes a delicate snore.

Till late in the morning he stays with Ivanov. Ivanov, the beginning of the unexpected, he thinks: let us see now where the unexpected takes us!

Never before has time passed so sluggishly, never has the air been so blank of revelation.

At last, bored, he rouses the man. 'Time to leave, your shift is over,' he says.

Ivanov seems oblivious of the irony. He is fresh, cheerful, well-rested. 'Ouf!' he yawns. 'I must pay a visit to the toilet!' And then, when he comes back: 'You don't have a scrap of breakfast to share, do you?'

He conducts Ivanov into the apartment. His breakfast is set out on the table, but he has no appetite. 'Yours,' he says curtly. Ivanov's eyes gleam, a dribble of saliva runs down his chin. Yet he eats decorously, and sips his tea with his little finger cocked in the air. When he is finished he sits back and sighs contentedly. 'How glad I am that our paths have crossed!' he remarks. 'The world can be a cold place, Fyodor Mikhailovich, as I am sure you know! I do not complain, mark you. We get what we deserve, in a higher sense. Nevertheless I sometimes wonder, do we not also deserve, each of us, a refuge, a haven, where justice will for a while relent and pity be taken on us? I pose that as a question, a philosophical question. Even if it isn't in Scripture, would it not be in the spirit of Scripture: that we deserve what we do not deserve? What do you think?'

'No doubt. This is unfortunately not my apartment. And now it is time for you to be leaving.'

'In a moment. Let me make one last observation. It was not just idle chatter, you know, what I said last night about God seeing into the crevices of our hearts. I may not be a proper holy simpleton, but that does not disqualify me from speaking the truth. Truth can come, you know, in winding and mysterious ways.' He taps his forehead meaningfully. 'You never dreamed – did you? – when you first clapped eyes on me, that one day we would be sitting down together, the two of us, and drinking tea in a civilized fashion. Yet here we are!'

'I am sorry, but I do not follow you, my mind is elsewhere. You really must leave now.'

'Yes, I must leave, I have my duties too.' He rises, tosses the blanket over his shoulders like a cape, holds out a hand. 'Goodbye. It has been a pleasure to converse with a man of culture.'

'Goodbye.'

It is a relief to be rid of him. But a frowzy, fishy smell lingers in his room. Despite the cold, he has to open the window.

Half an hour later there is a knock at the apartment door. Not that man again! he thinks, and opens the door with an angry frown.

Before him stands a child, a fat girl dressed in a dark smock such as novice nuns wear. Her face is round and unexpressive, her cheekbones so high that the little eyes are almost hidden, her hair drawn back tightly and gathered in a brief queue.

'Are you Pavel Isaev's stepfather?' she asks in a surprisingly deep voice.

He nods.

She steps inside, closing the door behind her. 'I was a friend of Pavel's,' she announces. He expects condolences to follow. But they do not come. Instead she takes up position squarely before him with her arms at her sides, measuring him, giving off an air of stolid, watchful calm, the calm of a wrestler waiting for the bout to begin. Her bosom rises and falls evenly.

'Can I see what he left behind?' she says at last.

'He left very little. May I know your name?'

'Katri. Even if there is very little, can I see it? This is the third time I have called. The first two times that stupid landlady of his wouldn't let me in. I hope you won't be the same.'

Katri. A Finnish name. She looks like a Finn too.

'I am sure she has her reasons. Did you know my son well?'

She does not answer the question. 'You realize that the police killed your stepson,' she says matter-of-factly.

Time stands still. He can hear his heart beating.

'They killed him and put out a story about suicide. Don't you believe me? You don't have to if you don't want to.'

'Why do you say that?' he says in a dry whisper.

'Why? Because it's true. Why else?'

It is not just that she is belligerent: she is beginning to grow restless too. She has begun to rock rhythmically from foot to foot, her arms swinging in time. Despite her squat frame she gives an impression of limberness. No wonder Anna Sergeyevna wanted nothing to do with her!

'No.' He shakes his head. 'What my son left behind is a private matter, a family matter. Kindly explain the point of your visit.'

'Are there any papers?'

'There were papers but they aren't here any more. Why do you ask?' And then: 'Are you one of Nechaev's people?'

The question does not disconcert her. On the contrary, she smiles, raising her eyebrows, baring her eyes for the first time, glaring, triumphant. Of course she is one of Nechaev's! A warrior-woman, and her swaying the beginnings of a war-dance, the dance of someone itching to go to war.

'If I were, would I tell you?' she replies, laughing.

'Do you know that the police are keeping watch on this house?'

She stares intently, swaying on her toes, as though willing him to see something in her gaze.

'There is a man downstairs this very minute,' he persists.

'Where?'

'You didn't notice him but you can be sure he noticed you. He pretends to be a beggar.'

Her smile broadens into true amusement. 'Do you think a police spy would be clever enough to spot me?' she says. And she does a surprising thing. Twitching the hem of her dress aside, she gives two little skips, revealing simple black shoes and white cotton stockings.

She is right, he thinks: one could take her for a child; but a child in the grip of a devil nevertheless. The devil inside her twitching, skipping, unable to keep still.

'Stop that!' he says coldly. 'My son didn't leave anything for you.'

'Your son! He wasn't your son!'

'He is my son and will always be. Now please go. I have had enough of this conversation.'

He opens the door and motions her out. As she leaves, she deliberately knocks against him. It is like being bumped by a pig.

There is no sign of Ivanov when he goes out later in the afternoon, nor when he returns. Should he care? If it is Ivanov's task to see without being seen, why should it be his task to see Ivanov? Even if, in the present charade, Ivanov is the one playing the part of God's angel – an angel only by virtue of being no angel at all – why should it be his role to seek out the angel? Let the angel come knocking at my door, he tells himself, and I will not fail, I will give him shelter: that is enough for the bargain to hold. Yet even as he says so he is aware that he is lying to himself, that it is in his power to deliver Ivanov wholly and absolutely from his cold watchpost.

So he frets and frets till at last there is nothing for it but to go downstairs and search for the man. But the man is not downstairs, is not in the street, is nowhere to be found. He sighs with relief. I have done what I can, he thinks.

But he knows in his heart he has not. There is more he could do, much more.

9

Nechaev

He is in the streets of the Haymarket the next day when ahead of him he glimpses the plump, almost spherical figure of the same Finnish girl. She is not alone. By her side is a woman, tall and slim, walking so fast that the Finn has to skip to keep up with her.

He quickens his pace. Though for moments he loses sight of them in the crowd, he is not far behind when they enter a shop. As she enters, the tall woman casts a glance up the street. He is struck by the blue of her eyes, the pallor of her skin. Her glance passes over him without settling.

He crosses the street and dawdles, waiting for them to emerge. Five minutes pass, ten minutes. He is getting cold.

The brass plate advertises Atelier La Fay or La Fée, Milliner. He pushes open the door; a bell tinkles. In a narrow, well-lit room, girls in uniform grey smocks sit at two long sewing-tables. A woman of middle age bustles forward to greet him.

'Monsieur?'

'An acquaintance of mine came in a few minutes ago

– a young lady. I thought – ' He glances around the shop, dismayed: there is no sign of either the Finn or the other woman. 'I am sorry, I must have made a mistake.'

The two young seamstresses nearest by are giggling at his embarrassment. As for Madame la Fay, she has lost interest. 'It must be students you are thinking of,' she says dismissively. 'We have nothing to do with the students.'

He apologizes again and begins to leave.

'There!' says a voice behind him.

He turns. One of the girls is pointing to a small door on his left. 'Through there!'

He passes into an alleyway walled off from the street. An iron staircase leads to the floor above. He hesitates, then ascends.

He finds himself in a dark passage smelling of cooking. From an upper floor comes the sound of a scratchy violin playing a gypsy tune. He follows the music up two more flights to a half-open garret door, and knocks. The Finnish girl comes to the door. Her stolid face shows no sign of surprise.

'May I speak to you?' he says.

She stands aside.

The violin is being played by a young man in black. Seeing the stranger, he stops in mid-phrase, casts a quick glance toward the tall woman, then picks up his cap and, without a word, leaves.

He addresses the Finn. 'I caught sight of you in the street and followed. Could we speak in private?'

She sits down on the couch but does not invite him to sit. Her feet barely reach the floor. 'Speak,' she says.

'You made a remark yesterday about the death of my

 son. I would like to know more. Not in any spirit of vengefulness. I am inquiring for my own relief. I mean, in order to relieve myself.'

She regards him quizzically. 'To relieve yourself?'

'I mean I did not come to Petersburg to involve myself in detection,' he continues doggedly; 'but now that you have said what you said about the manner of his death, I cannot ignore it, I cannot push it away.'

He pauses. His head is swimming, he is suddenly exhausted. Behind closed eyes he has a vision of Pavel walking towards him. There is a girl at his side, a girl he has chosen to be his bride. Pavel is about to speak, to introduce the girl; and he is about to think to himself: Good, at last all these years of fathering are at an end, at last he has other hands to fall into! He is about to smile at Pavel, in his smile rejoicing but also relief. But who can the bride be? Can she be this tall young woman (nearly as tall as Pavel himself) with the piercing blue eyes?

He tugs himself loose from the reverie. His own next sentence is already emerging, in what sounds to him like a drone. 'I have a duty towards him that I cannot evade,' he is saying.

That is all. The words come to an end, dry up. Silence falls, grows longer and longer. He makes an effort to revive the vision of Pavel and his bride, but of all people it is Ivanov who comes instead, or at least Ivanov's hands: pale, plump fingers emerging like grubs from green woollen mittens. As for the face, it bobs in a sulphurous mist, not keeping still long enough for his gaze to fix on it. The impression he has, however, is of a sly, insistent smile, as though the man knows something damaging to him and wants him to know that he knows.

He shakes his head, tries to gather his wits. But words seem to have fled him. He stands before the Finn like an actor who has forgotten his lines. The silence lies like a weight upon the room. A weight or a peace, he thinks: what peace there would be if everything were to fall still, the birds of the air frozen in their flight, the great globe suspended in its orbit! A fit is certainly on its way: there is nothing he can do to hold it back. He savours the last of the stillness. What a pity the stillness cannot last forever! From far away comes a scream that must be his own. *There will be a gnashing of teeth* – the words flash before him; then there is an end.

When he returns it is as if he has been away in a far country and grown old and grey there. But in fact he is in the room as before, still on his feet, with a hand half-raised. And the two women are there too, in the postures he remembers, though the Finn now has a wary air about her.

'May I sit down?' he mumbles, his tongue too large for his mouth.

The Finn makes space and he sits down beside her on the couch, dizzy, hanging his head. 'Is something wrong?' she asks.

He makes no reply. What is it he wants to say, and why is he so tired all the time? It is as though a fog has settled over his brain. If he were a character in a book, what would he say, at a moment like this when either the heart speaks or the page remains blank?

'I cannot tell you,' he says slowly, 'how sad and alien I feel in your company. The game you are playing is a game I cannot enter. What engages you, what must have engaged Pavel too, does not engage me. If I must be honest, it repels me.'

Without a word the tall girl leaves the room. The rustle of her dress and a waft of lavender as she passes awake in him an unexpected flutter of desire. Desire for what? For the girl herself? Surely not – or not only. For youth, rather, for the forever-lost, the freedom of loosened clothes, naked bodies. Even so, his response disturbs him. Why here, why now? Something to do with exhaustion, but perhaps to do with Pavel too – with finding himself in Pavel's world, Pavel's erotic surround.

'I have been shown the lists of people marked down for execution,' he says.

The Finn observes him narrowly.

'The police are in possession of those lists – I hope you realize that. They took them from Pavel's room. What I want to ask is: Does each of you simply have a certain number of people to kill, or are there particular persons marked down as yours, yours alone? And, if the latter, are you expected to study these persons beforehand, to familiarize yourselves with their daily lives? Do you spy on them at home?'

The Finn tries to speak, but he is beginning to come to life, and his voice rises above hers.

'*If so*, if so, don't you necessarily grow more familiar with your victims than you want to be? Don't you become like someone called in from the street, a beggar, for instance, offered fifty kopeks to dispose of an old, blind dog, who takes the rope and ties the noose and strokes the dog to calm it, and murmurs a word or two, and as he does so feels a current of feeling begin to flow, so that from that instant onward he and the dog are no longer strangers, and what should have been a mere job of work has turned into the blackest betrayal – such a betrayal, in fact, that the sound the dog makes as he strings it up, when he strings it up, haunts him for days afterwards – a yelp of surprise: *Why you?* Wouldn't it deter you, that thought?'

While he has been speaking the tall woman has returned. She is kneeling in the far corner of the room now, folding sheets, rolling up a mattress. The Finn, on the other hand, has positively come to life. Her eyes sparkle, she cannot wait to speak. Still he presses on.

'And if a mere dog can do that, what power will the men and women you propose to get rid of not have to haunt you? It seems to me that, however scientifically these enemies of the people are selected, you lack a means of killing them without peril to your soul. For instance: who was set down as Pavel's first victim? Whom was he allotted to kill?'

'Why do you ask? Why do you want to know?'

'Because I intend to go to that person's house and before the door, on my knees, give thanks that Pavel never arrived.'

'So you are happy that Pavel was killed?'

'Pavel is not dead. He would have died, but by great good fortune he escaped with his life.'

For the first time the other woman speaks. 'Won't you come and sit here, Fyodor Mikhailovich?' she says, indicating the table near the window, at which there are two chairs.

'My sister,' explains the Finn.

'Sisters, but not of the same parents,' says the other. Their laughter is easy, familiar.

Her accent belongs to Petersburg, her voice is deep. A trained voice. He has a feeling he has met her before. A singer? From his Opera days? Surely she is too young for that.

He takes one of the chairs; she sits down opposite him. The table is narrow. Her foot touches his; he shifts his foot.

Though she has her back to the window, he now understands why she is so heavily powdered. Her skin is pitted with smallpox scars. What a shame, he thinks: not a beauty, but a handsome creature all the same.

Her foot touches his again, rests against it, instep to instep.

A disturbing excitement creeps over him. Like chess, he thinks: two players across a small table making their deliberate moves. Is it the deliberateness that excites him – the opposite foot lifted like a pawn and placed against his? And the third person, the watcher who does not see, the dupe, looking in the wrong place: does she play her part too? Deliberateness and tawdriness, a tawdriness that has its own thrill. Where could they have learned so much about him, about his desires?

A singer, a contralto: a contralto queen.

'You knew my son,' he says.

'He was a follower. A mascot.'

He is familiar with the term, and it hurts him. A mascot: a hanger-on in student circles, useful for running errands.

'But was he a friend of yours?'

She shrugs. 'Friendship is effeminate. We don't need friendship.'

Effeminate: strange word for a woman to use! Already he has a feeling he knows more than he wants to know. The foot still rests against his, but now there is something inert about its pressure, inert and lumpish and even threatening. No longer a foot but a boot. Pavel would not be playing these games. The vision of Pavel returns, Pavel walking towards him. The girl at his side, his bride, is obscured. Pavel is smiling, and a glory of a kind breaks from that smile. *My friend!* he thinks. A fierce love wrings his heart. *And this*, he thinks, *is this what I must have in your place?*

'If you don't need friendship, God save you,' he whispers.

He gets up from the table and turns his back on the women. What does he look like, he wonders? There is no mirror. By the time he sits down again, the tears that had threatened have gone.

'What did you do with my son?' he asks thickly.

The woman leans across the table and fixes him with her blue stare. Through the coat of powder, from the craters of the chin, he spies hairs that the razor did not catch. And the eyebrows are too thick over the bridge of the nose. A woman would have had the sense to tell him to pluck them. So is the Finn a boy too, a fat little boy? All at once he is revolted by the pair of them.

She, or he, is speaking. Nechaev himself – no doubt about that. The disguise is all at once transparent. The memory comes back again with sudden clarity: in the hall of the Peace Congress, during an intermission between sessions, Nechaev all alone in a corner, wolfing down finger-sandwiches, glaring, challenging the roomful of grownups: *Yes, laugh if you dare, laugh at the schoolboy!* The look on his face that of a boy surprised at stool with his trousers around his knees, vulnerable but defiant. *Laugh, but one day I will get my own back!*

He remembers a remark made by Princess Obolenskaya, Mroczkowski's mistress: 'He may be the *enfant terrible* of anarchism, but really, he should do something about those pimples!'

 'Given what the police did to your son,' Nechaev is saying, 'I am surprised you are not incensed. As the Gospels say, an eye for an eye and a tooth for a tooth.'

'You wretch, that is not in the Gospels! What are you saying about Pavel? And why are you dressed up in this ridiculous costume?'

'Surely you don't believe the suicide story. Isaev didn't kill himself – that's just a fiction put out by the police. They can't use the law against us, so they perpetrate these obscene murders. But of course you must have your doubts – why else would you be here?'

All the man's affected softness has gone: the voice is his own. As he paces back and forth the blue dress swishes. What is underneath it, trousers or bare legs? What must it be like to walk about with one's legs naked yet hidden, brushing each other?

'Do you think we are not all in danger? Do you think I *want* to creep about in disguise in my own city, the city where I was born? Do you know what it is like to be a woman by yourself on the streets of Petersburg?' His voice rises, anger taking him over. 'Do you know what you have to listen to? Men dog your footsteps whispering filth such as you cannot imagine, and you are helpless against it!' He collects himself. 'Or perhaps you can imagine it only too well. Perhaps what I describe is only too familiar to you.'

The Finn has taken a bowl of potatoes on her lap, which she is peeling. Her face is peaceful; more than ever she looks like a little grandmother. 'It's getting colder,' she remarks.

Mad, both of them! he thinks. What am I doing here? I must find my way back to Pavel!

'Kindly repeat . . . Kindly repeat what you were saying about my son,' he says.

'Very well, let me tell you about your son. The official verdict will be that he killed himself. If you believe that, you are truly gullible, criminally gullible. Weren't you a revolutionary yourself in the old days, or am I mistaken? Surely you must be aware that the struggle has never ceased. Or have you made a separate peace? Those in the forefront of the struggle continue to be hunted down and tortured and killed. I would have expected you to know this and write about it. Particularly because people will never read the truth about your son and others like him in our shameful Russian press.'

Nechaev's voice becomes lower, more intense. 'What happened to your son can happen to me any day, or to other of our comrades. You say you know nothing about it. But go into the streets, go to the markets and the taverns where the people gather, and you will find that the people know. Somehow they know! And when the day of judgment comes, the people will not forget who suffered and died for them, and who did not lift a hand!'

Christ in his wrath, he thinks: that is who he models himself on. The Christ of the Old Testament, the Christ who scourged the usurers out of the temple. Even the costume is right: not a dress but a robe. An imitator; a pretender; a blasphemer.

'Don't threaten me!' he replies. 'By what right do you speak in the name of the people? The people aren't vengeful. The people don't spend their time scheming and plotting.'

'The people know who their enemies are, and the people don't waste tears on them when they meet their end! As for us, at least we know what has to be done and are doing it! Perhaps you used once to know, but now all you can do is mumble and shake your head and cry. That is soft. We aren't soft, we aren't crying, and we aren't wasting our time on clever talk. There are things that can be talked about and things that can't, that just have to be done. We don't talk, we don't cry, we don't endlessly think *on the one hand* and *on the other hand*, we just *do!*'

'Excellent! You just *do*. But where do you get your instructions? Is it the voice of the people you obey, or just your own voice, a little disguised so that you need not recognize it?'

'Another clever question! Another waste of time! We are sick and tired of cleverness. The days of cleverness are numbered. Cleverness is one of the things we are going to get rid of. The day of ordinary people is arriving. Ordinary people aren't clever. Ordinary people just want the job done. And once the job is done, it is ordinary people who will decide what is going to be what, and whether any more cleverness is going to be allowed!'

'And whether clever books and that kind of thing are going to be allowed!' chimes in the Finn, animated, even excited.

Is it possible, he thinks with disgust, that Pavel could have been friends with people like these, people ever-eager to whip themselves into frenzies of self-righteousness? This place is like a Spanish convent in the days of Loyola: well-born girls flagellating themselves, rolling about in ecstasies, foaming at the lips; or fasting, praying for hours on end to be taken into the arms of the Saviour. Extremists all of them, sensualists hungering for the ecstasy of death – killing, dying, no matter which. And Pavel among them!

Upon him bursts the thought of Pavel's last moment, of the body of a hot-blooded young man in the pride of life striking the earth, of the rush of breath from the lungs, the crack of bones, the surprise, above all the surprise, that the end should be real, that there should be no second chance. Under the table he wrings his hands in agony. A body hitting the earth: death, the measure of all things!

'Prove to me . . .' he says. 'Prove what you say about Pavel.'

Nechaev leans closer. 'I will take you to the place,' he says, enunciating each word slowly. 'I will take you to the very place and I will open your eyes for you.'

In silence he gets up and stumbles to the door. He finds the staircase and descends, but then loses the way to the alley. He knocks at random on a door. There is no answer. He knocks at a second door. A tired-looking woman in slippers opens it and stands aside for him to enter. 'No,' he says, 'I just want to know the way out.' Without a word she closes the door.

From the end of the passage comes the drone of voices. A door stands open; he enters a room so low-ceilinged that it feels like a birdcage. Three young men are lounging in armchairs, one reading aloud from a newspaper. A silence falls. 'I'm looking for the way out,' he says. '*Tout droit!*' says the reader, waving a hand, and returns to his newspaper. He is reading an account of a skirmish between students and gendarmes outside the Faculty of Philosophy. He glances up, sees the intruder has not stirred. '*Tout droit, tout droit!*' he commands; his companions laugh.

Then the Finnish girl is at his side. 'Heavens, you are poking your nose into the strangest places!' she remarks good-humouredly. Taking his arm, she guides him as if he were blind first down another flight of stairs, then along an unlit passageway cluttered with trunks and boxes, to a barred door which she opens. They are on the street. She holds out a hand to him. 'So we have an appointment,' she says.

'No. What appointment do we have?'

'Be waiting at the corner of Gorokhovaya on the Fontanka this evening at ten o'clock.'

'I won't be there, I assure you.'

'Very well, you won't be there. Or perhaps you will. Don't you have family feeling? You aren't going to betray us, are you?'

She puts the question jokingly, as if it were not really in his power to harm them.

'Because, you know, some people say you will betray us despite everything,' she goes on. 'They say you are treacherous by nature. What do you think?'

If he had a stick he would hit her. But with only a hand, where does one strike such a round, obtuse body?

'It doesn't help to be aware of one's nature, does it?' she continues reflectively. 'I mean, one's nature leads one on, no matter how much one thinks about it. What's the use of hanging a person if it's in his nature? It's like hanging a wolf for eating a lamb. It won't change the nature of wolves, will it? Or hanging the man who betrayed Jesus – that didn't change anything, did it?'

'No one hanged him,' he retorts irritably. 'He hanged himself.'

'The same thing. It doesn't help, does it? I mean, whether you hang him or he hangs himself.'

Something terrible is beginning to loom through this prattle. 'Who is Jesus?' he asks softly.

'Jesus?' It is dusk; they are the only people on this cold, empty back street. She regards him disbelievingly. 'Don't you know Jesus?'

'When you say I am Judas, who is Jesus?'

She smiles. 'It's just a way of speaking,' she says. And then, half to herself: 'They don't understand anything.' Again she proffers a hand. 'Ten o'clock, on the Fontanka. If no one is there to meet you, it means something has happened.'

He refuses the hand, sets off down the street. Behind him he hears a word half-whispered. What is it? *Jew? Judas?* He suspects it is *Jew*. Extraordinary: is that where they think the word comes from? But why his fastidiousness about touching her? Is it because she may have known Pavel, known him too well – carnally, in fact? Do they hold their women in common, Nechaev and the others? Hard to imagine this woman as held in common. More likely she who would hold men in common. Even Pavel. He resists the thought, then yields. He sees the Finn naked, enthroned on a bed of scarlet cushions, her bulky legs apart, her arms held wide to display her breasts and a belly rotund, hairless, barely mature. And Pavel on his knees, ready to be covered and consumed.

He shakes himself free. Envious imaginings! A father like an old grey rat creeping in afterwards upon the love-scene to see what is left for him. Sitting on the corpse in the dark, pricking his ears, gnawing, listening, gnawing. Is that why the police-pack hunts the free youth of Petersburg so vengefully, with Maximov, the good father, the great rat, at its head?

He recalls Pavel's behaviour after his marriage to Anya.

 Pavel was nineteen, yet obstinately would not accept that she, Anna Grigoryevna, would henceforth share his father's bed. For the year they all lived together Pavel maintained the fiction that Anya was simply his father's companion as an old woman may have a companion: someone to keep house, order the groceries, attend to the laundry. When – perhaps after an evening game of cards – he would announce that he was going to bed, Pavel would not allow Anya to follow him: he would challenge her to rounds of cribbage ('Just the two of us!'), and even when she blushingly tried to withdraw, refuse to understand ('This isn't the country, you don't have to get up at dawn to milk the cows!').

Is it always like this between fathers and sons: jokes masking the intensest rivalry? And is that the true reason why he is bereft: because the ground of his life, the contest with his son, is gone, and his days are left empty? Not the People's Vengeance but the Vengeance of the Sons: is that what underlies revolution – fathers envying their sons their women, sons scheming to rob their fathers' cashboxes? He shakes his head wearily.

10

The shot tower

Arriving home, he is met in the passageway by Matryona in a state of great excitement. 'The police have been here, Fyodor Mikhailovich, they are looking for a murderer!'

Time stops; he stands frozen. 'Why should they come here?' The words come from him but he seems to hear them from afar, the thin words of someone else.

'They are looking everywhere, all through the building!'

From Anna Sergeyevna he gets a fuller story. 'They are questioning people about a beggar who has been haunting the neighbourhood. I suppose I must have seen him, but I can't recall. They say he has been sheltering in this building.'

He could at this point reveal that Ivanov has spent a night in her apartment, but he does not. 'What is he accused of?' he asks instead.

'The police are being very tight-lipped. Matryosha says he killed somebody, but that is pure gossip.'

'It's not possible. I know the man, I spoke to him at length. He is not a killer.'

But, as it turns out, it is not just gossip. There has

 indeed been a crime; the body of the victim, the beggarman himself, was found in an alley just down the street. This he learns from the concierge, and is shaken. Ivanov: one of those bad-penny faces that turn up at one's deathbed, or at the graveside; not one to die first.

'Are they sure he didn't simply perish of cold?' he asks. 'Why does it have to be murder?'

'Oh, it's murder all right,' replies the old man, with a knowing look. 'What surprises me is that they are going to all this trouble over a nobody.'

Over supper Matryona will speak of nothing but the murder. She is overwrought: her eyes glisten, words tumble out of her. As for him, he has his own story to tell, but that must wait till her mother has calmed her and put her to bed.

When he thinks she is asleep, he begins to tell Anna Sergeyevna of his meeting with Nechaev. He speaks softly, conscious that the whisperings of adults – treacherous, fascinating – can pierce a child's deepest slumbers.

Anna recognizes Nechaev's name, but seems to have only the vaguest idea of who he is. Nevertheless she is ready to advise him, and her advice is firm. 'You must keep your appointment. You will not be able to rest till you know what really happened.'

'But I know what happened. There is nothing more I need to know.'

She makes an impatient gesture. His lack of zeal makes no sense to her: she sees it only as apathy. How can he make her understand? To make her understand he would have to speak in a voice from under the waters, a boy's clear bell-voice pleading out of the deep dark. 'Sing to me, dear father!' the voice would have to call, and she would have to hear. Somewhere within himself he would have to find not only that voice but the words, the true words. Here and now he does not have the words. Perhaps – he has an intimation – they may be waiting for him in one of the old ballads. But the ballad is in no book: it is somewhere in the breast of the Russian people, where he cannot reach it. Or perhaps in the breast of a child.

'Pavel is not vengeful,' he says at last, haltingly. 'Whoever killed him, it is past, the cord is cut, he is free of that person. I want to be taught by him. I don't want to be poisoned by vengefulness.'

There is more he might say, but cannot, now. That Pavel has no interest in the retelling of the story of how he fell. That Pavel is above all lonely, and in his loneliness needs to be sung to and comforted, to be reassured that he will not be abandoned at the bottom of the waters.

A silence falls between himself and the woman. It is the first time since Sunday they have been alone together. She looks tired. Her shoulders slump, her hands are slack, there are creases at her throat. Older than his wife, it comes home to him again: not quite of another generation, but almost so. He wishes he did not have to see it. He has too recently come from Nechaev, youthful, demonic in his energy, as all the lesser demons are youthful.

On an impulse he takes her hand. She looks up with surprise.

'I am not urging you to vengeance,' she says slowly. 'Of course you are right about Pavel: he did not have a vengeful nature. But he did have a sense of what was right and just. Keep your appointment. Find out what you can. Otherwise you will never have peace.'

 He is still holding her hand. From it he feels a pressure, answering his, that he can only call kindly.

'Justice,' he reflects. 'A large word. Can one really draw a line between justice and vengefulness?' And, when she seems uncomprehending: 'Isn't that the originality of Nechaev – that he calls himself the People's Vengeance, not the People's Justice? At least he is honest.'

'Is he? Is that what the people want to be told: that it is vengeance they are after, not justice? I don't think so. Why should the people take Nechaev seriously? Why should anyone take him seriously – a student, an excitable young man? What power does he have, after all?'

'Not the power of life, but the power of death, certainly. A child can kill as dead as a man can, if the spirit is in him. Perhaps that again is Nechaev's originality: that he speaks what we dare not even imagine about our children; that he gives a voice to something dumb and brutal that is sweeping through young Russia. We close our ears to it; then he comes with his axe and makes us hear.'

Her hand, that has been a living thing, has suddenly grown lifeless. A woman of feeling, he thinks, releasing it. Like her daughter. And perhaps as easily hurt.

He wants to embrace her, wants to take her in his arms and repair whatever is fractured. He ought to stop this talk, which only repels and estranges her. But he does not.

'After all, you will never recruit people to your cause by invoking a spirit that is alien to them, or means nothing to them. Nechaev has disciples among the young because a spirit in them answers to the spirit in him. Of course that is not how *he* explains it. He calls himself a materialist. But that is just fashionable jargon. The truth is, he has what the Greeks called a demon. It speaks to him. It is the source of his energy.'

Again he thinks: Now I must stop. But the dry, deathly words keep coming. He knows he has lost touch with her.

'The same demon must have been in Pavel, otherwise why would Pavel have responded to his call? It's nice to think that Pavel was not vengeful. It's nice to think well of the dead. But it just flatters him. Let us not be sentimental – in ordinary life he was as vengeful as any other young man.'

She gets to her feet. He believes he knows the words she is going to speak, and, if only for form's sake, is ready to defend himself. *You call yourself Pavel's father, but I do not believe you love him* – that is what he expects. But he is wrong.

'I know nothing about this anarchist Nechaev, I can only accept what you tell me,' she says; 'but as I listen it is hard to tell which of you, you or Nechaev, desires it more that Pavel should belong to the party of vengeance. I am nothing to Pavel, I am certainly not his mother, but I owe it to him – to him and his memory – to protest. You and Nechaev should fight your battles without dragging him in.'

'Nechaev is not an anarchist. That is the mistake people keep making. He is something else.'

'Anarchist, nihilist, whatever he is, I don't want to hear any more of it! I don't want strife and hatred brought into my home! Matryona is excited enough as it is; I don't want her further infected.'

'Not an anarchist, not a nihilist,' he continues doggedly. 'By giving him labels you miss what is unique about him. He does not act in the name of ideas. He acts when he feels action stirring in his body. He is a sensualist. He is an extremist of the senses. He wants to live in a body at the limits of sensation, at the limits of bodily knowledge. That is why he can say *everything is permitted* – or why he would say so if he were not so indifferent to explaining himself!'

He pauses. Again he believes he knows what she wants to say; or rather, knows what she wants to say even when she herself does not: *And you? Are you so different?*

'Why do you think he chooses the axe?' he says. 'If you think of the axe, if you think of what it means – ' He throws up his hands in despair. He cannot decently produce the words. The axe, instrument of the people's vengeance, weapon of the people, crude, heavy, unanswerable, swung with the full weight of the body behind it, the body and the life's-weight of hatred and resentment stored up in that body, swung with dark joy.

A silence falls between them.

'There are people to whom sensation does not come by natural means,' he says at last, more evenly. 'That is how Sergei Nechaev struck me from the beginning – as a man who could not have a natural connection with a woman, for instance. I wondered whether that might not underlie his manifold resentments. But perhaps that is how it will be in the future: sensation will not come by the old means any longer. The old means will be used up. I mean love. Love will be used up. So other means will have to be found.'

She speaks. 'That is enough. I don't want to talk any more. It is past nine. If you want to go – '

He rises, bows, leaves.

At ten o'clock he is at the rendezvous on the Fontanka.

A high wind blows scuds of rain before it and whips up the black waters of the canal. The lamp-posts along the bare embankment creak in a concert of jangling. From roofs and gutters comes the gurgle of water.

He takes shelter in a doorway, growing more and more testy. If I catch cold, he thinks, it will be the last straw. He catches cold easily. Pavel too, ever since childhood. Did Pavel catch cold while he was living with *her*? Did she nurse him herself, or was that left to Matryona? He imagines Matryona coming into the room with a steaming glass of lemon tea, stepping gingerly to keep the glass steady; he imagines Pavel, his hair dark against the white of the pillow, smiling. 'Thank you, little sister,' says Pavel in a hoarse boy's-voice. A boy's life, in all its ordinariness! With no one to overhear him, he lowers his head and groans like a sick ox.

Then she is before him, inspecting him curiously – not Matryona but the Finn. 'Are you unwell, Fyodor Mikhailovich?'

Embarrassed, he shakes his head.

'Then come,' she says.

She conducts him, as he feared she would, westward along the canal toward Stolyarny Quay and the old shot tower. Raising her voice above the wind, she chatters amicably. 'You know, Fyodor Mikhailovich,' she says, 'you did yourself no credit by talking about the people in the way you did this afternoon. We were disappointed in you – you, with your background. After all, you did go to Siberia for your beliefs. We respect you for that. Even Pavel Alexandrovich respected you. You shouldn't be relapsing now.'

'Even Pavel?'

'Yes, even Pavel. You suffered in your generation, and

 now Pavel has sacrificed himself too. You have every right to hold your head up with pride.'

She seems quite able to chatter while keeping up a rapid trot. As for him, he has a pain in his side and is breathing hard. 'Slower,' he pants.

'And you?' he says at last. 'What of you?'

'What of me?'

'What of you? Will you be able to hold your head up in the future?'

Under a crazily swinging lamp she stops. Light and shadow play across her face. He was quite wrong to dismiss her as a child playing with disguises. Despite her shapeless form, he recognizes now a cool, womanly quality.

'I don't expect to be here long, Fyodor Mikhailovich,' she says. 'Nor does Sergei Gennadevich. Nor do the rest of us. What happened to Pavel can happen to any of us at any time. So don't make jokes. If you make jokes about us, remember you are joking about Pavel too.'

For the second time this day he has an urge to hit her. And it is clear that she senses his anger: in fact, she pokes out her chin as if daring him to strike. Why is he so irascible? What is coming over him? Is he turning into one of those old men with no control over their temper? Or is it worse than that: now that his succession is extinct, has he become not only old but a ghost, an angry, abandoned spirit?

The tower on Stolyarny Quay has stood since Petersburg was built, but has long been disused. Though there is a painted sign warning off trespassers, it has become a resort for the more daring boys of the neighbourhood, who, via a spiral of iron hoops set in the wall, climb up to the furnace-chamber a hundred feet above ground level, and even higher, to the top of the brick chimney.

The great nail-studded doors are bolted and locked, but the small back door has long ago been kicked in by vandals. In the shadow of this doorway a man is waiting for them. He murmurs a greeting to the Finn; she follows him in.

Inside, the air smells of ordure and mouldering masonry. From the dark comes a soft stream of obscenities. The man strikes a match and lights a lamp. Almost under their feet are three people huddled together in a bed of sacking. He looks away.

The man with the lamp is Nechaev, wearing a grenadier officer's long black cloak. His face is unnaturally pale. Has he forgotten to wash off the powder?

'Heights make me dizzy, so I'll wait down here,' says the Finn. 'He will show you the place.'

A spiral staircase winds up the inner wall of the tower. Holding the lamp on high, Nechaev begins to climb. In the enclosed space their footsteps clatter loudly.

'They took your stepson up this way,' says Nechaev. 'They probably got him drunk beforehand, to make their task easier.'

Pavel. Here.

Up and up they go. The well of the tower beneath them is swallowed in darkness. He counts backwards to the day of Pavel's death, reaches twenty, loses track, starts again, loses track again. Can it be that *so many days ago* Pavel climbed these very stairs? Why is it that he cannot count them? The steps, the days – they have something to do with each other. Each step another day subtracted from Pavel's sum. A counting up and a counting down proceeding at the same time – is that what is confusing him?

They reach the head of the stairs and emerge on to a broad steel deck. His guide swings the lantern around. 'This way,' he says. He glimpses rusty machinery.

They emerge high above the quay, on a platform on the outside of the tower bounded by a waist-high railing. To one side a pulley mechanism and chain-hoist are set into the wall.

At once the wind begins to tug at them. He takes off his hat and grips the railing, trying not to look down. A metaphor, he tells himself, that is all it is – another word for a lapse of consciousness, a not-being-here, an absence. Nothing new. The epileptic knows it all: the approach to the edge, the glance downward, the lurch of the soul, the thinking that thinks itself crazily over and over like a bell pealing in the head: *Time shall have an end, there shall be no death*.

He grips the rail tighter, shakes his head to chase away the dizziness. Metaphors – what nonsense! There is death, only death. Death is a metaphor for nothing. Death is death. I should never have agreed to come. Now for the rest of my life I will have this before my eyes like ghost-vision: the roofs of St Petersburg glinting in the rain, the row of tiny lamps along the quayside.

Through clenched teeth he repeats the words to himself: *I should not have come*. But the *nots* are beginning to collapse, just as happened with Ivanov. *I should not be here therefore I should be here. I will see nothing else therefore I will see all*. What sickness is this, what sickness of reasoning?

His guide has left the lantern inside. He is intensely aware of the youthful body beside his, no doubt strong with a wiry, untiring kind of strength. At any moment he could grasp him about the waist and tip him over the edge into the void. But who is *he* on this platform, who is *him*?

Slowly he turns to face the younger man. 'If it is indeed the truth that Pavel was brought here to be killed,' he says, 'I will forgive you for bringing me. But if this is some monstrous trick, if it was you yourself who pushed him, I warn you, you will not be forgiven.'

They are not twelve inches apart. The moon is obscured, they are lashed by gusts of rain, yet he is convinced that Nechaev does not flinch from him. In all likelihood his opponent has already played the game through from beginning to end, in all its variations: nothing he can say will surprise him. Or else he is a devil who shrugs off curses like water.

Nechaev speaks. 'You should be ashamed to talk like that. Pavel Isaev was a comrade of ours. We were his family when he had no family. You went abroad and left him behind. You lost touch with him, you became a stranger to him. Now you appear from nowhere and make wild accusations against the only real kin he had in the world.' He draws the cloak tighter about his throat. 'Do you know what you remind me of? Of a distant relative turning up at the graveside with his carpet-bag, come out of nowhere to claim an inheritance from someone he has never laid eyes on. You are fourth cousin, fifth cousin to Pavel Alexandrovich, not father, not even stepfather.'

It is a painful blow. Roughly he tries to push past Nechaev, but his antagonist blocks the doorway. 'Don't shut your ears to what I am saying, Fyodor Mikhailovich!

 You lost Isaev and we saved him. How can you believe we could have caused his death?'

'Swear it on your immortal soul!'

Even as he speaks, he hears the melodramatic ring to the words. In fact the whole scene – two men on a moonlit platform high above the streets struggling against the elements, shouting over the wind, denouncing each other – is false, melodramatic. But where are true words to be found, words to which Pavel will give his slow smile, nod his approval?

'I will not swear by what I do not believe in,' says Nechaev stiffly. 'But reason should persuade you I am telling the truth.'

'And what of Ivanov? Must reason tell me you are innocent of Ivanov's death too?'

'Who is Ivanov?'

'Ivanov was the name employed by the wretched man whose job it was to watch the building where I live. Where Pavel lived. Where your woman-friend called on me.'

'Ah, the police spy! The one you made friends with! What happened to him?'

'He was found dead yesterday.'

'So? We lose one, they lose one.'

'They lose one? Are you equating Pavel with Ivanov? Is that how your accounting works?'

Nechaev shakes his head. 'Don't bring in personalities, it just confuses the issue. Collaborators have many enemies. They are detested by the people. This Ivanov's death doesn't surprise me in the least.'

'I too was no friend of Ivanov's, nor do I like the work he did. But those are not grounds for murdering him! As for *the people*, what nonsense! The people did not do it. The people don't plot murders. Nor do they hide their tracks.'

'The people know who their enemies are, and the people don't waste tears when their enemies die!'

'Ivanov wasn't an enemy of the people, he was a man with no money in his pocket and a family to feed, like tens of thousands of others. If he wasn't one of the people, who are the people?'

'You know very well that his heart wasn't with the people. Calling him one of the people is just talk. The people are made up of peasants and workers. Ivanov had no ties with the people: he wasn't even recruited from them. He was an absolutely rootless person, and a drunkard too, easy prey, easily turned against the people. I'm surprised at you, a clever man, falling into a simple trap like that.'

'Clever or not, I don't accept such monstrous reasoning! Why have you brought me to this place? You said that you were going to give me proof that Pavel was murdered. Where is the proof? Being here is not proof.'

'Of course it is not proof. But this is the place where the murder happened, a murder that was in fact an execution, directed by the state. I have brought you here so that you can see for yourself. Now you have had your chance to see; if you still refuse to believe, then so much the worse for you.'

He grips the railing, stares down *there* into the plummeting darkness. Between *here* and *there* an eternity of time, so much time that it is impossible for the mind to grasp it. Between *here* and *there* Pavel was alive, more alive than ever before. We live most intensely while we are falling – a truth that wrings the heart!

'If you won't believe, you won't believe,' Nechaev repeats.

Believe: another word. What does it mean, to believe? I believe in the body on the pavement below. I believe in the blood and the bones. To gather up the broken body and embrace it: that is what it means to believe. To believe and to love – the same thing.

'I believe in the resurrection,' he says. The words come without premeditation. The crazy, ranting tone is gone from his voice. Speaking the words, hearing them, he feels a quick joy, not so much at the words themselves as at the way they have come, spoken out of him as if by another. *Pavel!* he thinks.

'What?' Nechaev leans closer.

'I believe in the resurrection of the body and in life eternal.'

'That isn't what I asked.' The wind gusts so strongly that the younger man has to shout. His cloak flaps about him; he grips tighter to steady himself.

'Nevertheless, that is what I say!'

Though it is past midnight when he gets home, Anna Sergeyevna has waited up. Surprised at her concern, grateful too, he tells her of the meeting on the quay, tells her of Nechaev's words on the tower. Then he asks her to repeat again the story of the night of Pavel's death. Is she quite sure, for instance, that Pavel died on the quay?

'That is what I was told,' she answers. 'What else was I to believe? Pavel went out in the evening without mentioning where he was going. The next morning there was a message: he had had an accident, I should come to the hospital.'

'But how did they know to inform you?'

'There were papers in his pockets.'

'And?'

'I went to the hospital and identified him. Then I let Mr Maykov know.'

'But what explanation did they give you?'

'They did not give me an explanation, I had to give them an explanation. I had to go to the police and answer questions: who he was, where his family lived, when I had last seen him, how long he had lived with us, who his friends were – on and on! All they would tell me was that he was already dead when he was found, and that it had happened on Stolyarny Quay. That was the message I sent Mr Maykov. I don't know what he then told you.'

'He used the word *misadventure*. No doubt he had spoken to the police. *Misadventure* is the word they use for suicide. It was a telegram, so he could not elaborate.'

'That is what I understood. I mean, that is what I understood had happened. I have never understood why he did it, if he did it. He gave us no warning. There was no hint that it was coming.'

'One last question. What was he was wearing that night? Was he wearing anything strange?'

'When he went out?'

'No, when you saw him . . . afterwards.'

'I don't know. I can't remember. There was a sheet. I don't want to talk about it. But he was quite peaceful. I want you to know that.'

He thanks her, from his heart. So the exchange ends. But in his own room he cannot sleep. He remembers Maykov's belated telegram (why had he taken so long?). Anya had been the one to open it; Anya it was who came to his study and pronounced the words that even tonight beat in his head like dull bells, each pealing with its full and final weight: 'Fedya, *Pavel is dead!*'

He had taken the telegram in his hands, read it himself, staring stupidly at the yellow sheet, trying to make the French say something other than what it said. Dead. Gone forever from a world of light into the prison of the past. With no return. And the funeral already taken care of. The account settled, the account with life. The book closed. Dead matter, as the printers say.

Mésaventure: Maykov's code-word. Suicide. And now Nechaev wants to tell him otherwise! His inclination, his wholehearted inclination, is to disbelieve Nechaev, to let the official story stand. But why? Because he detests Nechaev – his person, his doctrines? Because he wants to keep Pavel, even in retrospect, out of his clutches? Or is his motive shabbier: to dodge as long as possible the imperative that he seek justice for his son?

For he recognizes an inertia in himself of which Pavel's death is only the immediate cause. He is growing old, becoming day by day what he will at the last undoubtedly be: an old man in a corner with nothing to do but pick over the pages of his losses.

I am the one who died and was buried, he thinks, Pavel the one who lives and will always live. What I am struggling to do now is to understand what form this is in which I have returned from the grave.

He recalls a fellow-convict in Siberia, a tall, stooped, grey man who had violated his twelve-year-old daughter and then strangled her. He had been found after the event sitting by the side of a duckpond with the lifeless body in his arms. He had yielded without a struggle, insisting only on carrying the dead child home himself and laying her out on a table – doing all of this with, it was reported, the greatest tenderness. Shunned by the other prisoners, he spoke to no one. In the evenings he would sit on his bunk wearing a quiet smile, his lips moving as he read the Gospels to himself. In time one might have expected the ostracism to relax, his contrition to be accepted. But in fact he continued to be shunned, not so much for a crime committed twenty years ago as for that smile, in which there was something so sly and so mad that it chilled the blood. The same smile, they said one to another, as when he did the deed: nothing in his heart has changed.

Why does it recur now, this image of a man at the water's edge with a dead child in his arms? A child loved too much, a child become the object of such intimacy that it dare not be allowed to live. Murderous tenderness, tender murderousness. Love turned inside out like a glove to reveal its ugly stitching. And what is love stitched from? He calls up the image of the man again, looks intently into the face, concentrating not on the eyes, closed in a trance, but on the mouth, which is working lightly. Not rape but rapine – is that it? Fathers devouring children, raising them well in order to eat them like delicacies afterwards. *Delikatessen*.

Does that explain Nechaev's vengefulness: that his eyes have been opened to the fathers naked, the band of fathers, their appetites bared? What sort of man must he be, the elder Nechaev, father Gennady? When one day the news comes, as it undoubtedly will, that his son is no more, will he sit in a corner and weep, or will he secretly smile?

He shakes his head as if to rid it of a plague of devils. What is it that is corrupting the integrity of his grieving, that insists it is nothing but a lugubrious disguise? Somewhere inside him truth has lost its way. As if in the labyrinth of his brain, but also in the labyrinth of his body – veins, bones, intestines, organs – a tiny child is wandering, searching for the light, searching to emerge. How can he find the child lost within himself, allow him a voice to sing his sad song?

Piping on a bone. An old story comes back to him of a youth killed, mutilated, scattered, whose thigh-bone, when the wind blows, pipes a lament and names his murderers. One by one, in fact, the old stories are coming back, stories he heard from his grandmother and did not know the meaning of, but stored up unwittingly like bones for the future. A great ossuary of stories from before history began, built up and tended by the people. Let Pavel find his way to my thigh-bone and pipe to me from there! *Father, why have you left me in the dark forest? Father, when will you come to save me?*

The candle before the icon is nothing but a pool of wax; the spray of flowers droops. Having put up the shrine, the girl has forgotten or abandoned it. Does she guess that Pavel has ceased to speak to him, that he has lost his way too, that the only voices he hears now are devil-voices?

He scratches the wick erect, lights it, goes down on his knees. The Virgin's eyes are locked on her babe, who stares out of the picture at him, raising a tiny admonitory finger.

11

The walk

In the week that has passed since their last intimacy, there has grown up between Anna Sergeyevna and himself a barrier of awkward formality. Her bearing toward him has become so constrained that he is sure the child, who watches and listens all the time, must conclude she wants him gone from the house.

For whose sake are they keeping up this appearance of distance? Not for their own, surely. It can only be for the eyes of the children, the two children, the present one and the absent one.

Yet he hungers to have her in his arms again. Nor does he believe she is indifferent to him. On his own he feels like a dog chasing its tail in tighter and tighter circles. With her in the saving dark, he has an intimation that his limbs will be loosened and the spirit released, the spirit that at present seems knotted to his body at shoulders, hips, and knees.

At the core of his hunger is a desire that on the first night did not fully know itself but now seems to have becomes centred on her smell. As if she and he were animals, he is drawn by something he picks up in the air around her: the smell of autumn, and of walnuts in particular. He has begun to understand how animals live, and young children too, attracted or repelled by mists, auras, atmospheres. He sees himself sprawled over her like a lion, rooting with his muzzle in the hair of her neck, burying his nose in her armpit, rubbing his face in her crotch.

There is no lock on the door. It is not inconceivable that the child will wander into the room at a time like this and glimpse him in a state of – he approaches the word with distaste, but it is the only right word – lust. And so many children are sleepwalkers too: she could get up in the night and stray into his room without even waking. Are they passed down from mother to daughter, these intimate smells? Loving the mother, is one destined to long for the daughter too? Wandering thoughts, wandering desires! They will have to be buried with him, hidden forever from all except one. For Pavel is within him now, and Pavel never sleeps. He can only pray that a weakness that would once have disgusted the boy will now bring a smile to his lips, a smile amused and tolerant.

Perhaps Nechaev too, once he has crossed the dark river into death, will cease to be such a wolf and learn to smile again.

So he is waiting opposite Yakovlev's shop the next evening when Anna Sergeyevna emerges. He crosses the street, savouring her surprise as she sees him. 'Shall we take a walk?' he proposes.

She draws the dark shawl tighter under her chin. 'I don't know. Matryosha will be expecting me.'

Nevertheless they do walk. The wind has dropped, the air is crisp and cold. There is a pleasing bustle about

them in the streets. No one pays them any attention.
They might be any married couple.

She is carrying a basket, which he takes from her. He likes the way she walks, with long strides, arms folded under her breasts.

'I will have to be leaving soon,' he says.

She makes no reply.

The question of his wife lies delicately between them. In alluding to his departure he feels like a chess-player offering a pawn which, whether accepted or refused, must lead into deeper complications. Are affairs between men and women always like this, the one plotting, the other plotted against? Is plotting an element of the pleasure: to be the object of another's intrigue, to be shepherded into a corner and softly pressed to capitulate? As she walks by his side, is she too, in her way, plotting against him?

'I am waiting only for the investigation to run its course. I need not even stay for the ruling. All I want is the papers. The rest is immaterial.'

'And then you will go back to Germany?'

'Yes.'

They have reached the embankment. Crossing the street, he takes her arm. Side by side they lean against the rail by the waterside.

'I don't know whether to hate this city for what it did to Pavel,' he says, 'or to feel even more tightly bound to it. Because it is Pavel's home now. He will never leave it, never travel as he wanted to.'

'What nonsense, Fyodor Mikhailovich,' she replies with a sidelong smile. 'Pavel is with you. You are his home. He is in your heart, he travels with you wherever you go. Anyone can see that.' And she touches his breast lightly with her gloved hand.

He feels his heart leap as though her fingertip had brushed the organ itself. Coquetry – is that what it is, or does the gesture spring from her own heart? It would be the most natural thing in the world to take her in his arms. He can feel his gaze positively devour her shapely mouth, on which a smile still lingers. And beneath that gaze she does not flinch. Not a young woman. Not a child. Gazing back at him over the body of Pavel, the two of them throwing out their challenges. The flicker of a thought: *If only he were not here!* Then the thought vanishes around a corner.

From a street-seller they buy little fish-pasties for their supper. Matryona opens the door, but when she sees who is with her mother, turns her back. At table she is in a fretful mood, insisting that her mother pay attention to a long, confused story of a squabble between herself and a classmate at school. When he intervenes to make the mildest of pleas for the other girl, Matryona snorts and does not deign to answer.

She has sensed something, he knows, and is trying to reclaim her mother. And why not? It is her right. *Yet if only she were not here!* This time he does not suppress the thought. If the child were away he would not waste another word. He would snuff out the light, and in the dark he and she would find each other again. They would have the big bed to themselves, the widow-bed, the bed widowed of a man's body for – how long did she say? – four years?

He has a vision of Anna Sergeyevna that is crude in its sensuality. Her petticoat is pushed high up, so that beneath it her breasts are bared. He lies between her legs: her long pale thighs grip him. Her face is averted, her eyes closed, she is breathing heavily. Though the man coupling with her is himself, he sees all of this somehow from beside the bed. It is her thighs that dominate the vision: his hands curve around them, he presses them against his flanks.

'Come, finish the food on your plate,' she urges her daughter.

'I'm not hungry, my throat is sore,' Matryona whines. She toys with her food a moment longer, then pushes it aside.

He rises. 'Good night, Matryosha. I hope you feel better tomorrow.' The child does not bother to reply. He retires, leaving her in possession of the field.

He recognizes the source of the vision: a postcard he bought in Paris years ago and destroyed together with the rest of his erotica when he married Anya. A girl with long dark hair lying underneath a mustachioed man. GYPSY LOVE, read the caption in florid capitals. But the legs of the girl in the picture were plump, her flesh flaccid, her face, turned toward the man (who held himself up stiffly on his arms), devoid of expression. The thighs of Anna Sergeyevna, of the Anna Sergeyevna of his memory, are leaner, stronger; there is something purposeful in their grip which he links with the fact that she is not a child but a fullgrown, avid woman. Fullgrown and therefore open (that is the word that insists itself) to death. A body ready for experience because it knows it will not live forever. The thought is arousing but disturbing too. To those thighs it does not matter who is gripped between them; beheld from somewhere above and to the side of the bed, the man in the picture both is and is not himself.

There is a letter on his bed, propped against the pillow. For a wild instant he thinks it is from Pavel, spirited into the room. But the handwriting is a child's. 'I tried to draw Pavel Aleskandrovich,' it reads (the name misspelled), 'but I could not do it right. If you want to put it on the shrine you can. Matryona.' On the reverse is a pencil-drawing, somewhat smudged, of a young man with a high forehead and full lips. The drawing is crude, the child knows nothing about shading; nevertheless, in the mouth and particularly in the bold stare, she has unmistakably captured Pavel.

'Yes,' he whispers, 'I will put it on the shrine.' He brings the image to his lips, then stands it against the candle-holder and lights a new candle.

He is still gazing into the flame when, an hour later, Anna Sergeyevna taps at the door. 'I have your laundry,' she says.

'Come in. Sit down.'

'No, I can't. Matryosha is restless – I don't think she is well.' Nevertheless she sits down on the bed.

'They are keeping us good, these children of ours,' he remarks.

'Keeping us good?'

'Seeing to our morals. Keeping us apart.'

It is a relief not to have the dining-table between them. The candlelight, too, brings a comforting softness.

'I am sorry you have to leave,' she says, 'but perhaps it will be better for you to get away from this sad city. Better for your family too. They must be missing you. And you must be missing them.'

'I will be a different person. My wife will not know me. Or she will think she knows me, and be wrong. A difficult time for everyone, I foresee. I shall be thinking of you. But as whom? – that is the question. Anna is my wife's name too.'

'It was my name before it was hers.' Her reply is sharp, without playfulness. Again it is borne home to him: if he loves this woman, then in part it is because she is not young. She has crossed a line that his wife has yet to come to. She may or may not be dearer, but she is nearer.

The erotic tug returns, even stronger than before. A week ago they were in each other's arms in this same bed. Can it be that at this moment she is not thinking of that?

He leans across and lays a hand on her thigh. With the laundry on her lap, she bows her head. He shifts closer. Between thumb and forefinger he grips her bared neck, draws her face toward his. She raises her eyes: for an instant he has the impression he is looking into the eyes of a cat, wary, passionate, greedy.

'I must go,' she murmurs. Wriggling loose, she is gone.

He wants her acutely. More: he wants her not in this narrow child's-bed but in the widow-bed in the next room. He imagines her as she lies there now beside her daughter, her eyes open and glistening. She belongs, he realizes for the first time, to a type he has never written into his books. The women he is used to are not without an intensity of their own, but it is an intensity all of skin and nerves. Their sensations are intense, electric, immediate, of the surface. Whereas with her he goes into a body that bleeds, a visceral body whose sensations occur deep within itself.

Is it a feature that can be translated to, or cultivated in, other women? In his wife? Is there a quality of sensation he has been freed to find elsewhere now that he has found it in her?

What treachery!

If he were more confident of his French he would channel this disturbing excitement into a book of the kind one cannot publish in Russia – something that could be finished off in a hurry, in two or three weeks, even without a copyist – ten signatures, three hundred pages. A book of the night, in which every excess would be represented and no bounds respected. A book that would never be linked to him. The manuscript mailed from Dresden to Paillard in Paris, to be printed clandestinely and sold under the counter on the Left Bank. *Memoirs of a Russian Nobleman.* A book that she, Anna Sergeyevna, its true begetter, would never see. With a chapter in which the noble memoirist reads aloud to the young daughter of his mistress a story of the seduction of a young girl in which he himself emerges more and more clearly as having been the seducer. A story full of intimate detail and innuendo which by no means seduces the daughter but on the contrary frightens her and disturbs her sleep and makes her so doubtful of her own purity that three days later she gives herself up to him in despair, in the most shameful of ways, in a way of which no child could conceive were the history of her own seduction and surrender and the manner of its doing not deeply impressed on her beforehand.

Imaginary memoirs. Memories of the imagination.

Is that the answer to his question to himself? Is that what she is setting him free to do: to write a book of evil? And to what end? To liberate himself from evil or to cut himself off from good?

Not once in this long reverie, it occurs to him (the

whole house has fallen into silence by now), has he given
a thought to Pavel. And now, here he returns, whining, pale, searching for a place to lay his head! Poor child! The festival of the senses that would have been his inheritance stolen away from him! Lying in Pavel's bed, he cannot refrain from a quiver of dark triumph.

Usually he has the apartment to himself in the mornings. But today Matryona, flushed, coughing drily, heaving for breath, stays away from school. With her in the apartment, he is less than ever able to give his attention to writing. He finds himself listening for the pad of her bare feet in the next room; there are moments when he can swear he feels her eyes boring into his back.

At noon the concierge brings a message. He recognizes the grey paper and red seal at once. The end of waiting: he is instructed to call at the office of Judicial Investigator Councillor P. P. Maximov in connection with the matter of P. A. Isaev.

From Svechnoi Street he goes to the railway station to make a reservation, and from there to the police station. The ante-room is packed; he gives in his name at the desk and waits. At the first stroke of four the desk-sergeant puts down his pen, stretches, douses the light, and begins to shepherd the remaining petitioners out.

'What is this?' he protests.

'Friday, early closing,' says the sergeant. 'Come back in the morning.'

At six o'clock he is waiting outside Yakovlev's. Seeing him there, Anna Sergeyevna is alarmed. 'Matryosha – ?' she asks.

'She was sleeping when I left. I stopped at a pharmacy

 and got something for her cough.' He brings out a little brown bottle.

'Thank you.'

'I have been summoned again by the police in connection with Pavel's papers. I am hoping that the business will be settled once and for all tomorrow.'

They walk for a while in silence. Anna Sergeyevna seems preoccupied. At last she speaks. 'Is there a particular reason why you must have those papers?'

'I am surprised that you ask. What else of himself has Pavel left behind? Nothing is more important to me than those papers. They are his word to me.' And then, after a pause: 'Did you know he was writing a story?'

'He wrote stories. Yes, I knew.'

'The one I am thinking of was about an escaped convict.'

'I don't know that one. He would sometimes read what he was writing to Matryosha and me, to see what we thought. But not a story about a convict.'

'I didn't realize there were other stories.'

'Oh yes, there were stories. Poems too – but he was shy about showing those to us. The police must have taken them when they took everything else. They were in his room a long time, searching. I didn't tell you. They even lifted the floorboards and looked under them. They took every scrap of paper.'

'Is that how Pavel occupied himself, then – with writing?'

She glances at him oddly. 'How else did you think?'

He bites back a quick reply.

'With a writer for a father, what do you expect?' she goes on.

'Writing does not go in families.'

'Perhaps not. I am no judge. But he need not have intended to write for a living. Perhaps it was simply a way of reaching his father.'

He makes a gesture of exasperation. *I would have loved him without stories!* he thinks. Instead he says: 'One does not have to earn the love of one's father.'

She hesitates before she speaks again. 'There is something I should warn you of, Fyodor Mikhailovich. Pavel made a certain cult of his father – of Alexander Isaev, I mean. I would not mention it if I did not expect you will find traces of it in his papers. You must be tolerant. Children like to romanticize their parents. Even Matryona – '

'Romanticize Isaev? Isaev was a drunkard, a nobody, a bad husband. His wife, Pavel's own mother, could not abide him by the end. She would have left him had he not died first. How does one romanticize a person like that?'

'By seeing him through a haze, of course. It was hard for Pavel to see you through a haze. You were, if I may say so, too immediate to him.'

'That was because I was the one who had to bring him up day by day. I made him my son when everyone else had left him behind.'

'Don't exaggerate. His own parents didn't leave him behind, they died. Besides, if you had the right to choose him as a son, why had he no right to choose a father for himself?'

'Because he could do better than Isaev! It has become a sickness of this age of ours, young people turning their backs on their parents, their homes, their upbringing, because they are no longer to their liking! Nothing will satisfy them, it seems, but to be sons and daughters of Stenka Razin or Bakunin!'

'You're being silly. Pavel didn't run away from home. You ran away from him.'

An angry silence falls. When they reach Gorokhovaya Street he excuses himself and leaves her.

Walking up and down the embankment, he broods on what she has said. Without a doubt he has allowed something shameful about himself to emerge, and he resents her for having been witness to it. At the same time he is ashamed of such pettiness. He is caught in a familiar moral tangle – so familiar, in fact, that it no longer disturbs him, and should therefore be all the more shameful. But something else is troubling him too, like the point of a nail just beginning to come through a shoe, that he cannot or does not care to define.

There is still tension in the air when he returns to the apartment. Matryona is out of bed. She is wearing her mother's coat over her nightdress but her feet are bare. 'I'm bored!' she whines, over and over. She pays him no attention. Though she joins them at table, she will not eat. There is a sour smell about her, she wheezes, every now and again she has a fit of harsh coughing. 'You shouldn't be up, my dear,' he remarks mildly. 'You can't tell me what to do, you're not my father!' she retorts. 'Matryosha!' her mother reproves her. 'Well, he isn't!' she repeats, and falls into pouting silence.

After he has retired, Anna Sergeyevna taps at his door and comes in. He rises cautiously. 'How is she?'

'I gave her some of the medicine you bought, and she seems to be more restful. She shouldn't be getting out of bed, but she is wilful and I can't stop her. I came to apologize for what I said. Also to ask about your plans for tomorrow.'

'There is no need to apologize. I was the one at fault. I have made a reservation on the evening train. But it can be changed.'

'Why? You will get your papers tomorrow. Why should anything be changed? Why stay longer than necessary? You don't want to become the eternal lodger, after all. Isn't that the name of a book?'

'The eternal lodger? No, not that I know of. All arrangements can be changed, including tomorrow's. Nothing is final. But in this case it is not in my hands to change them.'

'In whose hands then?'

'In yours.'

'In my hands? Certainly not! Your arrangements are in your hands alone, I have no part in them. We should say goodbye now. I won't see you in the morning. I have to get up early, it's market day. You can leave the key in the door.'

So the moment has come. He takes a deep breath. His mind is quite blank. Out of that blankness he begins to speak, surrendering to the words that come, going where they take him.

'On the ferry, when you took me to see Pavel's grave,' he says, 'I watched you and Matryosha standing at the rail staring into the mist – you remember the mist that day – and I said to myself, "She will bring him back. She is" ' – he takes another breath – ' "she is a conductress of souls." That was not the word that came to me at the time, but I know now it is the right word.'

She regards him without expression. He takes her hand between his.

'I want to have him back,' he says. 'You must help me. I want to kiss him on the lips.'

As he speaks the words he hears how mad they are. He seems to move into and out of madness like a fly at an open window.

She has grown tense, ready to flee. He grips her tighter, holding her back.

'That is the truth. That is how I think of you. Pavel did not arrive here by chance. Somewhere it was written that from here he was to be conducted . . . into the night.'

He believes and does not believe what he is saying. A fragment of memory comes back to him, of a painting he has seen in a gallery somewhere: a woman in dark, severe dress standing at a window, a child at her side, both of them gazing up into a starry sky. More vividly than the picture itself he remembers the gilded curlicues of the frame.

Her hand lies lifeless between his.

'You have it in your power,' he continues, still following the words like beacons, seeing where they will take him. 'You can bring him back. For one minute. For just one minute.'

He remembers how dry she seemed when he first met her. Like a mummy: dry bones wrapped in cerements that will fall to dust at a touch. When she speaks, the voice creaks from her throat. 'You love him so much,' she says: 'you will certainly see him again.'

He lets go her hand. Like a chain of bones, she withdraws it. *Don't humour me!* he wants to say.

'You are an artist, a master,' she says. 'It is for you, not for me, to bring him back to life.'

Master. It is a word he associates with metal – with

the tempering of swords, the casting of bells. A master blacksmith, a foundry-master. *Master of life*: strange term. But he is prepared to reflect on it. He will give a home to any word, no matter how strange, no matter how stray, if there is a chance it is an anagram for Pavel.

'I am far from being a master,' he says. 'There is a crack running through me. What can one do with a cracked bell? A cracked bell cannot be mended.'

What he says is true. Yet at the same time he recalls that one of the bells of the Cathedral of the Trinity in Sergiyev is cracked, and has been from before Catherine's time. It has never been removed and melted down. It sounds over the town every day. The people call it St Sergius's wooden leg.

Now there is exasperation in her voice. 'I feel for you, Fyodor Mikhailovich,' she says, 'but you must remember you are not the first parent to lose a child. Pavel had twenty-two years of life. Think of all the children who are taken in infancy.'

'So – ?'

'So recognize that it is the rule, not the exception, to suffer loss. And ask yourself: are you in mourning for Pavel or for yourself?'

Loss. An icy distance instals itself between him and her. 'I have not lost him, he is not lost,' he says through clenched teeth.

She shrugs. 'If he is not lost then you must know where he is. He is certainly not in this room.'

He glances around the room. That bunching of shadows in the corner – might it not be the trace of the breath of the shadow of the ghost of him? 'One does not live in a place and leave nothing of oneself behind,' he whispers.

 'No, of course one does not leave nothing behind. That is what I told you this afternoon. But what he left is not in this room. He has gone from here, this is not where you will find him. Speak to Matryona. Make your peace with her before you leave. She and your son were very close. If he has left a mark behind, it is on her.'

'And on you?'

'I was very fond of him, Fyodor Mikhailovich. He was a good and generous young man. As your son, he did not have an easy life. He was lonely, he was unsure of himself, he had to struggle to find his way. I could see all of that. But I am not of his generation. He could not speak to me as he could to Matryona. He and she could be children together.' She pauses. 'I used to get the feeling – let me mention it now, since we are being frank with each other – that the child in Pavel was put down too early, before he had had enough time to play. I don't know whether it occurred to you. Perhaps not. But I am still surprised at your anger against him for something as trivial as sleeping late.'

'Why surprised?'

'Because I expected more sympathy from you – from an artist. Some children dream at night, others wait for the morning to do their dreaming. You should think twice about waking a dreaming child. When Pavel was with Matryona the child in him had a chance to come out. I am glad now that it could happen – glad he did not miss it.'

An image of Pavel comes back to him as he was at seven, in his grey checked coat and ear-muffs and boots too large for him, galloping about in the snow, shouting crazily. There is something else looming too in the corner of the picture, something he thrusts away.

'Pavel and I first laid eyes on each other in Semipalatinsk when he was already seven years old,' he says. 'He did not take to me. I was the stranger he and his mother were coming to live with. I was the man who was taking his mother away from him.'

His mother the widow. A widow's son. Widowson.

What he has been thrusting away, what comes back insistently as he talks, is what he can only call a troll, a misshapen little creature, red-haired, red-bearded, no taller than a child of three or four. Pavel is still running and shouting in the snow, his knees knocking together coltishly. As for the troll, he stands to one side looking on. He is wearing a rust-coloured jerkin open at the neck; he (or it) does not seem to feel the cold.

'. . . difficult for a child . . .' She is saying something he can only half attend to. Who is this troll-creature? He peers more closely into the face. With a shock it comes home to him. The cratered skin, the scars swelling hard and livid in the cold, the thin beard growing out of the pock-marks — it is Nechaev again, Nechaev grown small, Nechaev in Siberia haunting the beginnings of his son! What does the vision mean? He groans softly to himself, and at once Anna Sergeyevna cuts herself short. 'I am sorry,' he apologizes. But he has offended her. 'I am sure you have packing to do,' she says, and, over his apologies, departs.

12

Isaev

He is conducted into the same office as before. But the official behind the desk is not Maximov. Without introducing himself this man gestures towards a chair. 'Your name?' he says.

He gives his name. 'I thought I was going to see Councillor Maximov.'

'We will come to that. Occupation?'

'Writer.'

'Writer? What kind of writer?'

'I write books.'

'What kind of books?'

'Stories. Story-books.'

'For children?'

'No, not particularly for children. But I would hope that children can read them.'

'Nothing indecent?'

Nothing indecent? He ponders. 'Nothing that could offend a child,' he responds at last.

'Good.'

'But the heart has its dark places,' he adds reluctantly. 'One does not always know.'

For the first time the man raises his eyes from his papers. 'What do you mean by that?' He is younger than Maximov. Maximov's assistant?

'Nothing. Nothing.'

The man lays down his pen. 'Let us get to the subject of the deceased Ivanov. You were acquainted with Ivanov?'

'I don't understand. I thought I was summoned here in connection with my son's papers.'

'All in good time. Ivanov. When did you first have contact with him?'

'I first spoke to him about a week ago. He was loitering at the door of the house where I am at present staying.'

'Sixty-three Svechnoi Street.'

'Sixty-three Svechnoi Street. It was particularly cold, and I offered him shelter. He spent the night in my room. The next day I heard there had been a murder and he was suspected. Only later – '

'Ivanov was suspected? Suspected of murder? Do I understand you thought Ivanov was a murderer? Why did you think so?'

'Please allow me to finish! There was a rumour to that effect going around the building, or else the child who repeated the rumour to me misunderstood everything, I don't know which. Does it matter, when the fact is the man is dead? I was surprised and appalled that someone like that should have been killed. He was quite harmless.'

'But he was not what he seemed to be, was he?'

'Do you mean a beggar?'

'He was not a beggar, was he?'

'In a manner of speaking, no, he wasn't, but in another manner of speaking, yes, he was.'

'You are not being clear. Are you claiming that you

 were unaware of Ivanov's responsibilities? Is that why you were surprised?'

'I was surprised that anyone should have put his immortal soul in peril by killing a harmless nonentity.'

The official regards him sardonically. 'A nonentity – is that your Christian word on him?'

At this moment Maximov himself enters in a great hurry. Under his arm is a pile of folders tied with pink ribbons. He drops these on the desk, takes out a handkerchief, and wipes his brow. 'So hot in here!' he murmurs; and then, to his colleague: 'Thank you. You have finished?'

Without a word the man gathers up his papers and leaves. Sighing, mopping his face, Maximov takes over the chair. 'So sorry, Fyodor Mikhailovich. Now: the matter of your stepson's papers. I am afraid we are going to have to keep back one item, namely the list of people to be, as our friends say, liquidated, which – I am sure you will agree – should not go into circulation, since it will only cause alarm. Besides, it will in due course form part of the case against Nechaev. As for the rest of the papers, they are yours, we have finished with them, we have, so to speak, extracted their honey from them.

'However, before I pass them over to you for good, there is one thing further I would like to say, if you will do me the honour of hearing me out.

'If I thought of myself merely as a functionary whose path of duty you have happened to cross, I would return these papers to you without more ado. But in the present case I am not a mere functionary. I am also, if you will permit me to use the word, a well-wisher, someone with your best interests at heart. And as such I have a severe reservation about handing them over. Let me state that reservation. It is that painful discoveries lie in store for you – painful and unnecessary discoveries. If it were possible that you could bring yourself to accept my humble guidance, I could indicate particular pages it would be better for you not to dwell on. But of course, knowing you as I do, that is, in the way one knows a writer from his books, that is to say, in an intimate yet limited way, I expect that my efforts would have only the contrary effect – of whetting your curiosity. Therefore let me say only the following: do not blame me for having read these papers – that is after all the responsibility laid on me by the Crown – and do not be angry with me for having correctly foreseen (if indeed I have) your response to them. Unless there is a surprising turn of events, you and I will have no further dealings. There is no reason why you should not tell yourself that I have ceased to exist, in the same way that a character in a book can be said to cease to exist as soon as the book is closed. For my part, you may be assured my lips are sealed. No one will hear a word from me about this sad episode.'

So saying, Maximov, using only the middle finger of his right hand, prods the folder across the desk, the surprisingly thick folder that holds Pavel's papers.

He rises, takes the folder, makes his bow, and is preparing to leave when Maximov speaks again. 'If I may detain you a moment longer in a somewhat different regard: you have not by any chance had contact with the Nechaev gang here in Petersburg, have you?'

Ivanov! Nechaev! So that is the reason why he has been called in! Pavel, the papers, Maximov's dance of compunctiousness – nothing but a side-issue, a lure!

'I do not see the bearing of your question,' he replies

 stiffly. 'I do not see by what right you ask or expect me to answer.'

'By no right at all! Set your mind at rest – you are accused of nothing. Simply a question. As for its bearing, I would not have thought that so difficult to work out. Having discussed your stepson with me, I reasoned, perhaps you would now find it easier to discuss Nechaev. For in our conversation the other day it seemed to me that what you chose to say sometimes had a double meaning. A word had another word hidden beneath it, so to speak. What do you think? Was I wrong?'

'Which words? What lay beneath them?'

'That is for you to say.'

'You are wrong. I do not speak in riddles. Every word I use means what it says. Pavel is Pavel, not Nechaev.'

With that he turns and takes his departure; nor does Maximov call him back.

Through the winding streets of the Moskovskaya quarter he bears the folder to Svechnoi Street, to No. 63, up the stairs to the third floor, to his room, and closes the door.

He unties the ribbon. His heart is hammering unpleasantly. That there is something unsavoury in his haste he cannot deny. It is as if he has been conveyed back to boyhood, to the long, sweaty afternoons in his friend Albert's bedroom poring over books filched from Albert's uncle's shelves. The same terror of being caught red-handed (a terror delicious in itself), the same passionate engrossment.

He remembers Albert showing him two flies in the act of copulating, the male riding on the female's back. Albert held the flies in his cupped hand. 'Watch,' he said. He pinched one of the male's wings between his fingertips and tugged lightly. The wing came off. The fly paid no attention. He tore off the second wing. The fly, with its strange, bald back, went on with its business. With an expression of distaste, Albert flung the couple to the ground and crushed it.

He could imagine staring into the fly's eyes while its wings were being torn off: he was sure it would not blink; perhaps it would not even see him. It was as though, for the duration of the act, its soul went into the female. The thought had made him shudder; it had made him want to annihilate every fly on earth.

A childish response to an act he did not understand, an act he feared because everyone around him, whispering, grinning, seemed to hint that he too, one day, would be required to perform it. 'I won't, I won't!' the child wants to pant. 'Won't what?' reply the watchers, all of a sudden wide-eyed, nonplussed – 'Goodness, what is this strange child talking about?'

The folder contains a leather-bound diary, five school exercise books, twenty or twenty-five loose pages pinned together, a packet of letters tied with string, and some printed pamphlets: feuilletons of texts by Blanqui and Ishutin, an essay by Pisarev. The odd item is Cicero's *De Officiis*, extracts with French translation. He pages through it. On the last page, in a handwriting he does not recognize, he comes upon two inscriptions: *Salus populi suprema lex esto*, and below it, in lighter ink, *Talis pater qualis filius*.

A message, messages; but from whom to whom?

He takes up the diary and, without reading, ruffles through it like a deck of cards. The second half is empty. Still, the body of writing in it is substantial. He glances at the first date. 29 June 1866, Pavel's name-day. The diary must have been a gift. A gift from whom? He cannot recall. 1866 stands out only as the year of Anya, the year when he met and fell in love with his wife-to-be. 1866 was a year in which Pavel was ignored.

As if touching a hot dish, alert, ready to recoil, he begins to read the first entry. A recital, and a somewhat laboured one at that, of how Pavel spent the day. The work of a novice diarist. No accusations, no denunciations. With relief he closes the book. When I am in Dresden, he promises himself, when I have time, I will read the whole of it.

As for the letters, all are from himself. He opens the most recent, the last before Pavel's death. 'I am sending Apollon Grigorevich fifty roubles,' he reads. 'It is all we can afford at present. Please do not press A.G. for more. You must learn to live within your means.'

His last words to Pavel, and what petty-minded words! And this is what Maximov saw! No wonder he warned against reading! How ignominious! He would like to burn the letter, to erase it from history.

He searches out the story from which Maximov read aloud to him. Maximov was right: as a character, Sergei, its young hero, deported to Siberia for leading a student uprising, is a failure. But the story goes on longer than Maximov had led him to believe. For days after the wicked landowner has been slain, Sergei and his Marfa flee the soldiers, sheltering in barns and byres, abetted by peasants who hide them and feed them and meet their pursuers' questions with blank stupidity. At first they sleep side by side in chaste comradeship; but love grows up between them, a love rendered not without feeling, not without conviction. Pavel is clearly working up to a scene of passion. There is a page, heavily crossed out, in which Sergei confesses to Marfa, in ardent juvenile fashion, that she has become more to him than a companion in the struggle, that she has captured his heart; in its place there is a much more interesting sequence in which he confides to her the story of his lonely childhood without brothers and sisters, his youthful clumsiness with women. The sequence ends with Marfa stammering her own confession of love. 'You may . . . You may . . .' she says.

He turns the leaves back. 'I have no parents,' says Sergei to Marfa. 'My father, my real father, was a nobleman exiled to Siberia for his revolutionary sympathies. He died when I was seven. My mother married a second time. Her new husband did not like me. As soon as I was old enough, he packed me off to cadet school. I was the smallest boy in my class; that was where I learned to fight for my rights. Later they moved back to Petersburg, set up house, and sent for me. Then my mother died, and I was left alone with my stepfather, a gloomy man who addressed barely a word to me from one day to the next. I was lonely; my only friends were among the servants; it was from them that I got to know the sufferings of the people.'

Not untrue, not wholly untrue, yet how subtly twisted, all of it! 'He did not like me' – ! One could be sorry for the friendless seven-year-old and sincerely wish to protect him, but how could one love him when he was so suspicious, so unsmiling, when he clung to his mother like a leech and grudged every minute she spent away from him, when half a dozen times in a single night they would hear from the next room that high, insistent little voice calling to his mother to come and kill the mosquito that was biting him?

 He lays aside the manuscript. A nobleman for a father indeed! Poor child! The truth duller than that, the full truth dullest of all. But who except the recording angel would care to write the full, dull truth? Did he himself write with as much dedication at the age of twenty-two?

There is something overwhelmingly important he wants to say that the boy will now never be able to hear. If you are blessed with the power to write, he wants to say, bear in mind the source of that power. You write *because* your childhood was lonely, *because* you were not loved. (*Yet that is not the full story*, he also wants to say – *you were loved, you would have been loved, it was your choice to be unloved*. What confusion! An ape on a harmonium would do better!) We do not write out of plenty, he wants to say – we write out of anguish, out of lack. Surely in your heart you must know that! As for your so-called true father and his revolutionary sympathies, what non-sense! Isaev was a clerk, a pen-pusher. If he had lived, if you had followed him, you too would have become nothing but a clerk, and you would not have left this story behind. (*Yes, yes*, he hears the child's high voice – *but I would be alive!*)

Young men in white playing the French game, croquet, *croixquette*, game of the little cross, and you on the green-sward among them, alive! Poor boy! On the streets of Petersburg, in the turn of a head here, the gesture of a hand there, I see you, and each time my heart lifts as a wave does. Nowhere and everywhere, torn and scat-tered like Orpheus. Young in days, *chryseos*, golden, blessed.

The task left to me: to gather the hoard, put together the scattered parts. Poet, lyre-player, enchanter, lord of resurrection, that is what I am called to be. And the truth? Stiff shoulders humped over the writing-table, and the ache of a heart slow to move. A tortoise heart.

I came too late to raise the coffin-lid, to kiss your smooth cold brow. If my lips, tender as the fingertips of the blind, had been able to brush you just once, you would not have quit this existence bitter against me. But bearing the name Isaev you have departed, and I, old man, old pilgrim, am left to follow behind, pursuing a shade, violet upon grey, an echo.

Still, I am here and father Isaev is not. If, drowning, you reach for Isaev, you will grasp only a phantom hand. In the town hall of Semipalatinsk, in dusty files in a box on the back stairs, his signature is still perhaps to be read; otherwise no trace of him save in this remembering, in the remembering of the man who embraced his widow and his child.

13

The disguise

The file on Pavel is closed. There is nothing to keep him in Petersburg. The train leaves at eight o'clock; by Tuesday he can be with his wife and child in Dresden. But as the hour approaches it becomes more and more inconceivable that he will remove the pictures from the shrine, blow out the candle, and give up Pavel's room to a stranger.

Yet if he does not leave tonight, when will he leave? 'The eternal lodger' – where did Anna Sergeyevna pick up the phrase? How long can he go on waiting for a ghost? Unless he puts himself on another footing with the woman, another footing entirely. But what then of his wife?

His mind is in a whirl, he does not know what he wants, all he knows is that eight o'clock hangs over him like a sentence of death. He searches out the concierge and after lengthy haggling secures a messenger to take his ticket to the station and have the reservation changed to the next day.

Returning, he is startled to find his door open and someone in the room: a woman standing with her back

to him, inspecting the shrine. For a guilty moment he
thinks it is his wife, come to Petersburg to track him down. Then he recognizes who it is, and a cry of protest rises in his throat: Sergei Nechaev, in the same blue dress and bonnet as before!

At that moment Matryona enters from the apartment. Before he can speak she seizes the initiative. 'You shouldn't sneak in on people like that!' she exclaims.

'But what are the two of you doing in my room?'

'We have just as much right – ' she begins vehemently. Then Nechaev interrupts.

'Someone led the police to us,' he says. He steps closer. 'I hope not you.'

Beneath the scent of lavender he can smell rank male sweat. The powder around Nechaev's throat is streaked; stubble is breaking through.

'That is a contemptible accusation to make, quite contemptible. I repeat: what are you doing in my room?' He turns to Matryona. 'And you – you are sick, you should be in bed!'

Ignoring his words, she tugs Pavel's suitcase out. 'I said he could have Pavel Alexandrovich's suit,' she says; and then, before he can object: 'Yes, he can! Pavel bought it with his own money, and Pavel was his friend!'

She unbuckles the suitcase, brings out the white suit. 'There!' she says defiantly.

Nechaev gives the suit a quick glance, spreads it out on the bed, and begins to unbutton his dress.

'Please explain – '

'There is no time. I need a shirt too.'

He tugs his arms out of the sleeves. The dress drops around his ankles and he stands before them in grubby cotton underwear and black patent-leather boots. He wears no stockings; his legs are lean and hairy.

Not in the least embarrassed, Matryona begins to help him on with Pavel's clothes. He wants to protest, but what can he say to the young when they shut their ears, close ranks against the old?

'What has become of your Finnish friend? Isn't she with you?'

Nechaev slips on the jacket. It is too long and the shoulders are too wide. Not as well built as Pavel, not as handsome. He feels a desolate pride in his son. The wrong one taken!

'I had to leave her,' says Nechaev. 'It was important to get away quickly.'

'In other words you abandoned her.' And then, before Nechaev can respond: 'Wash your face. You look like a clown.'

Matryona slips away, comes back with a wet rag. Nechaev wipes his face. 'Your forehead too,' she says. 'Here.' She takes the rag from him and wipes off the powder that has caked in his eyebrows.

Little sister. Was she like this with Pavel too? Something gnaws at his heart: envy.

'Do you really expect to escape the police dressed like a holidaymaker in the middle of winter?'

Nechaev does not rise to the gibe. 'I need money,' he says.

'You won't get any from me.'

Nechaev turns to the child. 'Have you got any money?'

She dashes from the room. They hear a chair being dragged across the floor; she returns with a jar full of coins. She pours them out on the bed and begins to count. 'Not enough,' Nechaev mutters, but waits nevertheless. 'Five roubles and fifteen kopeks,' she announces.

'I need more.'

'Then go into the streets and beg for it. You won't get it from me. Go and beg for alms in the name of the people.'

They glare at each other.

'Why won't you give him money?' says Matryona. 'He's Pavel's friend!'

'I don't have money to give.'

'That isn't true! You told Mama you had lots of money. Why don't you give him half? Pavel Alexandrovich would have given him half.'

Pavel and Jesus! 'I said nothing of the kind. I don't have lots of money.'

'Come, give it to me!' Nechaev grips his arm; his eyes glitter. Again he smells the young man's fear. Fierce but frightened: poor fellow! Then, deliberately, he closes the door on pity. 'Certainly not.'

'Why are you so *mean*?' Matryona bursts out, uttering the word with all the contempt at her command.

'I am not mean.'

'Of course you are mean! You were mean to Pavel and now you are mean to his friends! You have lots of money but you keep it all for yourself.' She turns to Nechaev. 'They pay him thousands of roubles to write books and he keeps it all for himself! It's true! Pavel told me!'

'What nonsense! Pavel knew nothing about money matters.'

'It's true! Pavel looked in your desk! He looked in your account books!'

'Damn Pavel! Pavel doesn't know how to read a ledger, he sees only what he wants to see! I have been carrying debts for years that you can't even imagine!' He turns to Nechaev. 'This is a ridiculous conversation. I don't have money to give you. I think you should leave at once.'

But Nechaev is no longer in a hurry. He is even smiling. 'Not a ridiculous conversation at all,' he says. 'On the contrary, most instructive. I have always had a suspicion about fathers, that their real sin, the one they never confess, is greed. They want everything for themselves. They won't hand over the moneybags, even when it's time. The moneybags are all that matter to them; they couldn't care less what happens as a consequence. I didn't believe what your stepson told me because I had heard you were a gambler and I thought gamblers didn't care about money. But there is a second side to gambling, isn't there? I should have seen that. You must be the kind who gambles because he is never satisfied, who is always greedy for more.'

It is a ludicrous charge. He thinks of Anya in Dresden scrimping to keep the child fed and clothed. He thinks of his own turned collars, of the holes in his socks. He thinks of the letters he has written year after year, exercises in self-abasement every one of them, to Strakhov and Kraevsky and Lyubimov, to Stellovsky in particular, begging for advances. *Dostoëvski l'avare* – preposterous! He feels in his pocket and brings out his last roubles. 'This,' he exclaims, thrusting them beneath Nechaev's nose, 'this is all I have!'

Nechaev regards the out-thrust hand coolly, then in a single swooping movement snatches the money, all save a coin that falls and rolls under the bed. Matryona dives after it.

He tries to take his money back, even tussles with the younger man. But Nechaev holds him off easily, in the same movement spiriting the money into his pocket.

'Wait . . . wait . . . wait,' Nechaev murmurs. 'In your heart, Fyodor Mikhailovich, in your heart, for your son's sake, I know you want to give it to me.' And he takes a step back, smoothing the suit as if to show off its splendour.

What a poseur! What a hypocrite! The People's Vengeance indeed! Yet he cannot deny that a certain gaiety is creeping into his own heart, a gaiety he recognizes, the gaiety of the spendthrift husband. Of course they are something to be ashamed of, these reckless bouts of his. Of course, when he comes home stripped bare and confesses to his wife and bows his head and endures her reproaches and vows he will never lapse again, he is sincere. But at the bottom of his heart, beneath the sincerity, where only God can see, he knows he is right and she is wrong. Money is there to be spent, and what form of spending is purer than gambling?

Matryona is holding out her hand. In the palm is a single fifty-kopek coin. She seems unsure to whom it should go. He nudges the hand toward Nechaev. 'Give it to him, he needs it.' Nechaev pockets the coin.

Good. Done. Now it is his turn to take up the position of penniless virtue, Nechaev's turn to bow his head and be scolded. But what has he to say? Nothing, nothing at all.

Nor does Nechaev care to wait. He is bundling up the blue dress. 'Find somewhere to hide this,' he instructs Matryona – 'not in the apartment – somewhere else.' He hands her the hat and wig too, tucks the cuffs of his trousers into his trim little boots, dons his coat, pats his head distractedly. 'Wasted too much time,' he mutters. 'Have you – ?' He snatches a fur cap from the chair and makes for the door. Then he remembers something and turns back. 'You are an interesting man, Fyodor Mikhailovich. If you had a daughter of the right age I wouldn't mind marrying her. She would be an exceptional girl, I am sure. But as for your stepson, he was another story, not like you at all. I'm not sure I would have known what to do with him. He didn't have – you know – what it takes. That's my opinion, for what it's worth.'

'And what does it take?'

'He was a bit too much of a saint. You are right to burn candles for him.'

While he speaks, he has been idly waving a hand over the candle, making the flame dance. Now he puts a finger directly into the flame and holds it there. The seconds pass: one, two, three, four, five. The look on his face does not change. He could be in a trance.

He removes his hand. 'That's what he didn't have. Bit of a sissy, in fact.'

He puts an arm around Matryona, gives her a hug. She responds without reserve, pressing her blonde head against his breast, returning his embrace.

'*Wachsam, wachsam!*' whispers Nechaev meaningfully, and, over her head, wags the burned finger at him. Then he is gone.

It takes a moment to make sense of the strange syllables. Even after he has recognized the word he fails to understand. Vigilant: vigilant about what?

Matryona is at the window, craning down over the street. There are quick tears in her eyes, but she is too excited to be sad. 'Will he be safe, do you think?' she asks; and then, without waiting for an answer: 'Shall I go with him? He can pretend he is blind and I am leading him.' But it is just a passing idea.

He stands close behind her. It is almost dark; snow is beginning to fall; soon her mother will be home.

'Do you like him?' he asks.

'Mm.'

'He leads a busy life, doesn't he?'

'Mm.'

She barely hears him. What an unequal contest! How can he compete with these young men who come from nowhere and vanish into nowhere breathing adventure and mystery? Busy lives indeed: she is the one who should be *wachsam*.

'Why do you like him so much, Matryosha?'

'Because he is Pavel Alexandrovich's best friend.'

'Is that true?' he objects mildly. 'I think I am Pavel Alexandrovich's best friend. I will go on being his friend when everyone else has forgotten him. I am his friend for life.'

She turns away from the window and regards him oddly, on the point of saying something. But what? 'You are only Pavel Alexandrovich's stepfather'? Or something quite different: 'Do not use that voice when you speak to me'?

Pushing the hair away from her face in what he has come to recognize as a gesture of embarrassment, she tries to duck under his arm. He stops her bodily, barring her way. 'I have to . . .' she whispers – 'I have to hide the clothes.'

He gives her a moment longer to feel her powerlessness. Then he stands aside. 'Throw them down the privy,' he says. 'No one will look there.'

She wrinkles her nose. 'Down?' she says. 'In . . . ?'

'Yes, do as I say. Or give them to me and go back to bed. I'll do it for you.'

For Nechaev, no. But for you.

He wraps the clothes in a towel and steals downstairs to the privy. But then he has second thoughts. Clothes among the human filth: what if he is underestimating the nightsoil collectors?

He notices the concierge peering at him from his lodge and turns purposefully toward the street. Then he realizes he has come without his coat. Climbing the stairs again, he is all at once face to face with Amalia Karlovna, the old woman from the first floor. She holds out a plate of cinnamon cakes as if to welcome him. 'Good afternoon, sir,' she says ceremoniously. He mutters a greeting and brushes past.

What is he searching for? For a hole, a crevice, into which the bundle that is so suddenly and obstinately *his* can disappear and be forgotten. Without cause or reason, he has become like a girl with a stillborn baby, or a murderer with a bloody axe. Anger against Nechaev rises in him again. *Why am I risking myself for you,* he wants to cry, *you who are nothing to me?* But too late, it seems. At the instant he accepted the bundle from Matryona's hands, a shift took place; there is no way back to before.

At the end of the corridor, where one of the rooms stands empty, lies a heap of plaster and rubble. He scratches at it halfheartedly with the toe of his boot. A workman stops his trowelling and, through the open door, regards him mistrustfully.

At least there is no Ivanov to follow him around. But perhaps Ivanov has been replaced by now. Who would the new spy be? Is this very workman paid to keep an eye on him? Is the concierge?

He stuffs the bundle under his jacket and makes for the street again. The wind is like a wall of ice. At the first corner he turns, then turns again. He is in the same blind alley where he found the dog. There is no dog today. Did the dog die the night he abandoned it?

He sets the bundle down in a corner. The curls, pinned to the hat, flap in the wind, both comical and sinister. Where did Nechaev get the curls – from one of his sisters? How many little sisters does he have, all itching to snip off their maiden locks for him?

Removing the pins, he tries in vain to tear the hat in two, then crumples it and stuffs it up the drainpipe to which the dog had been tied. He tries to do the same with the dress, but the pipe is too narrow.

He can feel eyes boring into his back. He turns. From a second-floor window two children are staring down at him, and behind them a shadowy third person, taller.

He tries to pull the hat out of the pipe but cannot reach it. He curses his stupidity. With the pipe blocked, the gutter will overflow. Someone will investigate, and the hat will be found. Who would push a hat up a pipe – who but a guilty soul?

He remembers Ivanov again – Ivanov, called Ivanov so often that the name has settled on him like a hat. Ivanov was murdered. But Ivanov was not wearing a hat, or not a woman's hat. So the hat cannot be traced to Ivanov. On the other hand, might it not be Ivanov's murderer's hat? How easy for a woman to murder a man: lure him down an alley, accept his embrace against a wall, and then, at the climax of the act, search his ribs and sink a hatpin into his heart – a hatpin, that leaves no blood and only a pinprick of a wound.

He goes down on his knees in the corner where he

 tossed the hatpins, but it is too dark to find them. He needs a candle. But what candle would stay alive in this wind?

He is so tired that he finds it hard to get to his feet. Is he sick? Has he picked up something from Matryona? Or is another fit on its way? Is that what it portends, this utter exhaustion?

On all fours, raising his head, sniffing the air like a wild animal, he tries to concentrate his attention on the horizon inside himself. But if what is taking him over is a fit, it is taking over his senses too. His senses are as dull as his hands.

14

The police

He has left his key behind, so has to knock at the door. Anna Sergeyevna opens it and stares in surprise. 'Have you missed your train?' she asks. Then she takes in his wild appearance – the shaking hands, the moisture dripping from his beard. 'Is something wrong? Are you ill?'

'Not ill, no. I have put off my departure. I will explain everything later.'

There is someone else in the room, at Matryona's bedside: a doctor evidently, young, cleanshaven in the German fashion. In his hand he has the brown bottle from the pharmacy, which he sniffs, then corks disapprovingly. He snaps his bag shut, draws the curtain to across the alcove. 'I was saying that your daughter has an inflammation of the bronchi,' he says, addressing him. 'Her lungs are sound. There is also – '

He interrupts. 'Not my daughter. I am only a lodger here.'

With an impatient shrug the doctor turns back to Anna Sergeyevna. 'There is also – I cannot neglect to say this – a certain hysterical element present.'

'What does that mean?'

'It means that as long as she is in her present excited state we cannot expect her to recover properly. Her excitement is part of what is wrong with her. She must be calmed down. Once that has been achieved, she can be back in school within days. She is physically healthy, there is nothing wrong with her constitution. So as a treatment I recommend quiet above all, peace and quiet. She should stay in bed and take only light meals. Avoid giving her milk in any of its forms. I am leaving behind an embrocation for her chest and a sleeping-draught for use as required, as a calmative. Give her only a child's dose, mind you – half a teaspoon.'

As soon as the doctor has left he tries to explain himself. But Anna Sergeyevna is in no mood to listen. 'Matryosha says you have been shouting at her!' she interrupts him in a tense whisper. 'I won't have that!'

'It's not true! I have never shouted at her!' Despite the whispering he is sure that Matryona, behind the curtain, overhears them and is gloating. He takes Anna Sergeyevna by the arm, draws her into his room, closes the door. 'You heard what the doctor said – she is over-excited. Surely you cannot believe every word she says in that state. Has she told you the entire story of what happened here this morning?'

'She says a friend of Pavel's called and you were very rude to him. Is that what you are referring to?'

'Yes – '

'Then let me finish. What goes on between you and Pavel's friends is none of my business. But you also lost your temper with Matryosha and were rough with her. That I won't stand for.'

'The friend she refers to is Nechaev, Nechaev himself,

no one else. Did she mention that? Nechaev, a fugitive from justice, was here today, in your apartment. Can you blame me for being cross with her for letting him in and then taking sides with him – that actor, that hypocrite – against me?'

'Nevertheless, you have no right to lose your temper with her! How is she to know that Nechaev is a bad person? How am I to know? You say he is an actor. What about you? What about your own behaviour? Do you act from the heart all the time? I don't think so.'

'You can't mean that. I do act from the heart. Once upon a time I may not have, but now I do – now above all. That is the truth.'

'Now? Why all of a sudden now? Why should I believe you? Why should you believe yourself?'

'Because I do not want Pavel to be ashamed of me.'

'Pavel? Pavel has nothing to do with it.'

'I don't want Pavel to be ashamed of his father, now that he sees everything. That is what has changed: there is a measure to all things now, including the truth, and that measure is Pavel. As for losing my temper with Matryona, I am sorry, I regret it and will apologize to her. As you must know, however' – he spreads his arms wide – 'Matryona does not like me.'

'She does not understand what you are doing here, that is all. She understood why Pavel should be living with us – we have had students before – but an older lodger is not the same thing. And I am beginning to find it difficult too. I am not trying to eject you, Fyodor Mikhailovich, but I must admit, when you announced you were leaving today, I was relieved. For four years Matryona and I have lived a very quiet, even life together. Our lodgers have never been allowed to disturb that.

 Now, ever since Pavel died, there has been nothing but turmoil. It is not good for a child. Matryona would not be sick today if the atmosphere at home were not so unpredictable. What the doctor said is true: she is excited, and excitement makes a child vulnerable.'

He is waiting for her to come to what is surely the heart of the matter: that Matryona is aware of what is passing between her mother and himself and is in a frenzy of possessive jealousy. But that, it seems, she is not yet prepared to bring into the open.

'I am sorry about the confusion, sorry about everything. It was impossible for me to leave tonight as I had planned – I won't go into the reasons, they are not important. I will be here for another day or two at most, till my friends help me with money. Then I will pay what I owe and be gone.'

'To Dresden?'

'To Dresden or to other lodgings – I can't say yet.'

'Very well, Fyodor Mikhailovich. But as for money, let us wipe the slate clean between the two of us right now. I don't want to belong to a long list of people you are in debt to.'

There is something about her anger he does not understand. She has never spoken so woundingly before.

He sits down at once to write to Maykov. 'You will be surprised to hear, dear Apollon Grigorevich, that I am still in Petersburg. This is the last time, I hope, that I will need to appeal to your kindness. The fact is, I find myself in such straits that, short of pawning my coat, I have no means of paying for my lodging, to say nothing of returning to my family. Two hundred roubles will see me through.'

To his wife he writes: 'I stupidly allowed a friend of

Pavel's to prevail on me for a loan. Maykov will again have to come to the rescue. As soon as my obligations are settled I will telegraph.'

So the blame is shifted again to Fedya's generous heart. But the truth is, Fedya's heart is not generous. Fedya's heart –

There is a loud knocking at the door of the apartment. Before Anna Sergeyevna can open it, he is at her side. 'It must be the police,' he whispers, 'only they would come at this hour. Let me try to deal with them. Stay with Matryona. It is best that they do not question her.'

He opens the door. Before him stands the Finnish girl, flanked by two blue-uniformed policemen, one of them an officer.

'Is this the man?' the officer asks.

The girl nods.

He stands aside and they enter, pushing the girl before them. He is shocked by the change in her appearance. Her face is a pasty white, she moves like a doll whose limbs are pulled by strings.

'Can we go to my room?' he says. 'There is a sick child here who shouldn't be disturbed.'

The officer strides across the room and whips open the curtain. Anna Sergeyevna is revealed, bending protectively over her daughter. She whirls around, eyes blazing. 'Leave us alone!' she hisses. Slowly he draws the curtain to.

He ushers them into his own room. There is something familiar about the way the Finn shuffles. Then he sees: her ankles are shackled.

The officer inspects the shrine and the photograph. 'Who is this?'

'My son.'

 There is something wrong, something has changed about the shrine. His blood runs cold when he recognizes what it is.

The questioning begins.

'Has a man named Sergei Gennadevich Nechaev been here today?'

'A person whom I suspect to be Nechaev, but who does not go under that name, has been here, yes.'

'What name does he go under?'

'Under a woman's name. He was disguised as a woman. He was wearing a dark coat over a dark-blue dress.'

'And why did this person call on you?'

'To ask for money.'

'For no other reason?'

'For no other reason that I am aware of. I am no friend of his.'

'Did you give him money?'

'I refused. However, he took what I had, and I did not stop him.'

'You are saying that he robbed you?'

'He took the money against my wishes. I did not think it prudent to try to recover it. Call that robbery if you wish.'

'How much was it?'

'About thirty roubles.'

'What else happened?'

He risks a glance at the Finn. Her lips quiver soundlessly. Whatever they have done to her in the time she has been in their hands has changed her demeanour entirely. She stands like a beast in the slaughterhouse waiting for the axe to fall.

'We spoke about my son. Nechaev was a friend of my son's, of a kind. That is how he came to know this house.

My son used to lodge here. Otherwise he would not have come.'

'What do you mean – "otherwise he would not have come"? Are you saying he expected to see your son?'

'No. None of my son's friends expects to see him again. I mean that Nechaev came not because he expected sympathy from me but because of that past friendship.'

'Yes, we know all about your son's culpable associations.'

He shrugs. 'Perhaps not culpable. Perhaps not associations – perhaps only friendships. But let it rest there. It is a question that will never come to trial.'

'Do you know where Nechaev went from here?'

'I have no idea.'

'Show me your papers.'

He hands over his passport – his own, not Isaev's. The officer pockets it and puts on his cap. 'You will report to the station on Sadovaya Street tomorrow morning to make a full declaration. You will report to the same station each day before noon, seven days a week, until further notice. You will not leave Petersburg. Is that clear?'

'And at whose expense am I to remain here?'

'That is not my concern.'

He signals to his companion to remove their prisoner. But at the front door the Finn, who has up to this point not uttered a word, balks. 'I'm hungry!' she says plaintively, and when her guard grasps her and tries to force her out, plants her feet and holds on to the door-jamb: 'I'm hungry, I want something to eat!'

There is something wailing and desperate about her cry. Though Anna Sergeyevna is nearer to her, it is an appeal unmistakably addressed to the child, who has quietly crept out of bed and, thumb in mouth, stands watching.

'Let me!' says Matryona, and in a flash has darted to the cupboard. She returns with a wedge of rye bread and a cucumber; she has brought her little purse too. 'You can have all of it!' she says excitedly, and thrusts food and money together into the Finn's hands. Then she takes a step back and, bobbing her head, drops an odd, old-fashioned curtsy.

'No money!' the guard objects fiercely, and makes her take the purse back.

Not a word of thanks from the Finn, who after her moment's rebellion has relapsed into passivity. As though, he thinks, the spark has been beaten out of her. Have they indeed been beating her – or worse? And does Matryona somehow know it? Is that the source of her pity? Yet how can a child know such things?

As soon as they are gone he returns to his room, blows out the candle, sets icon, pictures, candle on the floor, and removes the three-barred flag that has been spread over the dressing-table. Then he returns to the apartment. Anna Sergeyevna is sitting at Matryona's bedside, sewing. He tosses the flag on to the bed. 'If I speak to your daughter I am sure to lose my temper again,' he says, 'so perhaps you can ask on my behalf how this comes to be in my room.'

'What are you talking about? What is this?'

'Ask her.'

'It's a flag,' says Matryona sullenly.

Anna Sergeyevna spreads the flag out on the bed. It is over a metre in length and evidently well-used, for the colours – white, red, black in equal vertical bars – are weathered and faded. Where can they have been flying it – from the roof of Madame la Fay's establishment?

'Who does this belong to?' asks Anna Sergeyevna.

He waits for the child to answer.

'The people. It's the people's flag,' she says at last, reluctantly.

'That's enough,' says Anna Sergeyevna. She gives her daughter a kiss on the forehead. 'Time to sleep.' She draws the curtain shut.

Five minutes later she is in his room, bringing with her the flag, folded small. 'Explain yourself,' she says.

'What you have there is the flag of the People's Vengeance. It is the flag of insurrection. If you want me to tell you what the colours stand for, I will tell you. Or ask Matryona herself, I'm sure she knows. I can think of no act more provocative and more incriminating than to display it. Matryona spread it out in my room in my absence, where the police could see it. I don't understand what has got into her. Has she gone mad?'

'Don't use that word about her! She had no idea the police were coming. As for this flag, if it causes so much trouble I will take it away at once and burn it.'

'Burn it?' He stands astonished. How simple! Why did he not burn the blue dress?

'But let me tell you,' she adds, 'that is to be the end of the matter, the absolute end. You are drawing Matryona into affairs that are no concern of a child's.'

'I could not agree with you more. But it is not I who am drawing her in. It is Nechaev.'

'That makes no difference. If you were not here there would be no Nechaev.'

15

The cellar

It has snowed heavily during the night. Emerging into the open, he is dazzled by the sudden whiteness. He halts and crouches, overtaken by a sensation of spinning not from left to right but from above to below. If he tries to move, he feels, he will pitch forward and tumble.

This can only be the prelude to a fit. In spells of dizziness and palpitations of the heart, in exhaustion and irritability, a fit has been announcing itself for days without arriving. Unless the entire state in which he lives can be called a fit.

Standing at the entrance to No. 63, preoccupied with what is happening inside him, he hears nothing till his arm is gripped tight. With a start he opens his eyes. He is face to face with Nechaev.

Nechaev grins, showing his teeth. His carbuncles are livid from the cold. He tries to tug himself free, but his captor only holds him closer.

'This is foolhardy,' he says. 'You should have left Petersburg while you could. You will certainly be caught.'

With one hand gripping his upper arm and the other

his wrist, Nechaev turns him. Side by side, like a reluctant dog and its master, they walk down Svechnoi Street.

'But perhaps what you secretly want is to be caught.'

Nechaev wears a black cap whose flaps shake as he shakes his head. He speaks in a patient, sing-song tone. 'You are always attributing perverse motives to people, Fyodor Mikhailovich. People are not like that. Think about it: why should I want to be caught and locked away? Besides, who is going to look twice at a couple like us, father and son out for a walk?' And he turns upon him a distinctly good-humoured smile.

They have reached the end of Svechnoi; with a light pressure Nechaev guides him to the right.

'Have you any idea what your friend is going through?'

'My friend? You mean the Finnish girl? She will not break, I have confidence in her.'

'You would not say so if you had seen her.'

'You have seen her?'

'The police brought her to the apartment to point me out.'

'Never mind, I have no fear for her, she is brave, she will do her duty. Did she have a chance to speak to your landlady's little girl?'

'To Matryona? Why should she?'

'No reason, no reason. She likes children. She is a child herself: very simple, very straight.'

'I was questioned by the police. I will be questioned again. I concealed nothing. I will conceal nothing. I am warning you, you cannot use Pavel against me.'

'I don't need to use Pavel against you. I can use you against yourself.'

They are in Sadovaya Street, in the heart of the Haymarket. He digs in his heels and stops. 'You gave Pavel a list of people you wanted killed,' he says.

'We have talked about the list already – don't you remember? It was one of many lists. Many copies of many lists.'

'That is not my question. I want to know – '

Nechaev throws back his head and laughs. A gust of vapour leaves his mouth. 'You want to know whether you are included!'

'I want to know whether that was why Pavel fell out with you – because he saw I was marked down, and refused.'

'What a preposterous idea, Fyodor Mikhailovich! Of course you are not on any list! You are much too valuable a person. Anyhow, between ourselves, it makes no difference what names go on the lists. What matters is that *they* should know reprisals are on their way, and quake in their boots. The people understand something like that, and approve. The people aren't interested in individual cases. From time immemorial the people have suffered; now the people demand that *they* should have a turn to suffer. So don't worry. Your time hasn't come. In fact, we would be happy to have the collaboration of persons like yourself.'

'Persons like me? What persons are like me? Do you expect me to write pamphlets for you?'

'Of course not. Your talent is not for pamphlets, you are too sincere for that. Come, let us walk. I want to take you somewhere. I want to sink a seed in your soul.'

Nechaev takes his arm, and they resume their walk down Sadovaya Street. Two officers in the olive-green greatcoats of the Dragoons approach. Nechaev yields the way, cheerfully raising a hand in salute. The officers nod.

'I have read your book *Crime and Punishment*,' he resumes. 'It was that that gave me the idea. It is an excellent book. I have never read anything like it. There were times when it frightened me. Raskolnikov's illness and so forth. You must have heard it praised by many people. Still, I am telling you – ' He claps a hand to his breast, then, as though tearing out his heart, flings the hand forward. The oddity of his own gesture seems to strike him, for he blushes.

It is the first uncalculated act he has seen from Nechaev, and it surprises him. A virgin heart, he thinks, bewildering itself in its stirrings. Like that creature of Doctor Frankenstein's, coming to life. He feels a first touch of pity for this stiff, unprepossessing young man.

They are deep in the Haymarket now. Through narrow streets jammed with hucksters' tables and barrows, through a throng of smelly humanity, Nechaev conducts him.

In a doorway they halt. From his pocket Nechaev draws a blue woollen scarf. 'I must ask you to submit to being blindfolded,' he says.

'Where are you taking me?'

'There is something I want to show you.'

'But where are you taking me?'

'To where I at present live, among the people. It will be easier for both of us. You will be able to report in good conscience that you do not know where to find me.'

With the blindfold on, he is able to fall back into the luxury of dizziness. Nechaev leads him; he is knocked and jostled by passers-by; once he loses his footing and has to be helped up.

They turn off the street into a courtyard. From a tavern comes singing, the tinkling of a guitar, shouts of merriment. There is a smell of drains and fish-offal.

His hand is guided to a rail. 'Mind your step,' says Nechaev's voice. 'It's so dark here, it wouldn't help to take the blindfold off anyway.'

He shuffles down the steps like an old man. The air is dank and still. From somewhere comes the slow drip of water. It is like going into a cave.

'Here,' says Nechaev. 'Mind your head.'

They halt. He removes the blindfold. They are at the foot of an unlit wooden staircase. Before them is a closed door. Nechaev raps four times, then three. They wait. There is no sound but the dripping of water. Nechaev repeats the code. No response. 'We'll have to wait,' he says. 'Come.'

He taps on the door at the other side of the staircase, pushes it open, and stands aside.

They are in a cellar room so low that he has to stoop, lit only by a small papered window at head-height. The floor is of bare stone; even as he stands he can feel the cold creeping through his boots. Pipes run along the angle of the floor. There is a smell of damp plaster, damp brick. Though it cannot be so, sheets of water seem to be descending the walls.

Across the far end of the cellar a rope has been spanned, over which hangs washing as damp and grey as the room itself. Under the clothesline is a bed, on which sit three children in identical postures, their backs to the wall, their knees drawn up to their chins, their arms clasped around their knees. Their feet are bare; they wear linen smocks. The eldest is a girl. Her hair is greasy and unkempt; mucus covers her upper lip, which she licks at languidly. Of the others, one is a mere toddler. There is no movement, no sound from any of them. Through rheumy, incurious eyes they gaze back at the intruders.

Nechaev lights a candle and sets it in a niche in the wall.

'This is where you live?'

'No. But that is not important.' He begins to pace back and forth. Again he has the impression of caged energy. He imagines Pavel side by side with him. Pavel was not driven like this. It is no longer so hard to see why Pavel accepted him as his leader.

'Let me tell you why I have brought you here, Fyodor Mikhailovich,' Nechaev begins. 'In the room next door we have a printing press – a hand press. Illegal, of course. The idiot who has the key is unfortunately out, though he promised to be here. I am offering you the use of this press before you leave Petersburg. Whatever you choose to say we can distribute in a matter of hours, in thousands of copies. At a time like this, when we are on the brink of great things, a contribution from you can have an enormous effect. Yours is a respected name, particularly among the students. If you are prepared to write, under your own name, the story of how your stepson lost his life, the students will be bound to come out in the streets in just outrage.' He ceases his pacing and faces him squarely. 'I am sorry Pavel Isaev is dead. He was a good comrade. But we cannot look only to the past. We must use his death to light a flame. He would agree with me. He would urge you to put your anger to good use.'

As he says these words, he seems to realize he has

 gone too far. Lamely he corrects himself. 'Your anger and your grief, I mean. So that he will not have died for nothing.'

Light a flame: it is too much! He turns to go. But Nechaev grips him, holds him back. 'You can't leave yet!' he says through gritted teeth. 'How can you abandon Russia and return to a contemptible bourgeois existence? How can you ignore a spectacle like this' – he waves a hand over the cellar – 'a spectacle that can be multiplied a thousandfold, a millionfold across this country? What has become of you? Is there no spark left in you? Don't you *see* what is before your eyes?'

He turns and looks across the damp cellar-room. What does he see? Three cold, famished children waiting for the angel of death. 'I see as well as you do,' he says. 'Better.'

'No! You think you see but you don't! Seeing is not just a matter of the eyes, it is a matter of correct understanding. All you see are the miserable material circumstances of this cellar, in which not even a rat or a cockroach should be condemned to live. You see the pathos of three starving children; if you wait, you will see their mother too, who to bring home a crust of bread has to sell herself on the streets. You see how the poorest of our black poor of Petersburg have to live. But that is not seeing, that is only detail! You fail to recognize the *forces* that determine the lives to which these people are condemned! *Forces:* that is what you are blind to!'

With a finger he traces a line from the floor at his feet (he bends to touch the floor; his fingertip comes away wet) out through the dim window into the heavens.

'The lines end here, but where do you think they begin? They begin in the ministries and the exchequers and the stock exchanges and the merchant banks. They begin in the chancelleries of Europe. The lines of force begin there and radiate out in every direction and end in cellars like this, in these poor underground lives. If you wrote *that* you would truly awaken the world. But of course' – he gives a bitter laugh – 'if you wrote that you would not be allowed to publish. They will let you write stories of the mute sufferings of the poor to your heart's content, and applaud you for them, but as for the real truth, they would never let you publish it! That is why I am offering you the press. Make a start! Tell them about your stepson and why he was sacrificed.'

Sacrificed. Perhaps his mind has been wandering, perhaps he is just tired, but he does not understand how or for whom Pavel was sacrificed. Nor is he moved by this vehemence about lines. And he is in no mood to be harangued. 'I see what I see,' he says coldly. 'I don't see any lines.'

'Then you might as well still be blindfolded! Must I give you a lesson? You are appalled by the hideous face of hunger and sickness and poverty. But hunger and sickness and poverty are not the enemy. They are only ways in which *real* forces manifest themselves in the world. Hunger is not a force – it is a medium, as water is a medium. The poor live in their hunger as fish live in water. The real forces have their origin in the centres of power, in the collusion of interests that takes place there. You told me you were frightened that your name might be on our lists. I assure you again, I swear to you, it is not. Our lists name only the spiders and bloodsuckers who sit at the centres of the webs. Once the spiders and their webs are destroyed, children like these will be freed. All over Russia children will be able to emerge from their cellars. There will be food and clothes and housing, proper housing, for everyone. And there will be work to do – so much work! The first work will be to raze the banks to the ground, and the stock exchanges, and the government ministries, raze them so thoroughly that they will never be rebuilt.'

The children, who at first had seemed to be listening, have lost interest. The smallest has slid sideways and fallen asleep in his sister's lap. The sister younger than Matryona, but also, it strikes him, duller, more acquiescent. Has she already begun to say yes to men?

Something about their silent watching seems odd too. Nechaev has not spoken to them since they arrived, or given any sign of so much as knowing their names. Specimens of urban poverty – are they more to him than that? *Must I give you a lesson?* He remembers Princess Obolenskaya's malicious remark: that young Nechaev had wanted to be a schoolmaster, but had failed the qualifying examinations, and had then turned to revolution in revenge against his examiners. Is Nechaev just another pedagogue [illegible] heart, like his mentor Jean-Jacques?

And the lines. He is still not sure what Nechaev means by lines. He does not need to be told that bankers hoard money, that covetousness makes the heart shrivel. But Nechaev is insisting on something else. What? Strings of numbers passing through the window-paper and striking these children in their empty bellies?

His head is spinning again. *Give you a lesson*. He draws a deep breath. 'Do you have five roubles?' he asks.

Nechaev feels distractedly in his pocket.

'This little girl' – he nods toward the child – 'If you were to give her a good wash and cut her hair and put

a new dress on her, I could direct you to an establishment
where tonight, this very night, she could earn you a hundred roubles on your five-rouble investment. And if you fed her properly and kept her clean and didn't overuse her or allow her to get sick, she could go on earning you five roubles a night for another five years at least. Easily.'

'What – ?'

'Hear me out. There are enough children in the cellars of Petersburg, and enough gentlemen on the streets with money in their pockets and a taste for young flesh, to bring prosperity to all the poor folk of the city. All that is required is a cool head. On the backs of their children the cellar-folk could be raised into the light of day.'

'What is the point of this depraved parable?'

'I don't speak in parables. Like you, I am outraged by the suffering of innocents. I do not mistake you, Sergei Gennadevich. For a long while I was not prepared to believe that my son could have been a follower of yours. Now I begin to understand what he saw in you. You were born with the spirit of justice in you, and it is not yet stifled. I am sure that if this child, this little girl here, were to be enticed into an alley by one of our Petersburg libertines, and if you were to come upon them – if you had been keeping a guardian eye on her, for instance – you would not hesitate to plunge a knife into the man's back to save her. Or, if it is too late to save her, at least to revenge her.

'This is not a parable: it is a story about children and their uses. With the aid of a child the streets of Petersburg could be rid of a bloodsucker, perhaps even a bloodsucking banker. And in due course the dead man's wife and children might be turned out on the streets too, thus bringing about a further measure of levelling.'

'You swine!'

'No, you misplace me in the story. I am not the swine, I am not the man who is stuck like a swine in the alley. I say again: not a parable but a story. Stories can be about other people: you are not obliged to find a place for yourself in them. But if the spirit of justice does not permit you to ignore the suffering of innocent children, even in stories, there are many other ways of punishing the spiders who prey upon them. One does not have to be a child, for instance, to lead a man into a dark alley. One need only shave off one's beard and powder one's face and put on a dress and be careful to hug the shadows.'

Now Nechaev smiles, or rather bares his teeth. 'This is all out of one of your books! It is all part of your perverse make-believe!'

'Perhaps. But I still have a question to ask. If you are free today to dress up and be whom you wish and follow the promptings of the spirit of justice (a spirit still, I believe, resident in your heart), what will be the state of affairs tomorrow, once the tempest of the people's vengeance has done its work and everyone has been levelled? Will you still be free to be whom you wish? Will each of us be free to be whom we wish, at last?'

'There will be no more need for that.'

'No need for dressing up? Not even on carnival days?'

'This is a stupid conversation. There will be no need for carnival days.'

'No carnival days? No holidays?'

'There will be days of recreation. People will have a

choice of resting or going into the country to help with the harvest.'

'Yes, I have heard of harvest days. No doubt we will sing while we work. But I return to my question. What of me, what of my place in your utopia? Shall I still be allowed to dress up like a woman, if the spirit takes me, or like a young dandy in a white suit, or will I be allowed only one name, one address, one age, one parentage?'

'That is not for me to say. The people will give you their answer. The people will tell you what you are allowed.'

'But what do *you* say, Sergei Gennadevich? For if you are not one of the people, who are you and what future do you have? Shall I still have the freedom to pass myself off as whomever I wish – as a young man, for instance, who spends his idle hours dictating lists of people he doesn't like and inventing bloodthirsty punishments for them, or as the storekeeper whose job it is to order sawdust for the basket under the guillotine? Shall I be as free as that? Or should I bear in mind what I heard you say in Geneva: that we have had enough Copernicuses, that if another Copernicus were to arise he should have his eyes gouged out?'

'You are raving. You are not Copernicus.'

'You are right, I am not Copernicus. When I look up into the heavens I see only the stars that watched over us when we were born and will watch over us when we die, no matter how we disguise ourselves, no matter how deep the cellars in which we hide.'

'I am not hiding, I have simply merged with the invisible people of this city and with the conditions that produced me. Except that you cannot see those conditions.'

'May I be frank? You are speaking nonsense. I may not see lines and numbers in the sky, but I am not blind.'

'None so blind as he who will not see! You see children starving in a cellar; you refuse to see what determines the conditions of those children's lives. How can you call that seeing? But of course, you and the people who pay you have a stake in starving, hollow-eyed children. That is what you and they like to read about: soulful, hollow-eyed children with piping little voices. Well, let me tell you the truth about hunger. When they look at you, do you know what these hollow-eyed children see? Ask them! I'll tell you. They see fat cheeks and a juicy tongue. These innocents would fall upon you like rats and chew you up if they did not know you were strong enough to beat them off. But you prefer not to recognize that. You prefer to see three little angels on a brief visit to earth.

'The more I talk to you, Fyodor Mikhailovich, the less I understand how you could have written about Raskolnikov. Raskolnikov was at least alive, until he came down with the fever or whatever it was. Do you know how you strike me now? As an old, blinkered horse going round and round in a circle, rolling out the same old story day after day. What right have you to talk to me about dressing up? You couldn't dress up to save your life. You are nothing but a dry old man, a dry old work-horse near the end of its life. Isn't it time you tried to *share* the existence of the oppressed instead of sitting at home and writing about them and counting your money? But I see you are beginning to fidget. I suppose you want to hurry home and get this cellar and these children down in a notebook before the memory fades. You sicken me!'

He pauses, comes closer, peers. 'Do I go too far,

Fyodor Mikhailovich?' he continues more softly. 'Am I
overstepping the bounds of decency, uncovering what should not be uncovered – that we have *seen through you*, all of us, your stepson too? Why so silent? Has the knife come too close to the bone?' He brings the scarf out of his pocket. 'Shall we put on the blindfold again?'

Close to the bone? Yes, perhaps. Not the accusation itself but the voice he hears behind it: Pavel's. Pavel complaining to his friend, and his friend storing up the words like poison.

Dispiritedly he pushes the scarf aside. 'Why are you trying to provoke me?' he says. 'You didn't bring me here to show me your press, or to show me starving children. Those are just pretexts. What do you really want from me? Do you want to put me in such a rage that I will stamp off and betray you to the police? Why haven't you quit Petersburg? Instead of making your escape like a sensible person, you behave like Jesus outside Jerusalem, waiting for the arrival of an ass to carry you into the hands of your persecutors. Are you hoping I will play the part of the ass? You fancy yourself the prince in hiding, the prince and the martyr, waiting to be called. You want to steal Easter from Jesus. This is the second time you tempt me, and I am not tempted.'

'Stop changing the subject! We are talking about Russia, not about Jesus. And stop trying to put the blame on me. If you betray me it will only be because you hate me.'

'I don't hate you. I have no cause.'

'Yes you do! You want to strike back at me because I open people's eyes to what you are really like, you and your generation.'

'And what are we really like, I and my generation?'

'I will tell you. Your day is over. Only, instead of passing quietly from the scene, you want to drag the whole world down with you. You resent it that the reins are passing into the hands of younger and stronger men who are going to make a better world. That is what you are really like. And don't tell me the story that you were a revolutionary who went to Siberia for your beliefs. I know for a fact that even in Siberia you were treated like one of the gentry. You didn't share the sufferings of the people at all, it was just a sham. You old men make me sick! The day I get to be thirty-five, I'll put a bullet through my brains, I swear!'

These last words come out with such petulant force that he cannot hide a smile; Nechaev himself colours in confusion.

'I hope you have a chance to be a father before then, so that you will know what it is like to drink from this cup.'

'I will never be a father,' mutters Nechaev.

'How do you know? You can't be sure. All a man can do is sow the seed; after that it has a life of its own.'

Nechaev shakes his head decisively. What does he mean? That he does not sow his seed? That he is vowed to be a virgin like Jesus?

'You can't be sure,' he repeats softly. 'Seed becomes son, prince becomes king. When one day you sit on the throne (if you haven't blown out your brains by then), and the land is full of princelings, hiding in cellars and attics, plotting against you, what will you do? Send out soldiers to chop off their heads?'

Nechaev glowers. 'You are trying to make me angry with your silly parables. I know about your own father, Pavel Isaev told me – what a petty tyrant he was, how everyone hated him, till his own peasants killed him. You think that because you and your father hated each other, the history of the world has to consist of nothing but fathers and sons at war with each other. You don't understand the meaning of revolution. Revolution is the end of everything old, including fathers and sons. It is the end of successions and dynasties. And it keeps renewing itself, if it is true revolution. With each generation the old revolution is overturned and history starts again. *That* is the new idea, the truly new idea. Year One. *Carte blanche*. When everything is reinvented, everything erased and reborn: law, morality, the family, everything. When all prisoners are set free, all crimes forgiven. The idea is so tremendous that you cannot understand it, you and your generation. Or rather, you understand it only too well, and want to stifle it in the cradle.'

'And money? When you forgive the crimes, will you redistribute the money?'

'We will do more than that. Every so often, when people least expect it, we will declare the existing money worthless and print fresh money. That was the mistake the French made – to allow the old money to go on circulating. The French did not have a true revolution because they did not have the courage to push it all the way through. They got rid of the aristocrats but they didn't eliminate the old way of thinking. In our schools we will teach the people's way of thinking, that has been repressed all this time. Everyone will go to school again, even the professors. The peasants will be the teachers and the professors will be the students. In our schools we will make new men and new women. Everyone will be reborn with a new heart.'

'And God? What will God think of that?'

 The young man gives a laugh of the purest exhilaration. 'God? God will be envious.'

'So you believe?'

'Of course we believe! What would be the point otherwise? – one might as well set a torch to everything, turn the world to ash. No; we will go to God and stand before his throne and call him off. And he will come! He will have no choice, he will have to listen. Then we will all be together on the same footing at last.'

'And the angels?'

'The angels will stand around us in circles singing their hosannas. The angels will be in transports. They will be freed as well, to walk on the earth like common men.'

'And the souls of the dead?'

'You ask so many questions! The souls of the dead too, Fyodor Mikhailovich, if you like. We shall have the souls of the dead walking the earth again – Pavel Isaev too, if you like. There are no bounds to what can be done.'

What a charlatan! Yet he no longer knows where the mastery lies – whether he is playing with Nechaev or Nechaev with him. All barriers seem to be crumbling at once: the barrier on tears, the barrier on laughter. If Anna Sergeyevna were here – the thought comes unbidden – he would be able to speak the words to her that have been lacking all this time.

He takes a step forward and with what seems to him the strength of a giant folds Nechaev to his breast. Embracing the boy, trapping his arms at his sides, breathing in the sour smell of his carbuncular flesh, sobbing, laughing, he kisses him on the left cheek and on the right. Hip to hip, breast to breast, he stands locked against him.

There is a clatter of footsteps on the stairs. Nechaev struggles free. 'So they are here!' he exclaims. His eyes gleam with triumph.

He turns. In the doorway stands a woman dressed in black, with an incongruous little white hat. In the dim light, through his tears, it is hard to tell her age.

Nechaev seems disappointed. 'Ah!' he says. 'Excuse us! Come in!'

But the woman stays where she is. Under her arm she bears something wrapped in a white cloth. The children's noses are keener than his. All together, without a word, they slither down from the bed and slip past the two men. The girl tugs the cloth loose and the smell of fresh bread fills the room. Without a word she breaks off lumps and gives them into her brothers' hands. Pressed against their mother's skirts, their eyes blank and vacant, they stand chewing. Like animals, he thinks: they know where it comes from and do not care.

16

The printing press

He bows to the woman. From beneath the silly hat a rather timid, girlish, freckled face peers out. He feels a quick flicker of sexual interest, but it dies down. He should wear a black tie, or a black band around his arm in the Italian manner, then his standing would be clearer – to himself too. Not a full man any longer: half a man. Or on his lapel a medal with Pavel's image. The better half taken, the half that was to come.

'I must go,' he says

Nechaev gives him a scornful look. 'Go,' he says. 'No one is stopping you.' And then, to the woman: 'He thinks I don't know where he is going.'

The remark strikes him as gratuitous. 'Where do you think I am going?'

'Do you want me to spell it out? Isn't this your chance for revenge?'

Revenge: after what has just passed, the word is like a pig's bladder thumped into his face. Nechaev's word, Nechaev's world – a world of vengeance. What has it to do with him? Yet the ugly word has not been thrust at him without reason. Something comes back to him:

Nechaev's behaviour when they first met – the flurry of skirts against the back of his chair, the pressure of his foot under the table, the way he used his body, shameless yet gauche. Does the boy have any clear idea of what he wants, or does he simply try anything to see where it will lead? *He is like me, I was like him*, he thinks – *only I did not have the courage*. And then: *Is that is why Pavel followed him: because he was trying to learn courage? Is that why he climbed the tower in the night?*

More and more it is becoming clear: Nechaev will not be satisfied till he is in the hands of the police, till he has tasted that too. So that his courage and his resolution can be put to the test. And he will come through – no doubt of that. He will not break. No matter how he is beaten or starved, he will never give in, not even fall sick. He will lose all his teeth and smile. He will drag his broken limbs around, roaring, strong as a lion.

'Do you *want* me to take revenge? Do you *want* me to go out and betray you? Is that what it is meant to achieve, all this charade of mazes and blindfolds?'

Nechaev laughs excitedly, and he knows that they understand each other. 'Why should I want that?' he replies in a soft, mischievous voice, giving the girl a sidelong glance as if drawing her into the joke. 'I'm not a youth who has lost his way, like your stepson. If you are going to the police, be frank about it. Don't sentimentalize me, don't pretend you are not my enemy. I know about your sentimentalizing. You do it to women too, I'm sure. Women and little girls.' He turns to the girl. 'You know all about it, don't you? How men of that type drop tears when they hurt you, to lubricate their consciences and give themselves thrills.'

For someone of his age, extraordinary how much he

 has picked up! More even than a woman of the streets, because he has his own shrewdness. He knows about the world. Pavel could have done with more of that. There was more real life in the filthy, waddling old bear in his story – what was his name? Karamzin? – than in the priggish hero he so painfully constructed. Slaughtered too soon – a bad mistake.

'I have no intention of betraying you,' he says wearily. 'Go home to your father. You have a father somewhere in Ivanovo, if I remember. Go to him, kneel, ask him to hide you. He will do it. There are no limits to what a father will do.'

There is a wild snort of laughter from Nechaev. He can no longer remain still: he stalks across the cellar, pushing the children out of his way. 'My father! What do you know about my father? I'm not a ninny like your stepson! I don't cling to people who oppress me! I left my father's house when I was sixteen and I've never been back. Do you know why? Because he beat me. I said, "Beat me once more and you will never see me again." So he beat me and he never saw me again. From that day he ceased to be my father. I am my own father now. I have made myself over. I don't need any father to hide me. If I need to hide, the people will hide me.

'You say there are no limits to what a father will do. Do you know that my father shows my letters to the police? I write to my sisters and he steals the letters and copies them for the police *and they pay him*. Those are his limits. It shows how desperate the police are, paying for that kind of thing, clutching at straws. Because there is nothing I have done that they can prove – nothing!'

Desperate. Desperate to be betrayed, desperate to find a father to betray him.

'They may not be able to prove anything, but they know and you know and I know that you are not innocent. You have gone further than drawing up lists, haven't you? There is blood on your hands, isn't there? I'm not asking you to confess. Nevertheless, in the most hypothetical of senses, *why do you do it?*'

'Hypothetically? Because if you do not kill you are not taken seriously. It is the only proof of seriousness that counts.'

'But why be taken seriously? Why not be young and carefree as long as you can? There is time enough afterwards to be serious. And spare a thought for those weaker fellows of yours who made the mistake of taking you seriously. Think of your Finnish friend and of what she is going through at this very moment as a consequence.'

'Stop harping on my so-called Finnish friend! She has been looked after, she isn't suffering any more! And don't tell me to wait to be old before I am taken seriously. I have seen what happens when you grow old. When I am old I won't be myself any longer.'

It is an insight he could have imagined coming from Pavel, never from Nechaev. What a waste! 'I wish,' he says, 'I could have heard you and Pavel together.' What he does not say is: Like two swords, two naked swords.

But how clever of Nechaev to have forewarned him against pity! For that is just what he is on the point of feeling: pity for a child alone in the sea, fighting and drowning. So is he wrong to detect something a little too studied in Nechaev's sombre look (for he has, surprisingly, fallen silent), in his ruminative gaze – more than studied, in fact: sly? But when was it last that words could be trusted to travel from heart to heart? An age of acting, this, an age of disguise. Pavel too much of a child, and too old-fashioned, to prosper in it. Pavel's hero and heroine conversing in the funny, stammering, old-fashioned language of the heart. 'I wish... I wish...' – 'You may... You may...' Yet Pavel at least tried to project himself into another breast. Impossible to imagine Sergei Nechaev as a writer. An egoist and worse. A poor lover too, for sure. Without feeling, without sympathy. Immature in his feelings, stalled, like a midget. A man of the future, of the next century, with a monstrous head and monstrous appetites but nothing else. Lonely, lone. His proper place a throne in a bare room. The throne of ideas. A pope of ideas, dull ideas. God save the faithful then, God save the ruled!

His thoughts are interrupted by a clatter on the stairs. Nechaev darts to the door, listens, then goes out. There is a furious whispering, the sound of a key in a lock, silence.

Still wearing her little white hat, the woman has sat down on the edge of the bed with the youngest child at her breast. Meeting his eye, she colours, then lifts her chin defiantly. 'Mr Ishutin says you may be able to help us,' she says.

'Mr Ishutin?'

'Mr Ishutin. Your friend.'

'Why should he have said that? He knows my situation.'

'We're being put out because of the rent. I've paid this month's rent, but I can't pay the back rent too, it's too much.'

The child stops sucking and begins to wriggle. She lets him go; he slithers off her lap and leaves the room. They hear him relieving himself under the stairs, moaning softly as he does so.

'He's been sick for weeks,' she complains.

'Show me your breasts.'

She slips a second button and exposes both breasts. The nipples stand out in the cold. Lifting them up between her fingers, she softly manipulates them. A bead of milk appears.

He has five roubles that he has borrowed from Anna Sergeyevna. He gives her two. She takes the coins without a word and wraps them in a handkerchief.

Nechaev comes back. 'So Sonya has been telling you of her troubles,' he says. 'I thought your landlady might do something for them. She's a generous woman, isn't she? That was what Isaev said.'

'It's out of the question. How can I bring – ?'

The girl – can her name really be Sonya? – looks away in embarrassment. Her dress, which is of a cheap floral material quite inappropriate to winter, buttons all the way down the front. She has begun to shiver.

'We'll talk about that later,' says Nechaev. 'I want to show you the press.'

'I am not interested in your press.'

But Nechaev has him by the arm and is half-steering, half-dragging him to the door. Again he is surprised by his own passivity. It is as though he is in a moral trance. What would Pavel think, to see him being used thus by his murderer? Or is it in fact Pavel who is leading him?

He recognizes the press at once, the same old-fashioned Albion-of-Birmingham model that his brother kept for running off handbills and advertisements. No question of thousands of copies – two hundred an hour at most.

'The source of every writer's power,' says Nechaev, giving the machine a slap. 'Your statement will be distributed to the cells tonight and on the streets tomorrow. Or, if you prefer, we can hold it up till you are across the border. If ever you are taxed with it, you can say it was a forgery. It won't matter by then – it will have had its effect.'

There is another man in the room, older than Nechaev – a spare, dark-haired man with a sallow complexion and rather lustreless dark eyes, stooped over the composing table with his chin on his hands. He pays no attention to them, nor does Nechaev introduce him.

'My statement?' he says.

'Yes, your statement. Whatever statement you choose to make. You can write it here and now, it will save time.'

'And what if I choose to tell the truth?'

'Whatever you write we will distribute, I promise.'

'The truth may be more than a hand-press can cope with.'

'Leave him alone.' The voice comes from the other man, still poring over the text in front of him. 'He's a writer, he doesn't work like that.'

'How does he work then?'

'Writers have their own rules. They can't work with people looking over their shoulders.'

'Then they should learn new rules. Privacy is a luxury we can do without. People don't need privacy.'

Now that he has an audience, Nechaev has gone back to his old manner. As for him, he is sick and tired of these callow provocations. 'I must go,' he says again.

'If you don't write, we'll have to write for you.'

'What do you say? Write for me?'

'Yes.'

'And sign my name?'

'Sign your name too – we'll have no alternative.'

'No one will accept that. No one will believe you.'

'Students will believe – you have quite a following among the students, as I told you. Particularly if they don't have to read a fat book to get the message. Students will believe anything.'

'Come on, Sergei Gennadevich!' says the other man. His tone is not amused at all. There are rings under his eyes; he has lit a cigarette and is smoking nervously. 'What have you got against books? What have you got against students?'

'What can't be said in one page isn't worth saying. Besides, why should some people sit around in luxury reading books when other people can't read at all? Do you think Sonya next door has time to read books? And students chatter too much. They sit around arguing and dissipating their energy. A university is a place where they teach you to argue so that you'll never actually do anything. It's like the Jews cutting off Samson's hair. Arguing is just a trap. They think that by talking they will make the world better. They don't understand that things have to get worse before they can get better.'

His comrade yawns; his indifference seems to goad Nechaev. 'It's true! That is why they have to be provoked! If you leave them to themselves they will always slide back into chattering and debating, and everything will run down. Your stepson was like that, Fyodor Mikhailovich: always talking. People who are suffering don't need to talk, they need to act. Our task is to make them act. If we can provoke them to act, the battle is half won. They may be smashed, there may be new repression, but that will just create more suffering and more outrage and more desire for action. That's how things work. Besides, if some are suffering, what justice is there till all are suffering? And things will accelerate too. You will be surprised at how fast history can move once we get it moving. The cycles will grow shorter and shorter. If we act today, the future will be upon us before we know it.'

'So forgery is permitted. Everything is permitted.'

'Why not? There's nothing new in that. Everything is permitted for the sake of the future – even believers say so. I wouldn't be surprised if it's in the Bible.'

'It certainly isn't. Only the Jesuits say so, and they will not be forgiven. Nor will you.'

'Not be forgiven? Who will know? We are talking about a pamphlet, Fyodor Mikhailovich. Who cares who actually writes a pamphlet? Words are like the wind, here today, gone tomorrow. No one owns words. We are talking about crowds. Surely you have been in a crowd. A crowd isn't interested in fine points of authorship. A crowd has no intellect, only passions. Or do you mean something else?'

'I mean that if you knowingly bring down suffering on those wretched children next door, in the name of the future, you will not be forgiven, ever.'

'Knowingly? What does that mean? You keep talking about the insides of people's minds. History isn't thoughts, history isn't made in people's minds. History is made in the streets. And don't tell me I am talking *thoughts* right now. That is just another clever debating trick, the kind of thing they confuse students with. I'm not talking thoughts, and even if I am, it doesn't matter. I can think one thing at one minute and another thing at another and it won't matter a pin as long as I *act*. The people *act*. Besides, you are wrong! You don't know your theology! Haven't you heard of the pilgrimage of the

Mother of God? On the day after the last day, when everything has been decided, when the gates of hell have been sealed, the Mother of God will leave her throne in heaven and make a pilgrimage to hell to plead for the damned. She will kneel and she will refuse to rise till God has relented and everyone has been forgiven, even the atheist, even the blasphemer. So you are wrong, you are contradicted out of your own books.' And Nechaev casts him a blazing look of triumph.

Forgiveness of all. He has only to think of it and his head spins. *And they shall be united, father and son*. Because it comes from the foul mouth of a blasphemer, shall it therefore not be the truth? Who shall prescribe where she may make her home, the Mother of God? If Christ is hidden, why should he not hide here in these cellars? Why should he not be here at this moment, in the child at the breast of the woman next door, in the little girl with the dull, knowing eyes, in Sergei Nechaev himself?

'You are tempting God. If you gamble on God's mercy you will certainly be lost. Don't even think the thought – pay heed to me! – or you will fall.'

His voice is so thick that he can barely pronounce the words. For the first time Nechaev's comrade looks up, inspecting him with interest.

As if sensing his weakness, Nechaev pounces, worrying him like a dog. 'Eighteen centuries have passed since God's age, nearly nineteen! We are on the brink of a new age where we are free to think any thought. There is nothing we can't think! Surely you know that. You must know it – it's what Raskolnikov said in your own book before he fell ill!'

'You are mad, you don't know how to read,' he mutters. But he has lost, and he knows it. He has lost because, in this debate, he does not believe himself. And he does not believe himself because he has lost. Everything is collapsing: logic, reason. He stares at Nechaev and sees only a crystal winking in the light of the desert, self-enclosed, impregnable.

'Be careful,' says Nechaev, wagging a finger meaningfully. 'Be careful what words you use about me. I am of Russia: when you say I am mad, you say Russia is mad.'

'Bravo!' says his comrade, and claps his hands in languid mockery.

He tries a last time to rouse himself. 'No, that's not true, that's just sophistry. You are only part of Russia, only part of Russia's madness. I am the one' – he lays a hand on his breast, then, struck by the affectedness of the gesture, lets it drop again – 'I am the one who carries the madness. My fate, my burden, not yours. You are too much of a child to begin to bear the weight.'

'Bravo again!' says the man, and claps: 'He has got you there, Sergei!'

'So I will make a bargain with you,' he pushes on. 'I will write for your press after all. I will tell the truth, the whole truth in one page, as you require. My condition is that you print it as it stands, without changing a word, and send it out.'

'Done!' Nechaev positively glows with triumph. 'I like bargains! Give him pen and paper!'

The other man lays a board over the composing table and sets out paper.

He writes: 'On the night of October 12th, in the year of our Lord 1869, my stepson Pavel Alexandrovich Isaev fell to his death from the shot tower on Stolyarny Quay. A rumour has been circulated that his death was brought about by the Third Section of the Imperial Police. This rumour is a wilful fabrication. I believe that my stepson was murdered by his false friend Sergei Gennadevich Nechaev.

'May God have mercy on his soul.

'F. M. Dostoevsky.

'November 18th, 1869.'

Trembling lightly, he hands over the paper to Nechaev.

'Excellent!' says Nechaev, and passes it to the other man. 'The truth, as seen by a blind man.'

'Print it.'

'Set it,' Nechaev commands the other.

The other gives him a steady interrogative look. 'Is it true?'

'*Truth? What is the truth?*' Nechaev screams in a voice that makes the whole cellar ring. 'Set it! We have wasted enough time!'

In this moment it becomes clear that he has fallen into a trap.

'Let me change something,' he says. He takes the paper back, crumples it, thrusts it into his pocket. Nechaev makes no attempt to stop him. 'Too late, no recanting,' he says. 'You wrote it, before a witness. We'll print it as I promised, word for word.'

A trap, a devilish trap. He is not after all, as he had thought, a figure from the wings inconveniently intruding into a quarrel between his stepson and Sergei Nechaev the anarchist. Pavel's death was merely the bait to lure him from Dresden to Petersburg. He has been the quarry all the time. He has been lured out of hiding, and now Nechaev has pounced and has him by the throat.

He glares; but Nechaev does not give an inch.

17

The poison

The sun rides low in a pale, clear sky. Emerging from the warren of alleys on to Voznesensky Prospekt, he has to close his eyes; the tumbling dizziness is back, so that he almost longs for the comfort of a blindfold and a guiding hand.

He is tired of the maelstrom of Petersburg. Dresden beckons like an atoll of peace – Dresden, his wife, his books and papers, and the hundred small comforts that make up home, not least among them the pleasure of fresh underwear. And this when, without a passport, he cannot leave! 'Pavel!' he whispers, repeating the charm. But he has lost touch with Pavel and with the logic that tells him why, because Pavel died here, he is tied to Petersburg. What holds him is no longer the memory of Pavel, nor even Anna Sergeyevna, but the pit that has been dug for him by Pavel's betrayer. Turning not left towards Svechnoi Street but right in the direction of Sadovaya Street and the police station, he hopes testily that Nechaev is on his tail, spying on him.

The waiting-room is as crowded as before. He takes

his place in the line; after twenty minutes he reaches the desk. 'Dostoevsky, reporting as required,' he says.

'Required by whom?' The clerk at the desk is a young man, not even in police uniform.

He throws up his hands in irritation. 'How can I be expected to know? I am required to report here, now I am reporting.'

'Take a seat, someone will attend to you.'

His exasperation boils over. 'I don't need to be attended to, it is enough that I am here! You have seen me in the flesh, what more do you require? And how can I take a seat when there are no seats?'

The clerk is clearly taken aback by his vehemence; other people in the room are watching him curiously too.

'Write my name down and be finished!' he demands.

'I can't just write down a name,' replies the clerk reasonably. 'How do I know it is your name? Show me your passport.'

He cannot restrain his anger. 'You confiscate my passport and now you demand that I produce it! What insanity! Let me see Councillor Maximov!'

But if he expects the clerk to be overawed by Maximov's name, he is mistaken. 'Councillor Maximov is not available. Best if you take a seat and calm down. Someone will attend to you.'

'And when will that be?'

'How can I say? You are not the only person with troubles.' He gestures toward the crowded room. 'In any event, if you have a complaint, the correct procedure is to submit it in writing. We can't get moving until we have something in writing – something to get our teeth into, so to speak. You sound like a cultured person.

 Surely you appreciate that.' And he turns to the next in the line.

There is no doubt in his mind that, if he could see Maximov now, he would trade Nechaev for his passport. If he hesitated at all, it would only be because he is convinced that to be betrayed – and betrayed by him, Dostoevsky – is exactly what Nechaev wants. Or is it worse, is there a further twist? Is it possible that behind the all too many insinuations Nechaev has let fall about his, Dostoevsky's, potential for treachery lies an intent to confuse and inhibit him? At every turn, he feels, he has been outplayed, and outplayed, perhaps, because he wants to be outplayed – outplayed by a player who, from the day he met him or even before then, recognized the pleasure he took in yielding – in being plotted against, ensnared, seduced – and harnessed that knowledge to his own ends. How else can he explain this stupid passivity of his, the half-drugged state of his conscience?

Was it the same with Pavel? Was Pavel in his deepest being a son of his stepfather, seducible by the voluptuous promise of being seduced?

Nechaev spoke of financiers as spiders, but at this moment he feels like nothing so much as a fly in Nechaev's web. He can think of only one spider bigger than Nechaev: the spider Maximov sitting at his desk, smacking his lips, looking ahead to his next prey. He hopes that he will make a meal of Nechaev, will swallow him whole and crush his bones and spit out the dry remnants.

So, after all his self-congratulation, he has sunk to the pettiest vengefulness. How much lower can he fall? He recalls Maximov's remark: blessed, in an age like this, the father of daughters. If there must be sons, better to father them at a distance, like a frog or a fish.

He pictures the spider Maximov at home, his three daughters fussing about him, stroking him with their claws, hissing softly, and against him too feels the acutest resentment.

He has been hoping for a speedy answer from Apollon Maykov; but the concierge is adamant that there has been no message.

'Are you sure my letter was delivered?'

'Don't ask me, ask the boy who took it.'

He tries to find the boy, but no one knows where he is.

Should he write again? If the first appeal reached Maykov and was ignored, will a second appeal not seem abject? He is not yet a beggar. Yet the unpleasant truth is, he is living from day to day on Anna Sergeyevna's charity. Nor can he expect his presence in Petersburg to remain unremarked much longer. The news will get around, if it has not already, and when it does, any of half a dozen creditors could initiate proceedings to have him restrained. His pennilessness would not protect him: a creditor might easily reckon that, in the last resort, his wife or his wife's family or even his writer-colleagues would raise the money to save him from disgrace.

All the more reason, then, to get out of Petersburg! He must recover his passport; if that fails, he must risk travelling on Isaev's papers again.

He has promised Anna Sergeyevna to look in on the sick child. He finds the curtain across the alcove open and Matryona sitting up in bed.

'How are you feeling?' he asks.

She gives no reply, absorbed in her own thoughts.

 He comes nearer, puts a hand to her forehead. There are hectic spots on her cheeks, her breathing is shallow, but there is no fever.

'Fyodor Mikhailovich,' she says, speaking slowly and without looking at him, 'does it hurt to die?'

He is surprised at the direction her brooding has taken. 'My dear Matryosha,' he says, 'you are not going to die! Lie down, have a nap, and you will wake up feeling better. In just a few days you will be back at school – you heard what the doctor said.'

But even while he speaks she is shaking her head. 'I don't mean me,' she says. 'Does it hurt – you know – when a person dies?'

Now he knows she is serious. 'At the moment?'

'Yes. Not when you are completely dead, but just before that.'

'When you know you are dead?'

'Yes.'

He is overcome with gratitude. For days she has been closing herself off to him, retreating into obtuseness and childishness, indulging her resentments, refusing him the precious memory of Pavel she bears within her. Now she has become herself again.

'Animals don't find it hard to die,' he says gently. 'Perhaps we should take our lesson from them. Perhaps that is why they are with us here on earth – to show us that living and dying are not as hard as we think.'

He pauses, then tries again.

'What frightens us most about dying isn't the pain. It is the fear that we must leave behind those who love us and travel alone. But that is not so, it is simply not so. When we die, we carry our loved ones with us in our breast. So Pavel carried you with him when he died, and he carried me, and your mother. He still carries all of us. Pavel is not alone.'

Still with a sluggish, abstracted air, she says: 'I wasn't thinking of Pavel.'

He is unsettled, he does not understand; but a moment more has to pass before he can appreciate how comprehensively he does not understand.

'Who are you thinking of then?'

'Of the girl who was here on Saturday.'

'I don't know which girl you mean.'

'Sergei Gennadevich's friend.'

'The Finnish girl? You mean because the police brought her? You mustn't lie here worrying about that!' He takes her hand in his and pats it reassuringly. 'Nobody is going to die! The police don't kill people! They will send her back to Karelia, that is all. At worst they will keep her in prison for a while.'

She withdraws her hand and turns her face to the wall. It begins to dawn on him that even now, perhaps, he does not understand; that she may not be asking to be reassured, to be relieved of childish fears – may, in fact, in a roundabout way, be trying to tell him something he does not know.

'Are you afraid she is going to be executed? Is that what you are afraid of? Because of something you know she has done?'

She shakes her head.

'Then you must tell me. I can't guess any further.'

'They have all taken a vow they will never be captured. They vow they will kill themselves first.'

'It's easy to take vows, Matryosha, much harder to keep them, particularly when your friends have deserted you and you are all by yourself. Life is precious, she is right to hold on to it, you mustn't blame her.'

She ruminates again for a while, fiddling abstractedly with the bedsheets. When she speaks, she does so in a murmur, and with her head bent, so that he can barely catch the words: 'I gave her poison.'

'You gave her what?'

She brushes her hair aside, and he sees what she has been hiding: the slightest of smiles.

'Poison,' she says, just as softly. 'Does poison hurt?'

'And how did you do that?' he asks, marking time while his mind races.

'When I gave her the bread. No one saw it.'

He remembers the scene that had affected him so strangely: the old-fashioned curtsy, the offering of food to the prisoner.

'Did she know?' he whispers, his mouth dry.

'Yes.'

'Are you sure? Are you sure she knew what it was?'

She nods. And, recalling now how wooden, how ungrateful the Finn seemed at that moment, he cannot doubt her.

'But how did you lay your hands on poison?'

'Sergei Gennadevich left it for her.'

'What else did he leave?'

'The flag.'

'The flag and what else?'

'Some other things. He asked me to look after them.'

'Show me.'

The child clambers out of bed, kneels, gropes among the bedsprings, and comes up with a canvas-wrapped parcel. He opens it on the bed. An American pistol and cartridges. Some leaflets. A little cotton purse with a long drawstring.

'The poison is in there,' says Matryona.

He loosens the drawstring and pours the contents out: three glass capsules containing a fine green powder.

'This is what you gave her?'

She nods. 'She was supposed to have one around her neck, but she didn't.' Deftly she slips the drawstring around her own neck, so that the purse hangs between her breasts like a medallion. 'If she had had it they wouldn't have caught her.'

'So you gave her one of these.'

'She wanted it for her vow. She would do anything for Sergei Gennadevich.'

'Perhaps. That is what Sergei Gennadevich says, at any rate. Still, if you had not given her the poison it would have been easier for her not to keep the promise to Sergei Gennadevich that is so particularly hard to keep – wouldn't it?'

She wrinkles her nose in an expression he has come to recognize: she is being pushed into a corner and does not like it. Nevertheless, he goes on.

'Don't you think that Sergei Gennadevich deals out death rather too freely? Do you remember the beggar who was killed? Sergei Gennadevich did that, or told someone else to do it, and that person obeyed, just as you have obeyed.'

She wrinkles her nose again. 'Why? Why did he want to kill him?'

'To send a message into the world, I suppose – that he, Sergei Gennadevich Nechaev, is a man not to be trifled with. Or to test whether the person he ordered to do the killing would obey him. I don't know. I can't see into his heart, and I no longer want to.'

Matryona thinks awhile. 'I didn't like him,' she says at last. 'He stank of fish.'

He gives her an unblinking stare, which she candidly returns.

'But you like Sergei Gennadevich.'

'Yes.'

What he means to ask, what he cannot bring himself to ask, is: Do you love him? Would you too do anything for him? But she understands his meaning perfectly well, and has given him his answer. So that there is really only one question left to ask: 'More than Pavel?'

She hesitates. He can see her weighing them, the two loves, one in the right hand, one in the left, like apples. 'No,' she says at last with what he can only call grace, 'I still like Pavel best.'

'Because they couldn't be more different, could they, the two of them. Like chalk and cheese.'

'Chalk and cheese?' She finds the idea funny.

'Just a saying. A horse and a wolf. A deer and a wolf.'

She considers the new similitude dubiously. 'They both like fun – liked fun,' she objects, slipping up on the verb.

He shakes his head. 'No, you make a mistake there. There is no fun in Sergei Gennadevich. There is certainly a spirit of a kind in him, but it is not a spirit of fun.' He bends closer, brushes the wing of hair back from her face, touches her cheek. 'Listen, Matryosha. You cannot hide these from your mother.' He gestures towards the instruments of death. 'I will get rid of them for you as I got rid of the dress. No matter what Nechaev says, you can't keep them. It is too dangerous. Do you understand?'

Her lips part, the corners of her mouth quiver. She is going to cry, he thinks. But it is not like that at all. When she raises her eyes, he is enveloped in a glance that is at once shameless and derisive. She draws away from his hand, tossing her hair. 'No!' he says. The smile she wears is taunting, provocative. Then the spell passes and she is a child as before, confused, ashamed.

It is impossible that what he has just seen has truly taken place. What he has seen comes not from the world he knows but from another existence. It is as though for the first time he has been present and conscious during a seizure; so that for the first time his eyes have been open to where he is when he is seized. In fact, he must wonder whether *seizure* is any longer the right word, whether the word has not all along been *possession* – whether everything that for the past twenty years has gone under the name of seizure has not been a mere presentiment of what is now happening, the quaking and dancing of the body a long-drawn-out prelude to a quaking of the soul.

The death of innocence. Never in his life has he felt more alone. He is like a traveller on a vast plain. Overhead the storm-clouds gather; lightning flashes on the horizon; darkness multiplies, fold upon fold. There is no shelter; if once he had a destination, he has long since lost it; the longer the clouds mass, the heavier they grow. *Let it all break!* he prays: what is the use of delaying?

It is six o'clock and the streets are still thronged when he hastens out bearing his parcel. He follows Gorokhovaya Street to the Fontanka Canal, and joins the press of people crossing the bridge. Midway he stops and leans over the ledge.

The water is frozen over by now, all but a ragged channel in the centre. What a clutter there must be under the ice on the canal-bed! With the spring thaw one could trawl a veritable harvest of guilty secrets here: knives, axes, bloodstained clothing. Worse too. Easy to kill the spirit, harder to dispose of what is left after that. The burial service and its incantations directed, if the truth be told, not at the soul but at the obstinate body, conjuring it not to arise and return.

Thus, gingerly, like a man probing his own wound, he readmits Pavel to his thoughts. Under his blanket of earth and snow on Yelagin Island, Pavel, unappeased, still stubbornly exists. Pavel tenses himself against the cold, against the aeons he must outlast till the day of the resurrection when tombs shall be riven open and graves yawn, gritting his teeth as a bare skull does, enduring what he must endure till the sun will shine on him again and he can slacken his tensed limbs. Poor child!

A young couple have paused beside him, the man with his arm around the woman's shoulders. He edges away from them. Beneath the bridge the black water courses sluggishly, lapping around a broken crate festooned with icicles. On the ledge he cradles the canvas parcel, tied with string. The girl glances at him, glances away. At that instant he gives the parcel a nudge.

It falls on to the ice just to one side of the channel and lies there in full view of everyone.

He cannot believe what has happened. He is directly over the channel, yet he has got it wrong! Is it a trick of parallax? Do some objects not fall vertically?

'Now you're in trouble!' says a voice to his left, startling him. A man in a workman's cap, old, greybearded, winks broadly. What a devil's-face! 'Won't be safe to step on for another week at least, I'd say. What do you think you're going to do now?'

Time for a fit, he thinks. Then my cup will be full. He sees himself convulsing and foaming at the mouth, a crowd gathering around, and the greybeard pointing, for the benefit of all, to where the pistol lies on the ice. A fit, like a bolt from heaven to strike the sinner down. But the bolt does not come. 'Mind your own business!' he mutters, and hurries away.

18

The diary

This is the third time he has sat down to read Pavel's papers. What makes the reading so difficult he cannot say, but his attention keeps wandering from the sense of the words to the words themselves, to the letters on the paper, to the trace in ink of the hand's movements, the shadings left by the pressure of the fingers. There are moments when he closes his eyes and touches his lips to the page. Dear: every scratch on the paper dear to me, he tells himself.

But there is more to his reluctance than that. There is something ugly in this intrusion on Pavel, and indeed something obscene in the idea of the *Nachlass* of a child.

Pavel's Siberian story has been spoilt for him, perhaps forever, by Maximov's ridicule. He cannot pretend that the writing itself is not juvenile and derivative. Yet it would take so little to breathe life into it! He itches to take his pen to it, to cross out the long passages of sentiment and doctrine and add the lifegiving touches it cries out for. Young Sergei is a self-righteous prig who needs to be distanced, seen more humorously, particularly in his solemn disciplining of his body. What draws the peasant girl to him can surely not be the promise of connubial life (a diet of dry bread and turnips, as far as he can see, and bare boards to sleep on) but his air of holding himself ready for a mysterious destiny. Where does that come from? From Chernyshevsky, certainly, but beyond Chernyshevsky from the Gospels, from Jesus – from an imitation of Jesus as obtuse and perverted in its way as that of the atheist Nechaev, gathering together a band of disciples and leading them out on errands of death. A piper with a troop of swine dancing at his heels. 'She will do anything for him,' said Matryona of the swine-girl Katri. Do anything, endure any humiliation, endure death. All shame burnt away, all self-respect. What went on between Nechaev and his women in the room above Madame la Fay's? And Matryona – was she being groomed for the harem too?

He closes Pavel's manuscript and pushes it aside. Once he begins to write on it he will certainly turn it into an abomination.

Then there is the diary. Paging through it, he notices for the first time a trail of pencil-marks, neat little ticks that are not in Pavel's hand and can therefore only be in Maximov's. For whom are they intended? Probably for a copyist; yet in his present state he cannot but take them as directives to himself.

'Saw A. today,' reads the ticked entry for November 11, 1868, almost exactly a year ago. November 14: a cryptic 'A.' November 20: 'A. at Antonov's.' Each reference to 'A.' from there onward has a tick beside it.

He turns the pages back. The earliest 'A.' is on June 6, save for May 14, where there is an entry, 'Long talk to – –,' with a tick and a question-mark beside it.

September 14, 1869, a month before his death: 'Outline of a story (idea from A.). A locked gate, outside which we stand, hammering on it, crying to be let in. Every few days it is opened a crack and a guard beckons one of us in. The chosen one is stripped of everything he owns, even his clothes. He becomes a servant, learns to bow, to keep his voice down. As servants they select those they consider the most docile, the easiest to tame. To the strong they bar entry.

'Theme: spread of the spirit among the servants. First muttering, then anger, rebelliousness, at last a joining of hands, swearing of an oath of vengeance. Closes with a faithful old retainer, white-haired, grandfatherly, coming with a candelabrum "to do his bit" (as he says), setting fire to the curtains.'

An idea for a fable, an allegory, not for a story. No life of its own, no centre. No spirit.

July 6, 1869: 'In the mail, ten roubles from the Snitkina, for my name-day (late), with orders not to mention it to The Master.'

'The Snitkina': Anya, his wife. 'The Master': himself. Is this what Maximov meant when he warned against hurtful passages? If so, then Maximov should know this is a pygmy arrow. There is more he can bear, much more.

He leafs back further to the early days.

March 26, 1867: 'Bumped into F. M. in the street last night. He furtive (had he been with a whore?), so I had to pretend to be drunker than I was. He "guided my steps home" (loves to play the father forgiving the prodigal son), laid me out on the sofa like a corpse while he and the Snitkina had a long whispered fight. I had lost my shoes (perhaps I gave them away). It ended with F. M. in his shirtsleeves trying to wash my feet. All v.

embarrassing. This morning told the S. I *must* have my own lodgings, can't she twist his arm, use her wiles. But she's too frightened of him.'

Painful? Yes, painful indeed: he will concede that to Maximov. Yet if anything is going to persuade him to stop reading, it will be not pain but fear. Fear, for instance, that his trust in his wife will be undermined. Fears, too, for his trust in Pavel.

For whom were these mischievous pages intended? Did Pavel write them for his father's eyes and then die so as to leave his accusations unanswerable? Of course not: what madness to think so! More like a woman writing to a lover with the familiar phantom figure of her husband reading over her shoulder. Every word double: to the one, passion and the promise of surrender; to the other, a plea, a reproach. Split writing, from a split heart. Would Maximov have appreciated that?

July 2, 1867, three months later: 'Liberation of the serf! Free at last! Saw off F. M. and bride at the railway station. Then immediately gave notice at these *impossible* lodgings he has put me in (*own* cup, *own* napkin-ring, and a 10:30 curfew). V. G. has promised I can stay with him till I find another place. Must persuade old Maykov to let me have the money to pay my rent directly.'

He turns the pages back and forth distractedly. Forgiveness: is there no word of forgiveness, however oblique, however disguised? Impossible to live out his days with a child inside him whose last word is not of forgiveness.

Inside the lead casket a silver casket. Inside the silver casket a gold casket. Inside the gold casket the body of a young man clothed in white with his hands crossed on his breast. Between the fingers a telegram. He peers at the telegram till his eyes swim, looking for the word of forgiveness that is not there. The telegram is written in Hebrew, in Syriac, in symbols he has never seen before.

There is a tap at the door. It is Anna Sergeyevna, in her street clothes. 'I must thank you for looking after Matryosha. Has she been any trouble?'

It takes him a moment to collect himself, to remember that she knows nothing about the abominable uses Nechaev has put the child to.

'No trouble at all. How does she seem to you?'

'She's asleep, I don't want to wake her.'

She notices the papers spread out on the bed.

'I see you are reading Pavel's papers after all. I won't interrupt.'

'No, don't go yet. It is not a pleasant business.'

'Fyodor Mikhailovich, let me plead with you again, don't read things not meant for your eyes. You will only hurt yourself.'

'I wish I could follow your advice. Unfortunately that is not why I am here – to save myself from hurt. I have been going through Pavel's diary, and I came to an incident that I remember all too well, from the year before last. Illuminating, to see it now through another's eyes. Pavel came home in the middle of the night incapable – he had been drinking. I had to undress him, and I was struck by something I had never noticed before – how small his toenails were, as though they had not grown since he was a child. Broad, fleshy feet – his father's, I suppose – with tiny nails. He had lost his shoes or given them away; his feet were like blocks of ice.'

Pavel tramping the cold streets after midnight in his socks. A lost angel, an imperfect angel, one of God's castoffs. His feet the feet of a walker, a treader upon our great mother; of a peasant, not a dancer.

Then on the sofa, his head lolling, vomit all over his clothes.

'I gave him an old pair of boots, and watched him go off in the morning, very grumpily, with the boots in his hand. And that was that, I thought. An awkward age, though, eighteen, nineteen, awkward for everyone, when they are fullgrown but can't leave the nest yet. Feathered but unable to fly. Always eating, always hungry. They remind me of pelicans: gangling creatures, ungainliest of birds, till they spread those great wings of theirs and leave the ground.

'Unfortunately, that is not how Pavel remembered the night. In his account there is nothing about birds or angels. Nothing about parental care either. Parental love.'

'Fyodor Mikhailovich, you do no good by lacerating yourself like this. If you aren't prepared to burn these papers, at least lock them away for a while and come back to them once you have made your peace with Pavel. Listen to me and do what I tell you, for your own sake.'

'Thank you, my dear Anna. I hear your words, they go to my heart. But when I talk about saving myself from hurt, when I talk about why I am here, I do not mean here in this apartment or in Petersburg. I mean that I am not here in Russia in this time of ours to live a life free of pain. I am required to live – what shall I call it? – a Russian life: a life inside Russia, or with Russia inside me, and whatever Russia means. It is not a fate I can evade.

'Which does not mean that I claim some great importance for it. It is not a life that will bear much scrutiny.

In fact, it is not so much a life as a price or a currency. It is something I pay with in order to write. That is what Pavel did not understand: that I pay too.'

She frowns. He can see now where Matryona gets the mannerism. Little patience with the tearing out of entrails. Well, all honour to her for that! Too much tearing out of entrails in Russia.

Nevertheless, *I pay too*: he would say it again if she would suffer hearing it. He would say it again, and say more. I pay and I sell: that is my life. Sell my life, sell the lives of those around me. Sell everyone. A Yakovlev trading in lives. The Finn was right after all: a Judas, not a Jesus. Sell you, sell your daughter, sell all those I love. Sold Pavel alive and will now sell the Pavel inside me, if I can find a way. Hope to find a way of selling Sergei Nechaev too.

A life without honour; treachery without limit; confession without end.

She breaks his train of thought. 'Are you still planning to leave?'

'Yes, of course.'

'I ask because there has been an inquiry about the room. Where will you go?'

'To Maykov in the first place.'

'I thought you said you couldn't go to him.'

'He will lend me money, I'm sure of that. I'll tell him I need it to get back to Dresden. Then I'll find somewhere else to stay.'

'Why not just go back to Dresden? Won't that solve all your problems?'

'The police still have my passport. There are other considerations too.'

'Because surely you have done all you can, surely you are wasting your time in Petersburg.'

Has she not heard what he has said? Or is she trying to provoke him? He stands up, gathers the papers together, turns to face her. 'No, my dear Anna, I am not wasting my time at all. I have every reason to remain here. No one in the world has more reason. As in your heart I am sure you must know.'

She shakes her head. 'I don't know,' she murmurs; but in the voice of someone ready to be contradicted.

'There was a time when I was sure you would conduct me to Pavel. I pictured the two of us in a boat, you at the prow piloting us through the mist. The picture was as vivid as life itself. I put all my trust in you.'

She shakes her head again.

'I may have been wrong in the details, but the feeling was not wrong. From the first I had a feeling about you.'

If she were going to stop him, she would stop him now. But she does not. She seems to drink in his words as a plant drinks water. And why not?

'We made it difficult for ourselves, rushing into . . . what we rushed into,' he goes on.

'I was to blame too,' she says. 'But I don't want to talk about that now.'

'Nor I. Let me only say, over the past week I have come to realize how much fidelity means to us, to both of us. We have had to recover our fidelity. I am right, am I not?'

He examines her keenly; but she is waiting for him to say more, waiting to be sure that he knows what fidelity means.

'I mean, on your side, fidelity to your daughter. And

 on my side, fidelity to my son. We cannot love until we have their blessing. Am I right?'

Though he knows she agrees, she will not yet say the word. Against that soft resistance he presses on. 'I would like to have a child with you.'

She colours. 'What nonsense! You have a wife and child already!'

'They are of a different family. You are of Pavel's family, you and Matryona, both of you. I am of Pavel's family too.'

'I don't know what you mean.'

'In your heart you do.'

'In my heart I don't! What are you proposing? That I bring up a child whose father lives abroad and sends me an allowance in the mail? Preposterous!'

'Why? You looked after Pavel.'

'Pavel was a lodger, not a child!'

'You don't have to decide at once.'

'But I *will* decide at once! No! That is my decision!'

'What if you are already pregnant?'

She bridles. 'That is none of your business!'

'And what if I were not to go back to Dresden? What if I were to stay here and send the allowance to Dresden instead?'

'Here? In my spare room? In Petersburg? I thought the reason you can't stay in Petersburg is that you will be thrown in jail by your creditors.'

'I can wipe out my debts. It requires only a single success.'

She laughs. She may be angry but she is not offended. He can say anything to her. What a contrast to Anya! With Anya there would be tears, slammed doors; it would take a week of pleading to get back in her good books.

'Fyodor Mikhailovich,' she says, 'you will wake up tomorrow and remember nothing of this. It was just an idea that popped into your head. You have given it no thought at all.'

'You are right. That is how it came to me. That is why I trust it.'

She does not give herself into his arms, but she does not fight him off either. 'Bigamy!' she says softly, scornfully, and again quivers with laughter. Then, in a more deliberate tone: 'Would you like me to come to you tonight?'

'There is nothing on earth I want more.'

'Let us see.'

At midnight she is back. 'I can't stay,' she says; but in the same movement she is shutting the door behind her.

They make love as though under sentence of death, self-absorbed, purposeful. There are moments when he cannot say which of them is which, which the man, which the woman, when they are like skeletons, assemblages of bone and ligament pressed one into the other, mouth to mouth, eye to eye, ribs interlocked, leg-bones intertwined.

Afterwards she lies against him in the narrow bed, her head on his chest, one long leg thrown easily over his. His head is spinning gently. 'So was that meant to bring about the birth of the saviour?' she murmurs. And, when he does not understand: 'A real river of seed. You must have wanted to make sure. The bed is soaked.'

The blasphemy interests him. Each time he finds something new and surprising in her. Inconceivable, if he does leave Petersburg, that he will not come back. Inconceivable that he will not see her again.

'Why do you say saviour?'

'Isn't that what he is meant to do: to save you, to save both of us?'

'Why so sure it is *he*?'

'Oh, a woman knows.'

'What would Matryosha think?'

'Matryosha? A little brother? There is nothing she would like more. She could mother him to her heart's content.'

In appearance his question is about Matryosha; but it is only the deflected form of another question, one that he does not ask because he already knows the answer. Pavel would not welcome a brother. Pavel would take him by his foot and dash his brains out against the wall. To Pavel no saviour but a pretender, a usurper, a sly little devil clothed in chubby baby-flesh. And who could swear he was wrong?

'Does a woman always know?'

'Do you mean, do I know whether I am pregnant? Don't worry, it won't happen.' And then: 'I'm going to fall asleep if I stay any longer.' She throws the bedclothes aside and clambers over him. By moonlight she finds her clothes and begins to dress.

He feels a pang of a kind. Memories of old feelings stir; the young man in him, not yet dead, tries to make himself heard, the corpse within him not yet buried. He is within inches of falling into a love from which no reserve of prudence will save him. The falling sickness again, or a version of it.

The impulse is strong, but it passes. Strong but not

strong enough. Never again strong enough, unless it can find a crutch somewhere.

'Come here for a moment,' he whispers.

She sits down on the bed; he takes her hand.

'Can I make a suggestion? I don't think it is a good idea that Matryosha should be involved with Sergei Nechaev and his friends.'

She withdraws her hand. 'Of course not. But why say so now?' Her voice is cold and flat.

'Because I don't think she should be left alone when he can come calling.'

'What are you proposing?'

'Can't she spend her days downstairs at Amalia Karlovna's till you get home?'

'That is a great deal to ask of an old woman, to look after a sick child. Particularly when she and Matryosha don't get on. Why isn't it enough to tell Matryosha not to open the door to strangers?'

'Because you are not aware of the extent of Nechaev's power over her.'

She gets up. 'I don't like this,' she says. 'I don't see why we need to discuss my daughter in the middle of the night.'

The atmosphere between them is suddenly as icy as it has ever been.

'Can't I so much as mention her name without you getting irritable?' he asks despairingly. 'Do you think I would bring the matter up if I didn't have her welfare at heart?'

She makes no reply. The door opens and closes.

19

The fires

The plunge from renewed intimacy to renewed estrangement leaves him baffled and gloomy. He veers between a longing to make his peace with this difficult, touchy woman and an exasperated urge to wash his hands not only of an unrewarding affair but of a city of mourning and intrigue with which he no longer feels a living connection.

He is tumbling. *Pavel!* he whispers, trying to recover himself. But Pavel has let go his hand, Pavel will not save him.

All morning he shuts himself up, sitting with his arms locked around his knees, his head bowed. He is not alone. But the presence he feels in the room is not that of his son. It is that of a thousand petty demons, swarming in the air like locusts let out of a jar.

When at last he rouses himself, it is to take down the two pictures of Pavel, the daguerreotype he brought with him from Dresden and the sketch Matryona drew, to wrap them together face to face and pack them away.

He goes out to make his daily report to the police. When he returns, Anna Sergeyevna is home, hours earlier than usual, and in a state of some agitation. 'We had to close the shop,' she says. 'There have been battles going on all day between students and the police. In the Petrogradskaya district mainly, but on this side of the river too. All the businesses have closed – it's too dangerous to be out on the streets. Yakovlev's nephew was coming back from market in the cart and someone threw a cobblestone at him, for no reason at all. It hit him on the wrist; he is in great pain, he can't move his fingers, he thinks a bone is broken. He says that working-men have begun to join in. And the students are setting fires again.'

'Can we go and see?' calls Matryona from her bed.

'Of course not! It's dangerous. Besides, there's a bitterly cold wind.'

She gives no sign of remembering what passed the night before.

He goes out again, stops at a tea-house. In the newspapers there is nothing about battles in the streets. But there is an announcement that, because of 'widespread indiscipline among the student body,' the university is to be closed until further notice.

It is after four o'clock. Despite the icy wind he walks eastward along the river. All the bridges are barred; gendarmes in sky-blue uniforms and plumed helmets stand on guard with fixed bayonets. On the far bank fires glow against the twilight.

He follows the river till he is in sight of the first gutted and smouldering warehouses. It has begun to snow; the snowflakes turn to nothing the instant they touch the charred timbers.

He does not expect Anna Sergeyevna to come to him again. But she does, and with as little explanation as before. Given that Matryona is in the next room, her lovemaking surprises him by its recklessness. Her cries and pantings are only half-stifled; they are not and have never been sounds of animal pleasure, he begins to realize, but a means she uses to work herself into an erotic trance.

At first her intensity carries itself over to him. There is a long passage in which he again loses all sense of who he is, who she is. About them is an incandescent sphere of pleasure; inside the sphere they float like twins, gyrating slowly.

He has never known a woman give herself so unreservedly to the erotic. Nevertheless, as she reaches a pitch of frenzy he begins to retreat from her. Something in her seems to be changing. Sensations that on their first night together were taking place deep within her body seem to be migrating toward the surface. She is, in fact, growing 'electric' in the manner of so many other women he has known.

She has insisted that the candle on the dressing-table remain lit. As she approaches her climax her dark eyes search his face more and more intently, even when her eyelids tremble and she begins to shudder.

At one point she whispers a word that he only half-catches. 'What?' he demands. But she only tosses her head from side to side and grits her teeth.

Half-catches. Nevertheless he knows what it is: *devil.* It is a word he himself uses, though he cannot believe in the same sense as she. *The devil:* the instant at the onset of the climax when the soul is twisted out of the body and begins its downward spiral into oblivion. And, flinging her head from side to side, clenching her jaw, grunting, it is not hard to see her too as possessed by the devil.

A second time, and with even more ferocity, she throws herself into coupling with him. But the well is dry, and soon they both know it. 'I can't!' she gasps, and is still. Hands raised, palms open, she lies as if in surrender. 'I can't go on!' Tears begin to roll down her cheeks.

The candle burns brightly. He takes her limp body in his arms. The tears continue to stream and she does nothing to stop them.

'What is wrong?'

'I haven't the strength to go on. I have done all I can, I am exhausted. Please leave us alone now.'

'Us?'

'Yes, we, us, both of us. We are suffocating under your weight. We can't breathe.'

'You should have said so earlier. I understood things quite differently.'

'I am not blaming you. I have been trying to take everything upon myself, but I can't any more. I have been on my feet all day, I got no sleep last night, I am exhausted.'

'You think I have been using you?'

'Not using me in that way. But you use me as a route to my child.'

'To Matryona! What nonsense! You can't believe that!'

'It's the truth, clear for anyone to see! You use me as a route to her, and I cannot bear it!' She sits up in the bed, crosses her arms over her naked breasts, rocks back and forth miserably. 'You are in the grip of something quite beyond me. You seem to be here but you are not really here. I was ready to help you because of . . .' She heaves her shoulders helplessly. 'But now I can't any longer.'

'Because of Pavel?'

'Yes, because of Pavel, because of what you said. I was ready to try. But now it is costing me too much. It is wearing me down. I would never have gone so far if I weren't afraid you would use Matryosha in the same way.'

He raises a hand to her lips. 'Keep your voice down. That is a terrible accusation to make. What has she been saying to you? I would not lay a finger on her, I swear.'

'Swear by whom? By what? What do you believe in that you can swear by? Anyway, it has nothing to do with *laying fingers*, as you well know. And don't tell me to be quiet.' She tosses the bedclothes aside and searches for her gown. 'I must be by myself or I will go mad.'

An hour later, just as he is falling asleep, she is back in his bed, hot-skinned, gripping herself to him, winding her legs around his. 'Don't pay attention to what I said,' she says. 'There are times when I am not myself, you must get used to that.'

He wakes up once more during the night. Though the curtains are drawn, the room is as bright as if under a full moon. He gets up and looks out of the window. Flames leap into the night sky less than a mile away. The fire across the river rages so hugely that he can swear he feels its heat.

He returns to the bed and to Anna. This is how he and she are when Matryona finds them in the morning: her mother, wild-haired, fast asleep in the crook of his arm, snoring lightly; and he, in the act of opening his eyes on the grave child at the door.

An apparition that could very well be a dream. But he knows it is not. She sees all, she knows all.

20

Stavrogin

A cloud of smoke hangs over the city. Ash falls from the sky; in places the very snow is grey.

All morning he sits alone in the room. He knows now why he has not gone back to Yelagin Island. It is because he fears to see the soil tossed aside, the grave yawning, the body gone. A corpse improperly buried; buried now within him, in his breast, no longer weeping but hissing madness, whispering to him to fall.

He is sick and he knows the name of his sickness. Nechaev, voice of the age, calls it vengefulness, but a truer name, less grand, would be resentment.

There is a choice before him. He can cry out in the midst of this shameful fall, beat his arms like wings, call upon God or his wife to save him. Or he can give himself to it, refuse the chloroform of terror or unconsciousness, watch and listen instead for the moment which may or may not arrive – it is not in his power to force it – when from being a body plunging into darkness he shall become a body within whose core a plunge into darkness is taking place, a body which contains its own falling and its own darkness.

If to anyone it is prescribed to live through the madness of our times, he told Anna Sergeyevna, it is to him. Not to emerge from the fall unscathed, but to achieve what his son did not: to wrestle with the whistling darkness, to absorb it, to make it his medium; to turn the falling into a flying, even if a flying as slow and old and clumsy as a turtle's. To live where Pavel died. To live in Russia and hear the voices of Russia murmuring within him. To hold it all within him: Russia, Pavel, death.

That is what he said. But was it the truth or just a boast? The answer does not matter, as long as he does not flinch. Nor does it matter that he speaks in figures, making his own sordid and contemptible infirmity into the emblematic sickness of the age. The madness is in him and he is in the madness; they think each other; what they call each other, whether madness or epilepsy or vengeance or the spirit of the age, is of no consequence. This is not a lodging-house of madness in which he is living, nor is Petersburg a city of madness. He is the mad one; and the one who admits he is the mad one is mad too. Nothing he says is true, nothing is false, nothing is to be trusted, nothing to be dismissed. There is nothing to hold to, nothing to do but fall.

He unpacks the writing-case, sets out his materials. No longer a matter of listening for the lost child calling from the dark stream, no longer a matter of being faithful to Pavel when all have given him up. Not a matter of fidelity at all. On the contrary, a matter of betrayal – betrayal of love first of all, and then of Pavel and the mother and child and everyone else. *Perversion*: everything and everyone to be turned to another use, to be gripped to him and fall with him.

He remembers Maximov's assistant and the question

 he asked: 'What kind of book do you write?' He knows now the answer he should have given: 'I write perversions of the truth. I choose the crooked road and take children into dark places. I follow the dance of the pen.'

In the mirror on the dressing-table he catches a quick glimpse of himself hunched over the table. In the grey light, without his glasses, he could mistake himself for a stranger; the dark beard could be a veil or a curtain of bees.

He moves the chair so as not to face the mirror. But the sense of someone in the room besides himself persists: if not of a full person then of a stick-figure, a scarecrow draped in an old suit, with a stuffed sugar-sack for a head and a kerchief across the mouth.

He is distracted, and irritated with himself for being distracted. The very spirit of irritation keeps the scarecrow perversely alive; its mute indifference to his irritation doubles his irritation.

He paces around the room, changes the position of the table a second time. He bends towards the mirror, examines his face, examines the very pores of his skin. He cannot write, he cannot think.

He cannot think, *therefore what?* He has not forgotten the thief in the night. If he is to be saved, it will be by the thief in the night, for whom he must unwaveringly be on watch. Yet the thief will not come till the householder has forgotten him and fallen asleep. The householder may not watch and wake without cease, otherwise the parable will not be fulfilled. The householder must sleep; and if he must sleep, how can God condemn his sleeping? God must save him, God has no other way. Yet to trap God thus in a net of reason is a provocation and a blasphemy.

He is in the old labyrinth. It is the story of his gambling in another guise. He gambles because God does not speak. He gambles to make God speak. But to make God speak in the turn of a card is blasphemy. Only when God is silent does God speak. When God seems to speak God does not speak.

For hours he sits at the table. The pen does not move. Intermittently the stick-figure returns, the crumpled, old-man travesty of himself. He is blocked, he is in prison.

Therefore? Therefore what?

He closes his eyes, makes himself confront the figure, makes the image grow clearer. Across the face there is still a veil, which he seems powerless to remove. Only the figure itself can do that; and it will not do so before it is asked. To ask, he must know its name. What is the name? Is it Ivanov? Is this Ivanov come back, Ivanov the obscure, the forgotten? What was Ivanov's true name? Or is it Pavel? Who was the lodger who had this room before him? Who was P. A. I., owner of the suitcase? Did the P. stand for Pavel? Was Pavel Pavel's true name? If Pavel is called by a false name, will he ever come?

Once Pavel was the lost one. Now he himself is lost, so lost that he does not even know how to call for help.

If he let the pen fall, would the figure across the table take it up and write?

He thinks of what Anna Sergeyevna said: *You are in mourning for yourself.*

The tears that flow down his cheeks are of the utmost clarity, almost saltless to the taste. If there is a purging going on, what is being purged is strangely pure.

Ultimately it will not be given him to bring the dead

 boy back to life. Ultimately, if he wants to meet him, he will have to meet him in death.

There is the suitcase. There is the white suit. Somewhere the white suit still exists. Is there a way, starting at the feet, of building up the body within the suit till at last the face is revealed, even if it is the ox-face of Baal?

The head of the figure across the table is slightly too large, larger than a human head ought to be. In fact, in all its proportions there is something subtly wrong with the figure, something excessive.

He wonders whether he is not touched with a fever himself. A pity he cannot call in Matryona from next door to feel his brow.

From the figure he feels nothing, nothing at all. Or rather, he feels around it a field of indifference tremendous in its force, like a cloak of darkness. Is that why he cannot find the name – not because the name is hidden but because the figure is indifferent to all names, all words, anything that might be said about it?

The force is so strong that he feels it pressing out upon him, wave upon silent wave.

The third testing. His words to Anna Sergeyevna: I was sent to live a Russian life. Is this how Russia manifests itself – in this force, this darkness, this indifference to names?

Or is the name that is dark to him the name of the other boy, the one he repudiates: Nechaev? Is that what he must learn: that in God's eyes there is no difference between the two of them, Pavel Isaev and Sergei Nechaev, sparrows of equal weight? Is he going to have to give up his last faith in Pavel's innocence and acknowledge him in truth as Nechaev's comrade and follower, a restless young man who responded without reserve to all that Nechaev offered: not just the adventure of conspiracy but the soul-inflating ecstasies of death-dealing too? As Nechaev hates the fathers and makes implacable war on them, so must Pavel be allowed to follow him?

As he asks the question, as he allows Pavel his first taste of hatred and bloodlust, he feels something stir in himself too: the beginnings of a fury that answers Pavel, answers Nechaev, answers all of them. Fathers and sons: foes: foes to the death.

So he sits paralysed. Either Pavel remains within him, a child walled up in the crypt of his grief, weeping without cease, or he lets Pavel loose in all his rage against the rule of the fathers. Lets his own rage loose too, like a genie from a bottle, against the impiety and thanklessness of the sons.

This is all he can see: a choice that is no choice. He cannot think, he cannot write, he cannot mourn except to and for himself. Until Pavel, the true Pavel, visits him unevoked and of his free will, he is a prisoner in his own breast. And there is no certainty that Pavel has not already come in the night, already spoken.

To Pavel it is given to speak once only. Nonetheless, he cannot accept that he will not be forgiven for having been deaf or asleep or stupid when the word was spoken. What he listens for, therefore, is Pavel's second word. He believes absolutely that he does not deserve a second word, that there will be no second word. But he believes absolutely that a second word will come.

He knows he is in peril of gambling on the second chance. As soon as he lays his stake on the second chance, he will have lost. He must do what he cannot do: resign himself to what will come, speech or silence.

 He fears that Pavel has spoken. He believes that Pavel will speak. Both. Chalk and cheese.

This is the spirit in which he sits at Pavel's table, his eyes fixed on the phantasm opposite him whose attention is no less implacable than his own, whom it has been given to him to bring into being.

Not Nechaev – he knows that now. Greater than Nechaev. Not Pavel either. Perhaps Pavel as he might have been one day, grown wholly beyond boyhood to become the kind of cold-faced, handsome man whom no love can touch, even the adoration of a girl-child *who will do anything for him*.

It is a version that disturbs him. It is not the truth, or not yet the truth. But from this vision of Pavel grown beyond childhood and beyond love – grown not in a human manner but in the manner of an insect that changes shape entirely at each stage of its evolution – he feels a chill coming. Confronting it is like descending into the waters of the Nile and coming face to face with something huge and cold and grey that may once have been born of woman but with the passing of ages has retreated into stone, that does not belong in his world, that will baffle and overwhelm all his powers of conception.

Christ on Calvary overwhelms him too. But the figure before him is not that of Christ. In it he detects no love, only the cold and massive indifference of stone.

This presence, so grey and without feature – is this what he must father, give blood to, flesh, life? Or does he misunderstand, and has he misunderstood from the beginning? Is he required, rather, to put aside all that he himself is, all he has become, down to his very features, and become as a babe again? Is the thing before him the one that does the fathering, and must he give himself to being fathered by it?

If that is what must be, if that is the truth and the way to the resurrection, he will do it. He will put aside everything. Following this shade he will go naked as a babe into the jaws of hell.

An image comes to him that for the past month he has flinched from: Pavel, naked and broken and bloody, in the morgue; the seed in his body dead too, or dying.

Nothing is private any more. As unblinkingly as he can he gazes upon the body-parts without which there can be no fatherhood. And his mind goes again to the museum in Berlin, to the goddess-fiend drawing out the seed from the corpse, saving it.

Thus at last the time arrives and the hand that holds the pen begins to move. But the words it forms are not words of salvation. Instead they tell of flies, or of a single black fly, buzzing against a closed windowpane. High summer in Petersburg, hot and clammy; from the street below, noise, music. In the room a child with brown eyes and straight fair hair lying naked beside a man, her slim feet barely reaching to his ankles, her face pressed against the curve of his shoulder, where she snuggles and roots like a baby.

Who is the man? The body is as perfectly formed as a god's. But it gives off such marmoreal coldness that it is impossible a child in its grasp could not be chilled to the bone. As for the face, the face will not be seen.

He sits with the pen in his hand, holding himself back from a descent into representations that have no place in the world, on the point of toppling, enclosed within a moment in which all creation lies open at his feet, the moment before he loosens his grip and begins to fall.

 It is a moment of which he is becoming a connoisseur, a voluptuary. For which he will be damned.

Restlessly he gets up. From the suitcase he takes Pavel's diary and turns to the first empty page, the page that the child did not write on because by then he was dead. On this page he begins, a second time, to write.

In his writing he is in the same room, sitting at the table much as he is sitting now. But the room is Pavel's and Pavel's alone. And he is not himself any longer, not a man in the forty-ninth year of his life. Instead he is young again, with all the arrogant strength of youth. He is wearing a white suit, perfectly tailored. He is, to a degree, Pavel Isaev, though Pavel Isaev is not the name he is going to give himself.

In the blood of this young man, this version of Pavel, is a sense of triumph. He has passed through the gates of death and returned; nothing can touch him any more. He is not a god but he is no longer human either. He is, in some sense, beyond the human, beyond man. There is nothing he is not capable of.

Through this young man the building, with its stale-smelling corridors and blind corners, begins to write itself, this building in Petersburg, in Russia.

He heads the page, in neat capitals, THE APARTMENT, and writes:

> He sleeps late, rarely rising before noon, when the apartment has grown so hot that the bedsheets are soaked with his sweat. Then he stumbles to the little washroom on the landing and splashes water over his face and brushes his teeth with his finger and stumbles back to the apartment. There, unshaven, straggle-haired, he eats the breakfast his

landlady has set out for him (the butter by now melted, gnats floating in the milk); and then shaves and puts on yesterday's underwear, yesterday's shirt, and the white suit (the trouser-creases sharp as a knife from being pressed under the mattress all night), and wets his hair and slicks it down; and then, having prepared for the day, loses interest, loses motive power: sits down again at the table still cluttered with the breakfast things and falls into a reverie, or sprawls about, picking his nails with a knife, waiting for something to happen, for the child to come home from school.

Or else wanders around the apartment opening drawers, fingering things.

He comes upon a locket with pictures of his landlady and her dead husband. He spits on the glass and shines it with his handkerchief. Brightly the couple stare at each other across their tiny prison.

He buries his face in her underclothes, smelling faintly of lavender.

He is enrolled as a student at the university but he attends no lectures. He joins a *kruzhok*, a circle whose members experiment with free love. One afternoon he brings a girl back to his room. It occurs to him that he ought to lock the door, but he does not. He and the girl make love; they fall asleep.

A noise wakes him. He knows they are being watched.

He touches the girl and she is awake. The two of them are naked, beautiful, in the pride of their youth. They make love a second time.

Throughout, he is aware of the door open a crack, and the child watching. His pleasure is acute; it communicates itself to the girl; never before have they experienced such dark sweetness.

When he takes the girl home afterwards, he leaves the bed unmade so that the child, exploring, can familiarize herself with the smells of love.

Every Wednesday afternoon from then on, for the rest of the summer, he brings the girl to his room, always the same girl. Each time, when they depart, the apartment seems to be empty; each time, he knows, the child has crept in, has watched or listened, is now hiding somewhere.

'Do that again,' the girl will whisper.

'Do what?'

'That!' she whispers, flushed with desire.

'First say the words,' he says, and makes her say them. 'Louder,' he says. Saying the words excites the girl unbearably.

He remembers Svidrigailov: 'Women like to be humiliated.'

He thinks of all of this as *creating a taste* in the child, as one creates a taste for unnatural foods, oysters or sweetbreads.

He asks himself why he does it. The answer he gives himself is: History is coming to an end; the old account-books will soon be thrown in the fire; in this dead time between old and new, all things are permitted. He does not believe his answer particularly, does not disbelieve it. It serves.

Or he says to himself: It is the fault of the Petersburg summer – these long, hot, stuffy afternoons with flies buzzing against the windowpanes, these evenings thick with the hum of mosquitoes. Let me last through the summer, and through the winter too; then when spring comes I will go away to Switzerland, to the mountains, and become a different person.

He takes his meals with his landlady and her daughter. One Wednesday evening, pretending high spirits, he leans across the table and ruffles the child's hair. She draws away. He realizes he has not washed his hands, and she has picked up the after-smell of lovemaking. Colouring, covered in confusion, she bends over her plate, will not meet his eye.

He writes all of this in a clear, careful script, crossing out not a word. In the act of writing he experiences, today, an exceptional sensual pleasure – in the feel of the pen, snug in the crook of his thumb, but even more in the feel of his hand being tugged back lightly from its course across the page by the strict, unvarying shape of the letters, the discipline of the alphabet.

Anya, Anna Snitkina, was his secretary before she was his wife. He hired her to bring his manuscripts into order, then married her. A fairy-girl of a kind, called in to spin the tangle of his writing into a single golden thread. If he writes so clearly today, it is because he is no longer writing for her eyes. He is writing for himself. He is writing for eternity. He is writing for the dead.

Yet at the same time that he sits here so calmly, he is a man caught in a whirlwind. Torrents of paper, fragments of an old life torn loose by the roar of the upward spiral, fly all about him. High above the earth he is borne, buffeted by currents, before the grip of the wind slackens and for a moment, before he starts to fall, he is allowed utter stillness and clarity, the world opening below him like a map of itself.

Letters from the whirlwind. Scattered leaves, which he gathers up; a scattered body, which he reassembles.

There is a tap at the door: Matryona, in her nightdress, for an instant looking startlingly like her mother. 'Can I come in?' she says in a husky voice.

'Is your throat still sore?'

'Mm.'

She sits down on the bed. Even at this distance he can hear how troubled her breathing is.

Why is she here? Does she want to make peace? Is she too being worn down?

'Pavel used to sit like that when he was writing,' she says. 'I thought you were Pavel when I came in.'

'I am in the middle of something,' he says. 'Do you mind if I go on?'

She sits quietly behind him and watches while he writes. The air in the room is electric: even the dust-motes seem to be suspended.

'Do you like your name?' he says quietly, after a while.

'My own name?'

'Yes. Matryona.'

'No, I hate it. My father chose it. I don't know why I have to have it. It was my grandmother's name. She died before I was born.'

'I have another name for you. Dusha.' He writes the name at the head of the page, shows it to her. 'Do you like it?'

She does not answer.

'What really happened to Pavel?' he says. 'Do you know?'

'I think . . . I think he gave himself up.'

'Gave himself up for what?'

'For the future. So that he could be one of the martyrs.'

'Martyrs? What is a martyr?'

She hesitates. 'Someone who gives himself up. For the future.'

'Was that Finnish girl a martyr too?'

She nods.

He wonders whether Pavel had grown used to speaking in formulas too, by the end. For the first time it occurs to him that Pavel might be better dead. Now that he has thought the thought, he faces it squarely, not disowning it.

A war: the old against the young, the young against the old.

'You must go now,' he says. 'I have work to do.'

He heads the next page THE CHILD, and writes:

> One day a letter arrives for him, his name and address written out in slow, neat block letters. The child takes it from the concierge and leaves it propped against the mirror in his room.
>
> 'That letter – do you want to know who sent it?' he remarks casually when he and she are next alone together. And he tells her the story of Maria Lebyatkin, of how Maria disgraced her brother Captain Lebyatkin and became the laughing-stock of Tver by claiming that an admirer, whose identity she coyly refused to disclose, was asking for her hand.

'Is the letter from Maria?' asks the child.

'Wait and you will hear.'

'But why did they laugh at her? Why shouldn't someone want to marry her?'

'Because Maria was simple, and simple people should not marry for fear they will bear simple children, and the simple children will then have simple children themselves, and so forth, till the whole land is full of simple people. Like an epidemic.'

'An epidemic?'

'Yes. Do you want me to go on? It all happened last summer while I was visiting my aunt. I heard the story of Maria and her phantom admirer and decided to do something about it. First of all I had a white suit made, so that I would look gallant enough for the part.'

'This suit?'

'Yes, this suit. By the time it was ready, everyone knew what was up – in Tver news travels fast. I put on the suit and with a bunch of flowers went calling on the Lebyatkins. The captain was mystified, but his sister wasn't. She had never lost her faith. From then on I called every day. Once I took her for a walk in the forest, just the two of us. That was the day before I set off for Petersburg.'

'So were you her admirer all the time?'

'No, that's not how it was. The admirer was just a dream she had. Simple people can't tell the difference between dreams and the real thing. They believe in dreams. She thought I was the dream. Because I behaved, you know, like a dream.'

'And will you go back and see her?'

'I don't think so. In fact, certainly not. And if she comes looking for me, you must be sure not to let her in. Say I have changed lodgings. Say you don't know my address. Or give her a false address. Make one up. You'll recognize her at once. She is tall and bony and her teeth stick out, and she smiles all the time. In fact she's a kind of witch.'

'Is that what she says in the letter – that she is coming here?'

'Yes.'

'But why – ?'

'Why did I do it? For a joke. Summer in the country is so boring – you have no idea how boring.'

It takes him no more than ten minutes to write the scene, with not a word blotted. In a final version it would have to be fuller, but for present purposes this is enough. He gets up, leaving the two pages open on the table.

It is an assault upon the innocence of a child. It is an act for which he can expect no forgiveness. With it he has crossed the threshold. Now God must speak, now God dare no longer remain silent. To corrupt a child is to force God. The device he has made arches and springs shut like a trap, a trap to catch God.

He knows what he is doing. At the same time, in this contest of cunning between himself and God, he is outside himself, perhaps outside his soul. Somewhere he stands and watches while he and God circle each other. And time stands still and watches too. Time is suspended, everything is suspended before the fall.

I have lost my place in my soul, he thinks.

He picks up his hat and leaves his lodgings. He does not recognize the hat, has no idea whose shoes he is wearing. In fact, he recognizes nothing of himself. If he were to look in a mirror now, he would not be surprised if another face were to loom up, staring back blindly at him.

He has betrayed everyone; nor does he see that his betrayals could go deeper. If he ever wanted to know whether betrayal tasted more like vinegar or like gall, now is the time.

But there is no taste at all in his mouth, just as there is no weight on his heart. His heart, in fact, feels quite empty. He had not known beforehand it would be like this. But how could he have known? Not torment but a dull absence of torment. Like a soldier shot on the battlefield, bleeding, seeing the blood, feeling no pain, wondering: Am I dead already?

It seems to him a great price to pay. *They pay him lots of money for writing books*, said the child, repeating the dead child. What they failed to say was that he had to give up his soul in return.

Now he begins to taste it. It tastes like gall.

THE MASTER OF PETERSBURG

J.M. Coetzee's work includes *Waiting for the Barbarians*, *Life & Times of Michael K*, *Boyhood: Scenes from Provincial Life*, *Youth*, *Elizabeth Costello* and *Disgrace*, which won the Booker Prize, making him the first author to have won it twice. In 2003 he was awarded the Nobel Prize for Literature.

ALSO BY J. M. COETZEE

Dusklands
In the Heart of the Country
Waiting for the Barbarians
Life & Times of Michael K
Foe
White Writing
Age of Iron
Doubling the Point: Essays and Interviews
Giving Offense
Boyhood: Scenes from Provincial Life
The Lives of Animals
Disgrace
Stranger Shores: Essays 1986-1999
Youth
Elizabeth Costello
Slow Man